MW01717520

The Assassin of Gleam

The Assassin of Gleam

James Norcliffe

HAZARD PRESS
publishers

This book was completed during my tenure as Robert Burns Fellow at the University of Otago. I am very grateful to the University for this support.

I am grateful, too, for the support and friendship of Quentin Wilson, whose belief in this work has ensured its publication.

Publication of this book has been supported by a publishing grant from Creative New Zealand.

Published by Hazard Press Limited
P.O. Box 2151, Christchurch, New Zealand
Email: info@hazard.co.nz
www.hazardpress.co.nz

First published 2006

ISBN 1-877270-99-7

Cover illustration: *Monk* by Peter Bergting
Cover design: Fiona Gartland

Printed in New Zealand by Astra Print

CONTENTS

For Hamish Duncan, and in memory of Jan Duncan: friends.

Chapter One
THE TOWER OF GLEAM

It was dusk over the city of Gleam, but because the city was huddled beneath a range of hills behind which the blood-red sun was setting already, most of the streets and low buildings were gripped in a fist of darkness. Only the waters of the harbour and the quays to the north were still lit crimson by the sun's last lingering rays. Crouched against the iron balustrade of the upper platform of his tower, the Markgrave of Gleam scanned the mean streets and squares with his telescope. Soon it would be winter and at this time of the evening the lanterns would be lit, but now in late autumn grey figures merged into the deeper grey of cobbles and stone. His nightly watch had become a tiring and frustrating business.

Evan Twyll, the Markgrave, was the third of his line. Like his father, and his grandfather before him, he ruled Gleam with a cruel and unyielding authority, as if it were his personal kingdom – which, in a sense, ever since the empire had crumbled, it was. Such far-flung outposts had long retreated behind their walls and palisades and were beholden only to themselves or to whichever ruler managed to hold sway. The Twylls of Gleam had been more successful than most. Constant suspicion and the application of erratic terror had maintained their rule. Their people had been cowed and beaten, and such a network of spies and informants existed that none dared whisper the word 'revolt' or even think the idea 'rebellion'.

Until recently. Of late there had been whispers of hope, whispers of a change, and word of such whisperings, muted as they were, had reached the ears of the ever-vigilant agents of Gleam. There had been graffiti, too. Walls had been daubed with a simple whitewashed message; the sides of the small arched bridges had been chalked with the same single message. The word was MAIDEN, and what it signified had only been gradually made clear to the Markgrave's spies. They tended to discount its importance until, like mushrooms whose spore had been liberated by soft rain, the words began to proliferate; and as the words proliferated there had come a brightening in people's eyes, a straightening of backs and a readiness to suggest, behind a discreet hand, what could never have been suggested before: the end of the reign of the Twylls.

MAIDEN. The word was everywhere.

'What does it mean?' the Markgrave demanded, when he was finally told of this unprecedented phenomenon. Evan Twyll had lost his left eye in a fencing accident as a youth. He had a livid scar that stretched from his jaw-line to the vacant socket which over the years had clenched shut and gathered so that it looked like a length of dried fig. Whenever he wanted to hide his thoughts from his audience he presented this clenched socket to them. It was ugly and anonymous and invariably reduced even the most confident of his followers to nervousness.

He did so now, and Martin Sculldung, the Captain of the Watch who had been charged to inform the Markgrave of what was going on, swallowed. 'I'm not sure what it means,' he replied, then, rightly sensing that this would be considered an inadequate answer, added, 'but I think we would be unwise to ignore it.'

'Is it the same hand?' the Markgrave asked.

Martin Sculldung shook his head. 'I don't believe so, sir. The word seems to be written in many different hands. I don't think any one person is responsible.'

'Hmmph!'

The fig-like socket stared sightlessly at him, and the captain instinctively looked down. 'You must know more than this, man!' the Markgrave insisted irritably, and once again the captain swallowed. He did know more, but was extremely nervous of telling the Markgrave. It was a dilemma. Telling him risked one of the Markgrave's famous rages, something he'd give his pension to avoid; and yet if he did not tell him and was later found to be derelict in his duty, it would be far more than his pension he'd be risking. The citadel beneath the tower was a rambling building of small chambers and winding ways, and beneath the citadel, as the captain well knew, were smaller, danker, darker chambers furnished with chains, shackles, and branding irons and from whose stench-filled darkness few guests ever returned.

The hurried vision of the dungeons decided the captain. 'There seems to be some story,' he began.

'Story?'

'Connected with the passing of the century…'

'Go on, man!'

The end of the century was only a few months away. In most states and kingdoms such a milestone would have suggested new beginnings, a rebirth. The end of the old. Evan Twyll, however, had not expected that the citizens of Gleam would have given themselves to such thoughts, such hopes. Incredibly, though, this seemed to be happening. As the days fell away like dried leaves in the winter of the century there was a growing belief that new leaves would follow, and the new days would be fresh, green, different.

Falteringly, the captain of the guard told the Markgrave what the people of Gleam had come to believe. 'They say that your days are numbered, sir,' he muttered. 'Just as the century's days are numbered. That a maiden will come to replace you. A maiden of great strength and loveliness and that she will bring great changes.'

'What!'

In his astonishment the Markgrave turned to face Martin Sculldung and the captain flinched at the anger flashing in his eye.

'That's what they say,' he mumbled.

'Who says!'

The captain shrugged helplessly. 'The whole city, sir. The rumour seems to have spread throughout.'

Thus the Markgrave learned of the story of the Maiden. Not one of his spies or agents could discover her name, or where she was to come from, or when. In all probability she had no name, had no country, had no reality. She was a story. A myth. But she was none the less powerful for all that. Probably, the Markgrave reasoned sourly, all the more powerful *because* of it. For how could he fight an idea, a belief, a myth? He might as well have his men take out their swords and cut and thrust at the eddying mists of the morning. But, as each day of the century ebbed away, the Maiden's reality to the people of Gleam became stronger, and details, even contradictory were passed about and savoured and treasured and added to.

Now high on the upper platform of his tower the Markgrave lowered his telescope. As the last of the sun retreated from the inner harbour he turned and gazed out over the still-shining sea and the long line of the horizon. Soon the two small green moons that ever ruled the night sky in the world of Gleam would appear and begin again their eternal race. Their emerald glow would not afford enough light for spying and the night would be given over to the creatures of darkness. Twyll sighed.

At that moment, a small object caught his attention and Evan Twyll lifted his telescope again and focused on it. There wobbling in the middle of the circle of the lens was a small vessel, its square-rigged sails billowing, its thin pennants streaming. Evan Twyll sighed again, but this time bitterly. Such a boat, increasingly, would be an object of hope for his townspeople. They would peer out of their hillside houses and imagine it carrying a tall fair maiden who would start the world anew, and they would dream of a fleet of such ships, the sun shining on their wind-slapped sails, the spray spinning off their rigging.

He embroidered the thought. The ship as maiden lifting her white arms like sails, ready to embrace the lost city of Gleam. He saw the figurehead and the angelic face with its long rippling hair streaming behind like pennants, bearing towards him, her expression both just and grim, forgiving yet stern.

The fancy angered Evan Twyll, and he brought his telescope back to the city and swept about. A flicker of flames too bright to have come from a watchman's brazier or a chestnut vendor's barrel stopped him in mid-sweep and he peered through the darkness to try to discover what it was. He was able to make out two figures, dark shadows really, and they seemed to be prancing around the flames. Grotesque echoes of their shadows lunged about them. He could locate where they were easily: a small square in front of a grimy waterfront tavern mainly frequented by sailors and the hangers-on of the port. The Gut and Cuttle was its name. His spies found it a useful place to uncover information.

What were the figures doing? He tried to hold the telescope steady. The source of the flames was a long elongated object, an object that insisted on jiggling about in the middle of the picture. Long. Black, with an aureole of flames and the two fiendish figures prancing this way, that.

It couldn't be. It couldn't be an effigy. The sudden thought filled him with fury and he clawed at the rope that dangled beside him, jerking it angrily, repeatedly. Far below he could hear the wild ringing that would summon the watch. He did not pause to check again but immediately began clambering down the long spiral of stone stairs.

He wanted those two prancing figures captured. He wanted them flung into the deepest recesses of the citadel. If they had dared to burn the Markgrave of Gleam in effigy they themselves would surely burn, slowly, slowly, until they screamed for the balm of death.

Long before he reached the bottom step he was screaming hoarsely, 'Sculldung! Sculldung! To arms! To arms!'

The interior of the Gut and Cuttle tavern was smoky, cold and gloomy. The oil lamps dangling from the low heavy rafters flickered ineffectually, for the landlord was a mean man and he kept the wicks shortened. The fire, too, was ever meagre, a small heap of smoking coal which did little except draw the damp out of the blackened timbers. Certainly it did little to warm the cluster of huddled drinkers who usually sat morosely in the small bay surrounding the ingle, nursing their large tankards of the brown cloudy brew served by the miserable landlord.

These drinkers were for the most part seafaring men between voyages, wherrymen who plied the waters of the port in their long sharp-nosed boats, or those scavenging types of either sex who managed to eke some seagull-type existence about the wharves. Usually there was little conversation, for who knew who might be sitting a shoulder or two away, and who might overhear a rash comment, or a thought that should never have been put into words?

This evening, however, was different. An argument had broken out between those who maintained that the end of the century would bring about a wondrous new beginning, and those who held that all this talk of the Maiden was nothing more than a fairy tale, a foolish fancy, a sprinkle of spun sugar to disguise the taste of a bitter reality. Faces had become flushed and the landlord's murky brown brew had loosened tongues, raised voices and made the drinkers forget their customary discretion.

Perhaps the most excitable voice in the room belonged to a tall, slender young man with short-cropped fair hair and a wispy ginger moustache but no beard. He looked to be about twenty years old and he wore the clothes and short blue cape of a student. Despite the fact that he'd downed more than three tankards already he was a fluent speaker and his eloquence, if not his arguments, had earned him the grudging respect of the other drinkers. Two companions sat with him. One sat deep in the shadows far from the glow of the ingle nook, wrapped around in a cloak of deep green linen, taking no apparent interest in what was going on. The other was older with a dark wrinkled face, crinkled brown eyes creased with laugh-lines, silvered hair and beard. This man, while merry with the ale and always laughing at the excesses of his companion, nevertheless from time to time reached and pulled at the younger man's sleeve, as if to warn him of saying too much, and saying it too loudly.

Every so often, too, the older man's eyes would flicker about the room, trying to locate and assess the other drinkers. Who could be trusted? Which of the huddled figures might be the ears of the Markgrave of Gleam? Would it be more likely the silent observing ones, or the noisy provoking ones: those clever ones, trying to goad a tongue thickened by beer into betraying its owner? On the surface, none. All looked as they seemed: seamen; wherrymen; seagulls. But in Gleam nothing was as it seemed. Any one of these could be an agent of the citadel. All could. Hugh Cassin reached again for his companion's sleeve. Not so wild, he silently implored, all the while smiling and nodding amiably.

'The Maiden?' laughed a grizzled man who could be a sailor. There was scorn in his voice. 'You might as well believe in giants, or mermaids, or lizards that fly in the air. It's madness. There'll be no Maiden come to wrap her white bandages round the running sore of this place. On my oath – you're nothing but dreamers!'

'But, don't you see, it doesn't matter!' broke in the young student so excitedly that Cassin gripped his sleeve once more. 'It doesn't matter whether she exists or not. All that matters is that the *idea* of her exists!'

'Whattya mean?' asked the sailor, grinning in a befuddled way.

'It's the *idea* of the Maiden that's important, not the Maiden herself,' continued the student. 'And the idea of the Maiden certainly exists! Haven't we been arguing about her for the last hour?'

Grudgingly, the sailor nodded, and the other listeners grinned at each other.

The student drove the point home. 'It's the *idea* of the Maiden that will give people hope. And out of hope will come imagination!' Then, dramatically he paused then dropped his voice to a whisper. 'And out of imagination will come *action*!'

Hugh Cassin gripped the student's arm so fiercely at this point it must have pinched painfully, but the young man appeared not to notice. 'Oh, Tobias, Tobias Swallow,' Hugh groaned to himself, gazing around the circle of slack-jawed listeners in the sudden silence. 'If any one of these is an agent of the Markgrave we are in trouble, in direst trouble.'

Some time later the two men stumbled out onto the cobbled square which fronted the tavern. It was cold and twilight was merging into a deeper evening. The sky was cobalt and already spotted with stars. The larger green moon, Chaser, was already in hopeless pursuit of its smaller companion.

The third figure followed Hugh Cassin and Tobias Swallow, but slowly, and with more dignity. Now, out of the shadows of the tavern, it could be ascertained that she was a young woman, perhaps a little younger than Tobias and looking strikingly like him, with her corn-coloured hair and fine features.

She gathered her deep green cloak about her and shrugged her hood over her head to protect herself against the chill of the approaching night. Her name was Johanna and she was Tobias's only sister. As she stood, still framed by the tavern's archway, watching his lurching gait, a faint hopeless smile briefly touched her face. She loved Tobias dearly, but he was rash and impulsively irresponsible and needed a steadying hand. She was so glad Hugh was with them. The three had arrived in Gleam only that afternoon from their village some ten miles distant. Tobias was to set sail within a week to return to the city of Aser where he was studying medicine. Hugh, who was their mother's brother, had been given the job by his sister of making sure that her son climbed aboard the vessel in good time. The widow Swallow knew her son's unreliability well. Johanna had come to wave her brother goodbye and to visit her aunt in Gleam, where she would stay for a few days to help with a new baby.

'Tobias!' Her voice was sharp in the crisp night.

'Sister?'

'I am unhappy. Very unhappy.'

Tobias peered back in her direction. 'Unhappy? What has made you unhappy, Johanna?'

'You have, Tobias. You have! Can't you see even now what you have done?'

Tobias shook his head, then grinned foolishly at Hugh Cassin. 'What have I done? Johanna? Uncle, what have I done?'

His fatuous tone was more than Johanna could bear. 'Tobias,' she said angrily, 'I have had to sit beside you in a filthy tavern and put up with the idle buzzing of grubby bar-flies for the last two hours. It is now dark. And cold.' She drew her cloak closer. 'Very cold. The city gates will be locked by the guard by now and – have you forgotten? We have no lodgings.'

Tobias stared at her. 'Don't be angry, sister.'

This response only made Johanna more furious. 'How can I not be angry? What will we do?'

Hugh Cassin nodded. The girl was right. He should have been more insistent earlier. Somehow he should have managed to pry Tobias loose from his ale and chatter. Gleam was a cold and treacherous place. There would be a curfew. No doubt there would be patrols. And even were there no patrols, there would certainly be a cruel frost. And icy cobblestones would not make a comfortable bed. He had been a fool.

Tobias smiled and shook his head. 'Never fear!' he said confidently. 'Help is near. I will find us lodgings.' He turned about and promptly tripped and all but fell full length on to his face.

Hugh leapt after the young man and held him steady. Tobias lurched backward, peering at his feet. He had tripped over a long thin object that had been left lying on the stones of the square. Tobias swung down and swayed up again, holding the object up, then brandishing it like a sword.

It was a broom, or what was left of a broom. A long handle with a balding switch of bristles. Tobias broke free from Hugh and began lunging with it like a bumbling swordsman, giggling, as he stumbled about in a mad parody of a knight at arms.

'Never fear!' he cried. 'With this trusty sword I will save us all!'

While Johanna watched, alarmed, Hugh hurried towards Tobias to try to stop his mad antics. But immediately Tobias began chasing him and Hugh was forced to duck and weave out of the way of the flailing broom. Made a child again by the beer he had drunk, Tobias lurched back and forth on the cobbled square in front of the Gut and Cuttle thrusting and swinging at his protesting uncle.

Otherwise, the square was deserted. It was not wise to be found out of doors within the walls of Gleam after sunset. Citizens, at such times, hurried about their business for fear of the officers of the watch, or of those who materialised out of the dark shadows and evil lanes and made a savage living preying on stragglers. The square itself was surrounded by ancient weathered buildings leaning crookedly against each other, with one side opening to the harbour. Among the buildings in addition to the Gut and Cuttle was a shuttered chandlers and ships' merchant, an apothecary, two or three dubious lodging houses catering to seamen, and a scatter of dingy shop-houses. A street passed through the square and a number of narrow lanes emptied into it.

The cobblestones were wet and slippery, shining in the evening dew. The flying feet of the mock duellists made a ring and clatter in the still night air. Tobias could not help shouting and grunting in the excitement of the game.

'Stop him, Uncle!'

'I'm trying!'

Hugh Cassin was increasingly fearful of the racket they were making. He glanced a little apprehensively up the street that led from the harbour, through the square, to the portcullis of the citadel. When he glanced back over his shoulder, his eyes instinctively lifted from the portcullis to the upper storeys, the narrow slit windows dark strips against the dark stone, to the tall tower that overlooked the city. A tower of black stone, patterned with rusted iron diamonds and triangles and laced with filigree-work. It rose to a point seventy or eighty feet from base to tip. Hugh shivered at the brutal spike of the thing piercing the night sky, and turned away from its presence. It was like looking up the nostrils of God.

'Tobias!' cried Johanna. 'Tobias, stop it!'

The tower had eyes. Hugh knew that. All of Gleam knew it: knew that the Markgrave often climbed the tower to spy from its lower or upper gallery. And as he thought of that harsh one-eyed watcher, Hugh was glad of the protection of the enveloping darkness.

This sense of security evaporated, however, when Tobias, on a crazy impulse, was moved to an act of unsurpassed stupidity. There were two small cone-shaped cressets of iron clamped one on either side of the doorway of the Gut and Cuttle. These were filled with burning coals offering a soft orange glow to light up the entrance. Before the others had quite realised what he was up to, Tobias had thrust the broom into one of these and after a few seconds the ragged bristles caught fire. Laughing gleefully, Tobias now lunged with his burning brand that flamed and smoked like a tiny stubble-field. Hugh jumped back from one of the aerial sweeps and nearly fell. Now almost possessed, Tobias swung the broom round and round and streams of sparks followed like a comet's tail.

'Tobias!' cried Johanna. 'Tobias! Stop!'

Tobias seemed not to have heard her.

'Tobias!' hissed Hugh.

He was in anguish at the mad folly of their situation. First noise, and now light. What more did they have to do to draw attention to themselves? Light! Again Hugh had a sudden sense of the dark spectator in the tower and saw the increasing danger they were in.

'Tobias!' Hugh Cassin's desperate cry this time. The older man rushed forward and again tried to wrestle the broom handle out of his nephew's grasp, but Tobias, still wild with excitement, thought this was part of the game, and would not give it up. Panting, the two men grappled with the handle while sparks showered about them.

'Tobias!' cried Johanna once again. More urgent this time, almost a scream. Tobias heard and stopped. He glanced towards her. 'The gate!' she cried.

Hugh quickly looked up the street. No need to ask which gate Johanna meant. He heard rather than saw it, however. The sound was faint but unmistakable. The strained clanking sound of heavy chains being geared. The portcullis was being raised.

'Oh, my god,' he muttered. 'The watch. Quick, Johanna, quick! We have to get away from here!' He jerked the broom out of Tobias's now unresisting hands and flung it to one side, then raced back to gather Johanna. Pulling her after him, he shouted, 'Run!'

They ran. Hugh and Johanna in front, Tobias stumbling after them, ignoring the faint shouts and the clatter of running feet. They were able to move quickly, propelled by the slope of the street. Down towards the quay and along the waterfront, they ran, not daring to dart into any of the many dark lanes that offered themselves lest they should prove to be cul-de-sacs. Dead ends.

Suddenly, Hugh pulled up short, a searing stitch pain thrust though him like a hot needle. 'No!' he gasped. 'I can't!'

They had turned a bend, and were for the moment out of sight and well ahead of the watch. Beside them was an arched gateway of a solid-looking house of stone, too large for a private house unless it belonged to an exceptionally wealthy merchant. Johanna had an unreasoned inspiration it might be a holy house or infirmary. There could be shelter there, sanctuary. Pulling the other two after her she ran through the archway and banged furiously on the heavy wooden door.

None of them noticed, because of the dark and because of their desperation, that carved into the front of the arch in bas-relief was the figure of a crouching toad. An ancient wart-ridden toad, bloated at the neck.

Martin Sculldung was a fit man. Lean, sinewy, he had risen to his present position by insisting on his own fitness, mental as well as physical. While being a member of the Markgrave's watch was to be a member of a powerful and privileged élite in Gleam, it was also a dangerous occupation – for you were, of necessity, close to the Markgrave, and therefore close to the Markgrave's wrath. The Captain of the Watch was in an even more precarious position and it took a person of great art and cunning to last long in the office. Martin Sculldung had survived longer than most. He had learnt, as a master mariner learns the stars, skies and seas, to read the shifting surfaces and configurations of the Markgrave's moods, expressions, and tones. Thus far he had steered a long but always perilous course.

When he'd heard the tocsin ring with wild urgency and heard the angry voice and clamour of the Markgrave clambering and clattering down the stone steps, Martin Sculldung knew instinctively that there would be another rocky strait to negotiate. For the Markgrave had been incensed. From his tower he had witnessed a scene of sedition. There had been figures dancing like demons in the streets. There'd been a burning effigy. All this on top of the unsettling talk of the Maiden. Sculldung knew it would be more than his life was worth if he failed to seize and drag the perpetrators of these vile acts back and fling them, quailing and fearful, before the feet of his master.

So he'd roared to his men, and they'd leapt to arms. They, too, had heard the Markgrave, and they'd also heard the keen edge in Sculldung's roar. Within seconds, armed with pikestaffs and short swords, some swinging dripping lanterns, they'd swept beneath the clanking portcullis and onto the street. They ran in a clatter between overhanging buildings towards the Gut and Cuttle. Pausing in the square, Sculldung cursed as he saw the discarded broom, its bristles still smouldering. He picked it up and threw it to one of his men. The square itself was deserted.

'Did you see where they went?'

'Towards the quay.'

The watch, Martin Sculldung at the head of a dozen or so men, raced down the short sloping street to the waterfront. The black outlines of a number of sailing vessels, their sails furled, were silhouetted against the sky. There was a cool breeze off the sea for which Sculldung was grateful. There'd be no ice underfoot to make the street slippery. His keen eyes swung right and left and he could make out a movement a couple of hundred yards to the left. He made a decision instantly. 'That way! Quickly!'

As he raced towards the spot where he'd seen the shadowy outlines he was aware of a bend, and that somewhere beyond it the outlines had somehow disappeared. Martin Sculldung knew the waterfront well. There were no alleys on this particular stretch to hide in, no side streets at all for a quarter of a mile or so to confuse the issue. They could only have slipped into a doorway or gained admission to a house. Either that or jumped into the icy sea. Sculldung hastily checked his mental map of the district and felt somewhat relieved. This was not a place that opened its doors to those seeking refuge. It was a quay of locked warehouses, workshops and ships' chandlers, all firmly bolted and secured against the thieves and locksmiths of the night.

There was only one possible house. A large stone building with an arched entranceway. The watch paused outside it and looked one to another uneasily. One man held a lantern up and the stone toad stared malevolently down upon them.

'They wouldn't have gone in there,' murmured a grizzle-headed man, Sculldung's lieutenant.

Martin Sculldung nodded. Surely not. He was a fit man, and a brave man. But he was neither fit enough nor brave enough to demand entrance here. He would prefer the wrath of the Markgrave. He shivered in the darkness looking towards the black portico with its crouching stone.

There was nothing to be done.

'Come,' he ordered shortly. 'And bring the broom.'

Chapter Two
THE HOUSE OF THE STONE TOAD

Johanna Swallow stood anxiously by the heavy wooden door, which was knobbled with a pattern of iron studs like some great hobnailed boot. Having already knocked once, she willed whoever was inside to hurry and open it. That being ineffective, she banged again with her open hand with even greater urgency. Hugh and Tobias had instinctively placed themselves in the deeper shadows to one side of the porch. They were both straining to listen to hear how close the sounds of pursuit were, and Johanna gave a soft gasp as she clearly heard the clear sharp sounds of running footsteps coming down the cobblestones of the esplanade. The footsteps seemed only seconds away.

'Here, let me,' panted Tobias, suddenly sobered by the peril of their situation. He moved quickly to his sister's side and hammered desperately at the door's unwelcoming surface.

Tobias put his ear to the door. 'I think someone's coming,' he whispered. The others could hear nothing, but Tobias was sure he could make out soft shuffling footsteps.

Just then, a rattling at the door caused him to jump back, and moments later the door creaked open.

'Yes?'

The figure in the door was holding a lantern high and in its yellow light Tobias could see the long blue velvet robes of a scholar. He felt a surge of relief. This was apparently a House of Learning. Surely they would be admitted here. Tobias, as a student, could claim some fellowship. Trying to frame his request in the most appropriate way Tobias sought the eyes of the man before him and found himself looking at an elderly man with a shock of white hair squeezing out from under a blue skullcap. The man almost looked comical, but Tobias did not smile, and not only because of the peril of their situation.

Nothing in this man's eyes would have allowed smiling. His eyes were dark and grave, and stared incuriously at Tobias and his companions as if they were nothing more than pebbles on a beach, grains of inconsequential sand. It was a disconcerting feeling.

The noises of the pursuing watch seemed almost upon them. 'Good sir,' Tobias said softly, quickly, 'I fear my companions and I are in some danger. It would be an act of great kindness if you would allow us to seek shelter beneath your roof.'

The little man said nothing, but gave a small nod. Tobias had chosen his words and tone carefully. The scholar, even had he not noticed Tobias's undergraduate cape, could not have failed to miss from his words that here was a young man of some learning. He stepped to one side, beckoning them to enter. As soon as he had done so he pushed the door shut and made fast the heavy bolts. Tobias caught Johanna's eye and she smiled with the relief of those solid shafts of iron shutting out the world of dark streets, clattering footsteps, swords and pikes.

'Thank you,' she murmured to the little man.

'Not at all. Not at all,' he said, glancing at her. But there was little interest in the glance and he immediately turned his back on all three saying, 'Follow me, young lady, gentlemen.'

Then holding the lantern aloft he led the way down a hall of polished flagstones.

'What do you mean, you lost them?' demanded the Markgrave.

It took all of Martin Sculldung's years of cunning to hide his fear. Like most bullies the Markgrave, Sculldung knew, was roused to a pleasurable fury by any signs of nervousness in others. It was a matter of survival that he did not by any show of fear ignite that rage. Thus he spoke suavely, easily, reasonably: 'We did not exactly lose them, my Lord,' he said. 'We know where they are. It's just that we did not think it worthwhile pursuing them, or your wasting your time on them.'

'I asked you to bring them back!'

'My Lord, I know. I know. But they are not the fish you think they are. They are very small fry indeed.'

'Who are they?'

Martin Sculldung had done his work. Before returning to the citadel he had visited the Gut and Cuttle. The landlord, a sly slouching creature named Mulbert, had been in his pay for years. Mulbert had not been especially informative but had been able to tell Sculldung something of the people he was seeking. There was an older man, very quiet; a young man, some sort of student who had all the loudness and arrogance of youth. 'In love with his own hoiking cleverness,' Mulbert had growled. And there'd been a girl, too, who'd kept out of it completely. 'You'd hardly have known she was there. Quiet like. Hiding herself in her cape and tucked away in the dark.'

They were strangers, not regulars. Mulbert had never seen them before. Someone had said the older man was a musician, a player of the lute, but if so he'd had no instrument with him. Probably passing through on a journey. They'd paid good coin for their beer and the younger man had drunk plenty. Mulbert had laughed coarsely. 'What are you after him for? Pissing once-used beer in public?'

Sculldung had frowned and shaken his head. 'This student. Did he say anything subversive? Was there any treachery in anything he said?'

'Talk of the Maiden, like?'

Sculldung had nodded.

Mulbert had scratched at his greasy scalp, then rubbed his moustache thoughtfully. Sculldung had looked away as flakes of scurf had fallen on the dark surface of the dirty bench. 'There was some talk of that,' Mulbert had admitted.

He was a simple man, one without subtlety or imagination. He could remember words but not always their meaning. Tobias was fortunate in that his arguments had been obscure. The landlord's rheumy eyes had squeezed in concentration, then he'd shook his head. 'But there was no treachery in it, I reckon,' he'd added. 'It was just beer talk. He was saying it didn't matter whether the Maiden existed or not. That she was just an idea.' Mulbert had shrugged. 'Nothing more, really. Just student cock-a-doodle but with beer and onions on his breath just like ordinary folks.' He'd laughed again and had drawn himself a generous tankard of his own vile brew. Sculldung had winced as the laugh assailed him with the beer-sump breath of ordinary folk.

He hadn't been as confident as the landlord that the student's talk was harmless, however. The captain knew perfectly well that the idea, which existed, was far more dangerous than the actual person, who probably did not exist. He could imagine the argument. However, he'd sighed gratefully at the landlord's information for now he could tell the Markgrave that these were a party of innocent travellers.

'Any names?' the Markgrave asked.

Sculldung shook his head. 'No names. We could probably find them from the gatekeepers. I'm convinced they came from outside the wall. But I'm almost certain they're harmless.'

The Markgrave frowned at him, squinting his sightless socket. 'The effigy. From my tower I saw them burning something and dancing.'

The captain turned and snapped his fingers at one of the watch who was standing erect by the door of the Markgrave's private apartment. 'Bring me the broom,' he ordered.

Shortly afterwards, the broom was presented to the Markgrave. 'This is what you saw, my Lord.'

In the relatively bright light of the Markgrave's apartment the broom looked a pathetic thing. A length of birch wood with the bristles mere blackened stumps. The Markgrave inspected it carefully. 'Is this all?' he asked.

'My information is that they were drunk,' said Martin Sculldung easily.

'Someone must know who they are.'

'Nobody really knows. An older man, a musician most likely; a young woman; and a younger man who had a lot to say, apparently.'

'And you lost them?'

'Not really, my Lord.' Sculldung could not help swallowing. This time, however, it was not the wrath of the Markgrave which caused the sudden summoning of nervous saliva, but the memory of the dark portal, the iron-studded door, and above it the bulbous staring eyes of the stone toad. 'It could only be that they were admitted into the House of the Brothers.'

Evan Twyll, the Markgrave, looked startled. 'The devil!' he explained. 'Are you sure?'

The captain nodded. 'I'm certain,' he said. 'Either that or they had the power to disappear into the ether itself.'

The Markgrave scratched at the back of his head. Then he smiled tightly. The problem, such as it was, had probably been taken care of all by itself. He wrapped his rich red cloak about his shoulders and hunched in his high-backed chair. Standing before him, Sculldung was somehow reminded of a falcon deprived of its prey, yet not frustrated – secure in the knowledge that there would be other scared bundles of flesh later.

So, the Markgrave mused, they had been admitted into the House of the Brotherhood. He shrugged. It was really out of his hands. If they were not of the Brotherhood then they were innocent beyond belief or mad and, in any case, probably doomed; and if they were of the Brotherhood then it was far from his interest to give offence. He turned back to Sculldung.

'And in this tavern – was there any dangerous talk?' The Markgrave cocked his head at the Captain, so that the sightless socket was presented to him while his good eye observed him closely.

Sculldung knew what 'dangerous talk' meant. 'There was apparently some discussion of the Maiden, my Lord. Taproom chatter. My informant says it was only the younger man who did any talking.'

The glittering dark eye waited. 'He was wearing the cape of a student,' continued the captain. 'They were strangers. Passing through. In fact, he was actually denying the existence of the Maiden. Showing off with the beer and his learning.' The captain had to force himself not to glance away from the relentless dark eye. It seemed to know there was more to tell, and for his own safety the captain was compelled to explain. 'He was arguing that the Maiden was nothing more than an idea.'

Nothing more than an idea. The phrase seemed resonant. It was still ringing in the air when the Markgrave abruptly flicked his fingers in a gesture of dismissal and Martin Sculldung, bowing slightly and slowly, steadily, turned and left the chamber. Never move quickly. Never scurry, however much your very being craves to run.

The Markgrave of Gleam stood up from the heavy high-backed chair, and moved to his fireplace. He backed towards the flames and lifted his cloak, warming himself. Another alarm. Another waste of anger and apprehension. Was there really more restlessness abroad, or was he merely more touchy? This wild talk of maidens. Even the idea of a Maiden. An alternative. A focus. *Nothing more than an idea.* That was a loaded phrase. An idea is never nothing. Is always something. Something he would need to kill, to root out. He would have to have the idea killed. He could not rest until then.

The tight little smile returned as the Markgrave considered this necessity, and he remembered the brooding portals of the House of the Brotherhood and its sign of the toad.

The cottage lay a mile or so outside the walls of the city. It had been built near the rippling waters of the Flint, a small river fed from the hills behind Gleam. Its position was handy as Mistress Beet took in washing from the city, rinsed the dirt from Gleam in a clear pool behind the house, beat the dirt out on the smooth flat rocks, and dried the garments on lines strung between the willow trees. As she did this her husband, Gabriel Beet, would wait patiently for her to come and prepare his meals as he whiled away the hours whittling little wooden figures, whistles, or toys. He was a woodcutter, but had little inclination to follow his trade in the woods and forests, preferring to sit in the shade of a willow on the riverbank, especially now that he had a little daughter to dandle and at whom he could make kissing noises.

From time to time Mistress Beet would look up and wonder how she came to marry such a man. Even when young he had the reputation of an idler, sitting on the riverbank watching his mother slap and squeeze the dirt of Gleam as he fashioned delicate, useless little wooden objects. His mother had owned the cottage so ideally suited to her profession, and now her son owned the cottage and had a wife who could take advantage of its position. She supposed it was because Gabriel had not only the bones of an idler, but the charm of an idler as well. And if his woodcutting didn't bring in shillings, his whittling sometimes earned them pennies.

This morning Mistress Beet was troubled. She knew she should not be bending and pushing, squeezing and wringing out the bitterly cold water so soon after her confinement. Reaching once more into the large willow basket of clothes, she glanced up at the little bundle slung on a cradle hammock between two branches on the riverbank. Beside the little one Gabriel lay, attempting to find a tune on a small whistle he'd made from an elder stem. Mistress Beet grimaced and felt her side. Moreover, she had been expecting her brother, Hugh Cassin, and her sister's children. The widow Swallow, knowing how feckless Gabriel Beet was likely to be in the circumstances, had promised her the help of Johanna, and Mistress Beet was concerned they had yet to arrive. Tobias, she knew, was off again to Aser to continue his studies.

It was odd they had not arrived yet, vaguely disturbing. They were now a day overdue. If, yesterday, they'd been late into Gleam they could have been trapped by the curfew and forced to find lodging in the city, but even so that could not explain their present late arrival. She hoped they were not in trouble. Waylaid by thieves, perhaps. Again, Tobias was a hothead and prone to trouble. Even as a boy… But he should have settled down by now. He was a student at a most respectable House of Learning, would be a doctor some day and, of course, Hugh was with them. Hugh was a most cautious and considerate man, not given to silly excesses. She could not imagine Hugh Cassin allowing Tobias to lead them into trouble.

Yet why were they not here? The sun was now high in the sky. Her husband lay on the riverbank while the shadow of her daughter's crib gently swung back and forth over him. The ineffectual squeaks of the primitive whistle seemed not to be disturbing the little one, which surprised Mistress Beet. He was no musician. Not like Hugh. Hugh would make that little stem sing like a linnet.

But where was Hugh? The washerwoman straightened and flung the jerkin she'd been beating into the basket. She was a tall woman and had once been as slender as her niece, but now was thickening, with broad shoulders and muscular forearms. After walking heavily up the gravelled bank she stood by the little hammock and checked her baby, still sleeping, swaddled about like a parcel. Gabriel, for his part, did not stop squeaking on the pipe and nor did he open his eyes, although he must have heard her.

She nudged him with her foot and he looked up at her, his brown eyes shining. 'Such a lovely day,' he murmured. 'Is it time to eat already?'

Mistress Beet ignored this. 'Gabriel, I'm worried that my brother and my sister's children have not arrived. I want you to go to the city and make inquiries. They should have passed through one of the gates. Discover what you can from the gatekeepers.'

Gabriel's eyes clouded. 'Do you think it really necessary?' he said.

'I do.'

'After we have eaten?'

'Now. I want you to go right now. I'm worried.'

'But who will look after the little one?' Sitting up, and blinking in the light, Gabriel nodded up at the crib.

His wife was becoming irritated. 'I want you to go,' she snapped.

Gabriel stood up hurriedly. He had rarely heard Posy Beet talk in such a determined and angry way, and felt vulnerable on the ground. From the expression on his wife's face he could well have received a swift and painful kick.

'Will I need money?' he asked craftily. Sometimes gatekeepers, like their gates, needed oiling; and if they didn't he could use some of the oil for himself.

'Fill a basket with your wooden trinkets and sell them!' snapped his wife, and then mumbling lovingly, her face close to her little daughter, she gently rocked the hanging crib back and forth. Gabriel's face fell. He had been dismissed, but the manner of his dismissal was new and steely and he didn't like it. After he'd filled his basket, he gathered his cap, muttered a quick goodbye, and hurried out on to the dusty road to Gleam.

Chapter Three
MISPRISION

So you are fugitives?' said the man in the dark blue gown and skullcap.

The question took Hugh Cassin back. He had not thought of it that way. He was a musician, yes, a traveller, yes, an uncle, a hundred things he supposed, but never before a fugitive. Yet a few minutes previously they had been hammering for sanctuary on the door of this calm cold house while running footsteps and urgent shouts had demanded their surrender.

The four were sitting in a small chamber, a sitting room or study. The old man who looked as if he were a scholar of some sort evidently did not want to waste money on oil or wax for the room was gloomy, illuminated only by the flickering light of three tapers and a small wood fire which glowed in its dying embers. As soon as they had entered he had extinguished the lantern. They had apparently interrupted his study, for a thick book lay open on the table by the nearest candle, a book the scholar had snapped shut before he'd asked them to sit down on the wooden benches clustered about the table.

Like the benches and table, the furnishings were dark and heavy. Shelves lined two walls, shelves stacked with leather-bound volumes whose titles Hugh could not make out. There were cabinets, too, and unusual objects. One small table which Hugh at first took to be fashioned from the trunk of a tree now looked to be a stuffed leg of some monstrous animal, and in a far corner another table contained a collection of bottles, flasks and vials. Only the light faintly reflected off their gleaming surfaces indicated their presence and Hugh could not tell whether they contained liquor or some other fluid.

The manner of the man was strange. It was abrupt and oddly scientific. He had admitted them but was neither welcoming nor unwelcoming. He had led them into his private chamber, but was neither friendly nor unfriendly: it was as if either feeling were unknown to him. His voice was dry, lacking in expression, and he spent his words sparingly as a miser with money. Hugh suspected he led a solitary, largely silent existence, and wondered about its nature but was nervous of asking.

Hugh Cassin swallowed. 'I suppose we are,' he said. 'Fugitives…' The word sounded odd in his mouth, and tasted like a bad berry. 'But I don't know why.'

'You have no doubt committed some offence,' said the man. It was neither a question nor a statement, but something which hovered between the two.

Tobias spoke. 'It was nothing really,' he said, with more cheerfulness than he felt. 'We were playing a foolish game in the square, you know how it is – full of ale and good spirits. But it seems good spirits aren't allowed in Gleam for the Watch shouted at us.'

The scholar stared at him. He made no comment, and Hugh Cassin felt wryly that this man did not know how it was to be full of ale and high spirits and to cavort about with a burning broom.

'It was stupid, I suppose, but we ran away. And when we ran away they chased us,' Tobias concluded a little lamely.

'Then you have committed an offence,' repeated the scholar in the same dry tone.

How precise he is, thought Hugh. How correct. Perhaps he is a magistrate.

Tobias shook his head, but without conviction, and his attempt at cheerfulness faded. He glanced at his sister. He knew he had disappointed, even angered, her by getting them all into this predicament. He knew by the cast of her head and shoulders that she was almost certainly still angry with him. Johanna, once again, had retreated to the shadows and was holding herself against the cold and was staring downwards. She looked resigned and resentful and Tobias knew he should move to her side to apologise, somehow make amends, but he felt pinioned to the spot. He looked up again at the dark figure of the scholar with his fluffy white hair under the skullcap lit up by the firelight.

'And now I, too, have committed an offence,' said the man. Hugh Cassin looked at him. 'I am guilty of misprision.'

'Misprision?' asked Tobias.

'Misprision,' repeated the scholar. 'Of harbouring fugitives.'

Hugh sighed. The man was right. Of course he was right. But in the murky night running from the angry torches you don't think of such things. Nothing was simple.

'You see how it is,' said the scholar. 'You beat on my door, and when I admit you, you reward me by turning me into a criminal.'

There was no accusation in the voice. It seemed merely to be reciting a litany of cold facts. 'What should we do?' asked Hugh. He would have asked, 'What should we have done?' But he knew the answer to that now. For the moment he felt confused and embarrassed, his head was heavy with the effects of ale, and he felt a tightness in the chest still from the stitch pain.

Somehow the man was able to understand all this for he replied, 'Do now? I shall put you to bed. And the maiden, too. She is cold and worried, and feeling strange. You will both feel better after a sleep.'

Hugh nodded in some surprise, but felt grateful all the same. He rose and moved to Johanna, and plucked at her elbow. 'Come, niece,' he said. 'We are being offered shelter.'

Tobias looked up at the others as they stood. He looked at the old man. He had never known a person with so much unstated authority. He had been courteous without courtesy, honest without giving anything away, and ever completely in command. The thought that startled him most was his sense that the old man had no curiosity about them because somehow he knew all there was to know of them already. It was at once a frightening and an exhilarating thought. And then, as the others began to leave, another, much more down-to-earth thought occurred to him 'But,' he began. He was trying to find the words to explain that the offer of a bed had not been extended to him.

The old man turned to him with a faint humourless smile. 'You are wearing the robes of a student. I too am a student. I would like to talk to you. It is not much to ask you in return for the changing of my rank from citizen to felon, is it?'

Tobias shook his head. It was not much to ask.

Kill the idea. Kill the idea.

Evan Twyll could not sleep. He was not averse to killing. At times it even gave him pleasure. His authority to rule was underpinned by his ruthlessness, his unpredictable willingness to have enemies, or those he merely suspected of being enemies, put to death. But how to kill an idea? It was not something he was able to comprehend easily. An idea was not flesh, as his noisily sleeping wife beside him was flesh. An idea did not snore, sigh or mumble. An idea did not smell of stale perfume and garlic, or twitch and toss or fling an arm across a bolster.

You could not put an idea on a rack and stretch it to eternity, or put it on a gibbet and hang it jerking as its tongue protruded and its eyes bulged. You could not stick a length of pointed steel into an idea and have it bleed its life away on the stones.

Evan Twyll shut his eyes against the images. The idea of killing an idea was in his head and he could not kill it. However, he was a dispenser of death, not an artist in death. This problem required expertise, artistry. Again the picture of the stone toad came before him. He well knew of the grim house on the waterfront: he had lived with it in uneasy tension all the years of his rule, as all rulers of Gleam had tolerated its presence. No ruler of Gleam would have dared to interfere with the house or any of its inhabitants, for the Brotherhood was ancient and mysterious and its reach was long. For its part, though, the Brotherhood was not interested in affairs of state or any of the trappings of power or wealth. Like hermits or monks, its members seemed only interested in a spare and simple life and the pursuit of knowledge. But the knowledge they pursued was of the darkest and most secret passages of existence.

Thus it was that when Martin Sculldung had reported that the three felons had gained admittance to the House of the Toad, the Markgrave had accepted there was nothing more to be done. If, as was possible, the three were Brothers themselves then they were inviolable: to capture them, or worse, would be like eating toads. If, on the other hand, the Brotherhood had simply opened their doors to them as strangers, the story would be quite different. At some point they might just be released; but, more likely, the Markgrave reflected again with grim satisfaction, they would never be seen again. No person in their right mind would seek sanctuary in that fearsome house. You might as well seek safety in a pit of vipers.

The Markgrave climbed out of his bed and walked across the stone floor to the heavily draped window. He pulled the drape aside and gazed over the rooftops of Gleam. Dawn was still some hours away but the moonlight shone on the slate and tiles, and on the waters of the harbour. Along the waterfront to the left the Markgrave could make out the brooding shape of the House of the Toad.

Suddenly it did not matter that his Captain and the Watch had failed to capture the felons. The events reported by Martin Sculldung tumbled together. First of all, the loud-mouthed student had given him the insight that the importance of the Maiden was not in her reality, but rather in the idea of her. And then the student had led his men a mad chase to the very place that offered him his solution: to the House of the Toad. The House of the Toad, where could be found experts, artists in death – who would surely know how to kill an idea.

Evan Twyll let the drape fall and returned to his bed. He shoved his sleeping wife to one side and lay in the warmth her body had left behind. On the morrow he would make delicate contact with the inhabitants of the House of the Toad. He would have a commission to offer them.

Gabriel Beet entered the Gut and Cuttle tavern wearily. He had walked a great distance, it seemed to him, and he was thirsty and hungry. He was sure Posy would not object to his having a tankard of Tobit Mulbert's dark ale and perhaps a slice or two of gammon or a pork pie, for he would have some success to report when he finally returned home. She should have prepared him a little something, anyway. Earlier he had traipsed around the gatehouses and questioned the gatekeepers, but without learning anything of Johanna, Tobias or Hugh Cassin. The difficulty was that the watch had changed. None of the watchmen had been on duty when his wife's relations would have sought to enter Gleam.

Just when he was about to think his journey had been a waste of time, however, he had discovered something. At the third gatehouse, the one under the east tower, a young girl, a gatekeeper's daughter, scampered after him. She'd heard him questioning the guard and had seen the pretty little objects he'd been carrying in his basket. The girl caught at Gabriel Beet's sleeve. 'Did you say an older man, a student and a maiden?' she'd asked of him, her eager eyes leaving his and concentrating on the shallow basket.

'I did,' Gabriel replied, smiling. 'Did you see them, little lady?'

'I might have,' the girl replied, glancing up at him calculatingly, and then glancing back at the basket. Her meaning was so plain that Gabriel laughed before reaching in and holding up the little figurine of a huntress.

'Would this little doll help jog your memory?' he asked.

The girl nodded, reaching for her prize. It had been delicately carved: a girl frozen in the act of running, her bow outstretched. Gabriel had been very pleased with it. But now he held it back and the girl paused, uncertain. 'Where?' Gabriel insisted. 'And when?'

'Last evening,' the girl replied. 'My father was on the gate and my mother had sent me to him with his supper. He was laughing with the older man, the one with the silver beard. There was a tall man with a little moustache and a green cape and a fair-haired maiden with a dark green cloak. She was very beautiful,' the little girl added.

Gabriel Beet tugged at his ear thoughtfully. It had been some years since he'd seen Hugh Cassin and his wife's sister's children. They were children then, of course. Little Johanna so self-contained and quiet, and Tobias with a hint of reckless devilry in him. Hugh Cassin had been dark in those days, but already greying, a grey that could well have turned into silver.

'Was the man with the silver hair carrying a lute?' he asked. 'Or some other musical instrument?'

The little girl shrugged. 'I don't know,' she replied. 'He could have been. I didn't see them leave.' She stared at him hopefully, and Gabriel Beet tousled her hair.

'What's your name, little lady?' he asked, and when the little girl replied 'Fritha, sir,' he handed her the wooden figurine with a smile. 'Well, Fritha, I thank you for your help. This little one's called "Chaser". I know you'll like her, she's the goddess of the large moon.'

Leaning on the bar of the tavern, Gabriel Beet smiled at the memory of the little girl's pleasure. Now that he had a daughter of his own, he enjoyed the idea of spreading a little kindness towards daughters in general. He felt pleased with the pleasure of a good deed done.

'You're looking satisfied with yourself, Master Beet,' grunted Tobit Mulbert as he slowly drew Gabriel's tankard of beer. The creamy head sat like a wobbly cauliflower on top of the dark ale and Gabriel wet his lips in anticipation.

'A job well done, Tobit,' said Gabriel, 'a job well done.'

The publican, not sure whether Gabriel Beet was referring to the beer or to something else, asked what he meant. 'I mean I was given a job and I performed it,' said Gabriel proudly, 'and I spread a little happiness as I did so.'

'Did you then?' Mulbert asked, wiping at a puddle of beer with his jerkin sleeve. 'And what'd that be then?'

Gabriel tilted back his head and took a draught of the bitter brew. 'Mistress Beet was worried about some her kinsfolk, and wanted to know whether they'd arrived in Gleam for they'd not come out to the Flint side,' he explained, blowing froth from his lips. Tobit Mulbert glanced at him. He was not especially interested in Mistress Beet's kinsfolk, but he knew that a show of fellowship could encourage a customer later to pass money over for a further tankard. 'And you found them then?' he asked.

'Not exactly,' he said, 'but I did have a stroke of luck.' And he told the publican about how the little girl had overheard his questions and had been able to volunteer the information he wanted. In doing so he described his wife's relations and at that point, Tobit Mulbert stiffened and looked at the woodcutter with more interest.

'Mistress Beet's kin, were they?' he asked carefully. 'What were their names then?'

Innocently, Gabriel burbled on. He told the publican the names of the travellers and all he knew of them. How Hugh Cassin was his wife's brother and was a famous musician in his own village and was passing through Gleam on his way to the valley of Lamaria to talk to the lute-makers there, how he was accompanying his niece and nephew, the children of the widow Swallow – Tobias who was on his way to the university in Aser, Tobias, the clever one who was studying to be a doctor and who would one day wear a furred cloak, Tobias who had been a wild boy but who was settling down, touch wood; and Johanna, who was going to stay with them, little Johanna, now almost a grown woman who was going to help Mistress Beet and himself now that they had a daughter of their own, just a baby mind, and who…

All of this Tobit Mulbert listened to keenly and craftily. To oil the talk he drew another foaming tankard, and yet another, and set one before Gabriel Beet and one before himself, and did not seem to notice that no coin had passed across the counter. This information would more than pay for the cost of the ale. Gabriel smiled and laughed and continued talking as Tobit Mulbert plied him with his brew and asked a question here, passed a comment there, and seemed no more than a pleasant and amiable fellow, although one with an unfortunate stoop, which gave him the appearance in the gloomy taproom of a hunched raven. All in all, though, Gabriel was most pleased to have made the journey into Gleam.

As she lay struggling for sleep in her cold narrow bed, Johanna Swallow wondered how it was that they had found themselves in this strange and dangerous situation. All of her life she had heard of the cruelties of the Markgrave of Gleam, of the injustices and mysterious disappearances, of how in Gleam you said nothing, listened to nothing, and tried your hardest not to be seen. Yet now somehow her madcap brother, cheekily blowing raspberries in the Markgrave's face, had filled himself with beer and shouted catch-me-if-you-can. For they would be caught, surely, thought Johanna. They had drawn attention to themselves, had fled from the Markgrave's watch. They would be captured, though. Like his stone and iron tower that could observe every street and courtyard, the dark eye of the Markgrave could peer into every cranny of every house, and room, and human heart. Soon his men would work out where they were sheltering and then not even these thick stone walls could save them from being dragged out to be flung before the Markgrave and forced to answer for their impudence.

Earlier she had followed the flickering yellow lantern light up stone stairs and down stone corridors and had then been shown into this small chamber. There was a bench with a straw mattress smelling of must and damp and she had been given a candlestick and a thin blanket. Apart from a clumsy chair the room was empty. She'd wondered again about the house and decided it must have been a monastery of some sort, fallen on hard times. The room had the air of a monk's cell.

Now, huddled on the mattress with her cloak and the blanket wrapped about her, Johanna thought of their journey and of her mother back in their quiet village, and of her aunt in the little house by the River Flint. She thought of the little cousin she was going to help look after. Neither woman could yet know of the danger she, Tobias, and Uncle Hugh were in, and it was best they didn't know. A sudden fear took possession of her: what if they had been recognised? Identified? If that were the case then her mother and aunt too could be in danger. The more these racing fears insinuated themselves the further away sleep seemed, and the more the cold penetrated through the flimsy blanket and long green cloak.

Stupid, stupid Tobias! She tossed on the narrow bed, her resentment building up again. Had they followed their timetable they should have now been close to Posy Beet's little cottage. But, no. Tobias must needs slake his thirst in that vile tavern, and then must needs stay to eat the landlord's foul mutton and then must continue into the evening in order to impress the assorted sots and leering tavern flies with his great learning and vocabulary. Two years in the city of Aser and he thought himself a prince of learning. He had always been proud and headstrong, a trouble to his mother and a pain to his grandfather, but he had always been tender with her and would do nothing to distress her. Now, though, he had such an arrogance he no longer cared. She feared for him, and in fearing for him she feared for herself. Tobias, what is to become of you? What is to become of us? Poor dear uncle, sweet as he is, he's of no earthly use. Not when you kick around like a wild horse.

And that strange man, their host. He was a man with an unnerving way of seeming to know your very thoughts, of seeing into your very soul. He would be able to, she knew. He could control Tobias. He would know what to do. However, far from comforting Johanna, that thought brought a sense of such foreboding her eyes opened, and she stared terrified through the darkness above her.

Sleep must have eventually found her, however, for Johanna found herself once more running through shiny cobbled streets, between dark walls and overhanging gables. She was pursued by faceless figures carrying burning brooms which they swung like broadswords around their heads spraying constellations of red and yellow sparks about the blackness. Every time Johanna turned into a street or alley to escape from the figures she would see before her another group approaching, more burning brooms, more trails of sparks, until she found herself back in the centre of the square turning round and round like a broom herself and every street and alley disgorging the shadowy figures, the burning brooms, the accusing sparks…

The dream was such a violent, rowdy thing she did not even hear the click of a heavy key locking her chamber door.

Chapter Four
SERPENT WINE

While their mysterious host was showing Johanna and Hugh Cassin to their rooms, Tobias waited in the chamber with growing anxiety, wondering whether he should have accepted at face value the man's explanation that he was putting the others to bed. Was he? Or was he simply separating them? *Splitting them up*? The idea alarmed him somewhat, as did the man's suggestion that he and Tobias had much to speak about. Eventually the man returned, closing the heavy door behind him. He did not sit down immediately, going instead to a tall wooden cabinet, opening it and peering inside, holding his lantern aloft. The unsteady light threw jagged bouncing shadows about the room, further adding to Tobias's sense of unease. Throughout this time the man remained silent, apart from breathing wheezily as he bent over. It was not until he returned to the table with a dusty jeroboam with a cork stopper that he uttered his first words.

'I have been waiting for you,' he said in his flat dispassionate voice.

This seemed quite wrong to Tobias. He wanted to say, lightly, 'No – *I*'ve been waiting for *you*,' but he felt constrained and unable to be flippant in the sombre gloom of the room. Instead, he simply nodded, looking at the man, wondering what he had meant. He found himself being looked at in return. Again the eyes seemed to know all there was to know about him, all there could possibly be to know about him, and Tobias felt suddenly exposed, cold.

The man put the huge bottle on the table, then went back to the cabinet and returned with two pewter goblets. 'We will take some wine,' he announced.

Tobias glanced idly at the bottle. It was large and rounded at the bottom, with a fine layer of dust concealing its contents and a blackened cork in the top. The man watched him. In the candlelight the bottle seemed full of a deep honey-coloured liquid, but through the dusty glass Tobias could make out something else within, some solid something which seemed coiled about in the bottom. The man reached out and rubbed at the glass, removing the layers of dust, then turned the jeroboam towards Tobias and the object came into focus. It was a snake, wrapped around itself in the bottom of the bottle, its pale body so unnaturally whitened by the alcohol that it looked albino.

'It is serpent wine,' said his host.

Tobias nodded, unable to speak. He felt a spasm of nausea. The scales on the white body were slightly enlarged by the glass and perfectly formed, their tessellations beautifully real on the ghostly bleached body. The head was lifted, the eyes white and blind, but the jaws open, with the fangs in the striking position. The man said nothing, examining him, gauging his reaction. Finally he said, 'My name is Manfred Bufo.'

Tobias inclined his head and told the man his name. 'We're from Blackfell,' he added. And he explained about Johanna and Hugh Cassin.

'You are, I take it, from your cloak, a student?'

Tobias nodded. 'At Aser. The university there. I'm on my way back.'

'Of medicine?'

It was a reasonable assumption. Aser was an ancient university, most famous for its faculty of medicine.

'I'm studying under Master Portcullis.'

For the first time his host showed some emotion: he gave a low chuckle. 'Jonah Portcullis? Nothing more than a common leech!'

'You know him?' asked Tobias. He wasn't accustomed to hearing the august master of the college spoken of in such familiar and unflattering terms. At the same time, Tobias felt a stirring of fellow-feeling. He privately felt that the good Doctor Portcullis was a pompous old fool and he yearned one day to be able to prick the bloated bladder of his pomposity.

'I know him,' said Manfred Bufo, but did not explain. Instead he grasped the cork and pulled it out, then lifted the jeroboam, gripping it at the neck with one hand and steadying it on the base with the other. Then he tilted it carefully above each goblet in turn. Tobias watched, fascinated, as the golden liquid trickled into the goblets and the bleached snake slid slowly down the bottle towards the neck. He stared horrified at its open jaw, the two bone-white fangs curved like tiny scimitars. Manfred Bufo carefully placed the bottle back down on the table, and lifted up his goblet in salutation.

'I am pleased you have come to me, Tobias Swallow of Aser. Let me raise a toast to this meeting.'

This was very formal. In turn, Tobias held his goblet up and stared over its brim at the dark eyes of the man watching him. Who would drink first? Tobias maintained his steady gaze, refusing to let his eyes glance back at the jeroboam and its pickled serpent. What was it? A viper? An adder? An asp? It was as long as a man's arm and thick as an infant's wrist. Had it been milked of its venom before it had been drenched in the wine, or had its venom slowly leached out, like its colour, to become part of the golden liquor? The pause became unbearable, and Tobias suddenly realised that this was a test. A test of his nerve, or his foolhardiness, he was not sure which. Manfred Bufo did not help him. He merely stared expressionlessly over the brim of the glass, waiting for the younger man to drink.

Finally, Tobias did put the goblet to his lips, and Manfred Bufo echoed his movement. It was a mirror game. He could never be sure who, in fact, took the first sip, but as soon as he was certain Bufo was also about to take a draught of the wine, Tobias did the same.

The liquor was cold at first, with an unusual bittersweet flavour, like wild gooseberries painted with honey, and with a smoky after-taste. However, soon after it began to trickle down his throat, a burning warmth took over every other sensation and Tobias all but coughed with the fiery heat of it. Poison? But Manfred Bufo had taken a deeper draught and was already taking another. Was he inured to it? Tobias had heard of poisoners who had developed a resistance to their poisons in order to allay the fears of their victims. Now he did glance back at the bottle and at the drawn-back fangs of the grimacing snake. Suddenly it seemed to bear an expression of frozen mockery.

Manfred Bufo spoke: 'Drink up,' he said. 'You are right to be cautious. I respect that. But, believe me, Tobias Swallow, this wine is no more dangerous than any wine in the wrong mouth.'

Tobias drank again. The gooseberries. The honey. The woodland smoke and then the magical fire. He had never drunk such a spirit. None of the taverns of Aser could have boasted of such a wine. He could feel the golden fire twisting and twining around his being like an insinuating serpent, searching out his extremities, flushing his face and dampening his brow.

'It is a very special wine,' murmured Manfred Bufo.

Tobias nodded again, but more confidently, having been emboldened by the drink. 'You said you'd been waiting for me?' he asked.

The scholar stared at him carefully. 'I think you are the one,' he explained. 'Although one can never be quite sure. Mistakes are possible, but the signs are there.'

Tobias had no idea what the man meant. Manfred Bufo was strange and vaguely unnerving with his deep blue skullcap and his shock of white hair, with his dark staring eyes and expressionless voice. A magician? A magus? Certainly he had power of some sort.

'Come,' said Manfred Bufo, standing up. 'I want to show you something of the House of the Stone Toad. As a medical student there are things which should interest you…'

Tobias Swallow was twenty years old. The Swallows of Blackfell were an ancient family fallen on rather hard times. They were the descendants of landowners and minor nobility reduced to the ranks of small, albeit fiercely independent, farmers. Tobias's grandfather still carried himself with pride as if he were the lord of the manor, rejoicing in his grandson's spirit and the quiet intelligence and great beauty of his granddaughter. His only son, Tobias's father, had been killed in a riding accident, and the young widow Swallow had been left to raise the two children as best she could.

Hugh Cassin had helped in his own way, but Hugh was ever a gentle dreamer, his head filled with songs and stories for which he had earned a local reputation. It was Tobias's grandfather, old Titus Swallow, who had tried to direct the course of the family stream. It was he who had seen in Tobias's wildness a strength, a strength that could possibly restore the family's fading fortunes; and when Tobias's teachers had reported that the boy, despite his madcap ways, had wit and a love of learning, had seen that the way to greatness could lie in Tobias becoming a famous scholar and master. Accordingly the boy had been sent to the grammar school at Aser, and thence to the university to study under the famous Master Portcullis.

All the same, old Titus Swallow had often had misgivings. There was a strain in Tobias that troubled him. It came he suspected from the Cassin line. They were ever a-dream, strange folk with a suggestion of magic and necromancy, and a liking for the music of the night. So far, however, Tobias had done well. He had a quick and effortless mastery of his subjects, great charm and an easy-going nature. It was this charm that had allowed him to escape serious trouble after the many misadventures and wild escapades he could not help but get involved in. He'd rapidly earned a reputation as a drinker, a frequenter of taverns and ill houses, and when full of ale would bluster and find himself in arguments and, occasionally, fights. He was given to practical jokes and tomfoolery, and, his imagination let loose by liquor, he had caused many of his teachers embarrassment and humiliation.

When accused, however, he had the ability to get his teachers to laugh at his follies and smile at their own embarrassment. He could, too, get away with crazy excesses which would have had lesser students expelled, by the flattery his teachers felt when he learnt their lessons so thoroughly and so well. It seemed Tobias had a charmed life. *When he settles down*, his teachers would murmur, and Master Portcullis would nod in agreement. *When he settles down* Master Swallow's brilliance will shine, he will end up as an ornament to the university, a light to attract learning and scholarship from cities and towns from near and far. *When he settles down…*

How much of this Manfred Bufo knew or was able to guess could not be told. Perhaps there was something in the young man's manner. Some spark that indicated recklessness tempered by intelligence. Whatever, Bufo's keen eyes had discovered something and, with a certainty born of instinct, had acted on it.

Serpent wine. The spirit of the serpent or the serpent in the spirit. Tobias could not be sure which of these it was which had heated his blood to a fever of excitement and anticipation. He could still feel the sinuous liquid twisting and writhing, declaring its burning presence.

As Manfred Bufo lifted the lantern that Tobias was following down a dark corridor, his wide sleeve fell down to reveal a strange tattoo on his lower arm. A crouching toad, yellow and bulbous with large knobbed eyes in a hunched head on top of which was a scarlet asterisk denoting the spot, Tobias knew, where the toadstone could be found. It was the same device as that carved in bas-relief on the porch of the building, but whereas that stone toad was grey and weathered to vagueness, this tattooed toad was brilliantly coloured and sharply defined.

'I am so used to this house,' murmured Bufo, 'I wouldn't ordinarily bother with a lantern. I have become something of a creature of the darkness, you might say.'

Tobias mumbled some response. Somehow Manfred Bufo had made being a creature of the darkness sound like a most desirable thing to be.

'When I was first admitted to the order,' the old scholar explained, 'there were quite a number of us in the house. Some died. Some were called elsewhere – to other houses, you know. There are few of us here today.' He did not elaborate.

'A quiet existence,' observed Tobias, and Bufo gave a short humourless laugh.

At this point Bufo stopped, opened a door, and stepped aside for Tobias to enter. 'This is the House's library,' he explained. He lit a number of lanterns fixed to the walls and then stood back to see Tobias's reaction.

Of all the rooms in the house, this was by far the largest of any Tobias had seen. Fluted arches high above him supported a ceiling that disappeared into darkness, and narrow oriel windows looked out over where a black sea would be. The walls were lined with shelves, and the shelves were packed with volumes. Calf-bound. Expensive vellum. Heavy. Eagerly Tobias moved forward to examine the gilt-lettered titles. Asplenius. Oxalides. Dr Cabra of Flagen. Ancient texts by the masters of medicine, books on anatomy, alchemy, pharmacopoeias, herbals and mystic lore, cabalistic texts and books on the occult. Shelves upon shelves of them. Tobias turned to his host in awe.

'I had no idea such a library existed in Gleam!'

Manfred Bufo inclined his head modestly.

'This is better…' began Tobias. 'Far better,' he added expansively, 'than the library in my university.' He turned back to the shelves, scanning the rows of books with growing astonishment. 'But why?' he asked. Once again the nature of the house eluded him. He had begun to think it might have been a religious order of some sort fallen on hard times. The so-called 'Brotherhood'. Now it seemed his first impression had been correct. It must be some kind of House of Learning. But with no students? And a staff of one?

'Naturally,' replied Bufo simply, 'the Brotherhood has need of knowledge.'

The room seem suffused in an amber glow from the lamps on the wall brackets, a glow that reflected off the dark polished wood of the refectory tables and lecterns. It shimmered with an atmosphere of parchment and beeswax and learning, a learning as deep and mysterious as the resinous light.

'Wonderful,' breathed Tobias.

He turned, aware that Manfred Bufo's eyes were studying him carefully, aware that there was a more profound reason for his showing him this room. For a full second the two men stared at each other. Nothing was said but in that time an understanding passed between them. Finally, Bufo nodded. 'I am inclining to the opinion that you are the one,' he said drily. 'And you know,' he added. 'We in the Brotherhood are students of medicine too, and I venture to suggest that you will learn far more with us than with a mountebank and charlatan like Master Jonah Portcullis.'

Tobias did not respond. He turned back to the shelves. The Masters of Egon's *Book of the Dead*. Azimuth the Elder. The *Hierographia Morticia*. The Crimson *Cabbala* of Stent. He knew what Bufo was suggesting and was excited. He turned again to the old man whose blue robe and skullcap were almost black in the golden light, and a sudden fancy overtook him: the man in the golden light; the white snake in the golden wine. There was a sudden writhing again within him and Tobias, in the midst of his excitement, felt a stabbing fear.

In his small cell Hugh Cassin had slept restlessly. At some stage a wild screeching woke him up and he lay rigidly awake. At first he thought it was an angry shout from the night watch, demanding he give himself up, but then the screech came again and he realised it was an owl. A scream of triumph, he guessed. Already high on a black branch the warm flesh of some small creature was being torn apart.

He had not done well, thought Hugh miserably. Not at all well. His sister, Joan, would be angry with him, justifiably so, for not being able to better protect his niece and nephew. And what of his other sister? Posy Beet would be expecting them and would be worried. She had problems enough of her own with that good-for-nothing whittler and tavern fly she'd married without having to grow grey hair because her own family were carousing in taverns and had fled from the watch. Felons, the old man had said. Felons... He should never have allowed Tobias to persuade him into that low taproom, and once there he should have insisted on their keeping themselves to themselves. But Tobias loved to debate. And all that talk of the Maiden. All that sailing so close to the wind of treason and sedition. Why not throw torches into kegs of gunpowder? Fire arrows into the fair? And Gleam so full of spies and informers.

Hugh groaned with the stupidity of it. And then that insane struggle with the burning broom, attracting the attention of the watch, and then running away from them. That made it worse. They'd be bound to be recognised, too. Strangers. Three of them. How could they now walk through the streets of Gleam in daylight? Hugh turned over and groaned again. The folly. The folly...

The members of the watch would be looking for them. The gatehouses would have been alerted. How could they hope to get on to the other side of those great grey city walls?

This should have been so uncomplicated. A walk to Gleam to accompany his niece, a visit to his sister, seeing Tobias on to the barque which would sail him back to Aser, and then the four-day walk to Lamaria, where his old friend, the master-craftsman Abel Larch, was building him a new lute. Hugh loved the visits he made to Lamaria. The narrow valley with its dancing streams, the birch woods and green meadows, the white goats with bells about their necks. He loved sitting in Abel's workshop with its smells of oil and fragrant shavings, the light glinting off the sharply honed tools as the old man carefully thumbed in the marvellous inlays of goat horn. Would he ever see the new lute, run his fingers over its strings, hear the ripple of its arpeggios?

But, most of all on his visits to Lamaria, Hugh loved to sit near Abel's dark-haired daughter, Alissa. He loved to hear her soft voice with its oddly different accent, her laugh which came easily and often, and he loved it especially when she provided a sweet harmony whenever he sang one of the old airs to the rippling music of his lute. Their voices sounded well together, Abel often told him. And when he told him this he'd often wink and nod and smile, but Hugh was shy and conscious of his own silver hair and white beard and pretended not to understand.

And now everything was complicated. They were trapped and in trouble in this grim city. The most likely end to their cursed journey would be a dungeon deep within the citadel of Gleam, and God knew what unspeakable horrors beforehand.

'Could I ask what your feelings were as you were running from the watch?' asked Bufo.

They had returned to the small chamber. The jeroboam of serpent wine sat on the table as they had left it, the serpent within still baring its frozen fangs.

Tobias considered the question carefully: Bufo's manner allowed for nothing less than careful consideration. He allowed himself to recall in detail those earlier events from the clatter of the rising portcullis to the first sounds of pursuit, the wildly flashing lanterns, and the gleam of helmets, breastplates and pikes.

He had felt alarm, and then a rush of guilt as he'd realised the danger he had brought upon Johanna and Hugh Cassin, a guilt made deeper by Johanna's distress and her look of helpless fury at his stupidity. Then he remembered his lurching chase after the others, his mind still fuddled by the ale and empty of everything except the need to get away. He glanced up at the old man. 'At first I felt fright,' he said, 'and then I felt a wave of foolishness at my bringing this trouble on the heads of my sister and uncle.'

Bufo nodded. 'But,' he insisted, 'as the pursuit continued?'

Tobias closed his eyes to recall those fevered minutes.

'Go back!' whispered Bufo sharply. 'Go there!'

All at once Tobias was back in the lane and stumbling in a half-run half-gallop on to the esplanade that ran alongside the sea wall. Beyond was the dark crashing sea. He heard its gravelly hiss and roar and caught the salt-cold wind in his nostrils. Just ahead of him were the fleeing figures of Hugh, already lagging a little and beginning to be gripped by stitch, and Johanna who had had a head start. Over his shoulder he could just make out the jumping lights and he could hear the clatter of iron-nailed boots and the muffled shouts of the guard. So many guards, and they were so few. A sense of their impotence overwhelmed him and he felt a rising resentment that he, Tobias Swallow, should be forced to run in fear like some panicky rabbit before a pack of yelping hounds. Tobias Swallow of Blackfell, and of the Academy of Master Portcullis of Aser, trying to scurry out of harm's way like some low-life. Somehow things had been reversed. The lowlife were doing the pursuing – the oafs and violent clod-poles who had taken the Markgrave's miserable shilling. The injustice of this offended him and, gasping with remembered resentment, Tobias suddenly realised precisely what he had been feeling at that moment.

'I felt anger,' he said.

'Anger?'

'Rage, I suppose.'

Bufo nodded. 'And what exactly did you want to do?'

Tobias thought again, recalling his impotent fury.

'I wanted to destroy them,' he said slowly.

Once more Bufo nodded. 'Very good,' he said drily. 'I had hoped as much.

When Johanna awoke, a watery light filtered through the high window of her tiny cell. The straw palliasse on which she had been lying was hard and prickly and, almost gratefully, she rolled over it and swung her feet onto the floor. The night had been long and her sleep had been restless, long periods of wakefulness punctuated by short violent dreams. And she had been cold. There had only been a thin bolster and a thinner rug of what may have been dog-hair furnishing the bed. Only this and her long cloak had been her defence against the numbing cold of the stone walls and flagstones of her cell-like chamber. Her cloak she now drew tightly around her as she crouched on the edge of the cot, her mind still tumbling with the events of the night before. She could not tell what hour it was, but there was daylight of a sort so it must have passed eight. She stood up. She must find Tobias and her uncle. It was important that they not delay any longer. Aunt Posy Beet would be worried.

Again, she felt a surging bitterness towards her rash and irresponsible brother. If it weren't for Tobias they would now be at Creekside. There would be a hot pot bubbling on the stove and pitchers of warm milk. Instead, they had all but been arrested by the evil Markgrave's watch and been compelled to spend the night in this creeping strange and dark house. Grateful as she was to its odd proprietor, she didn't trust him and longed to be gone, longed to be out of the house's gloomy confines, beyond Gleam's dark walls and on their way along the high road to Creekside.

She quickly crossed to the heavily timbered door and twisted at the iron door handle. The door did not move, and Johanna quickly realised that she had, sometime during the night, been locked in. At first, this filled her with some alarm. Then she stepped back, frustrated and angry. 'Hey!' she shouted. 'Hey! Let me out!'

Taking a deep breath, she stepped forward again and began pounding at the door.

The noise she was making woke Hugh Cassin who had been given a chamber on the other side of the narrow corridor.

'Johanna?' he called.

'I'm locked in!'

'Wait a bit. I'm coming!'

Hugh rolled off his bed and stumbled to his feet. Johanna waited until she heard the rattling and shaking of his door.

'Uncle?'

'I can't. I'm locked in as well.'

Through her door, Johanna then heard Hugh's muffled cries and angry banging. She waited for some moments, then joined in the cries and once again began to pound at her own door. For a long time there seemed to be absolutely no response. From time to time she would stop and listen intently, then she would begin again. Hugh too would stop and start, listen and shout. Just when she thought they were to be ignored completely and with ever more light shafting through the narrow window, Johanna heard a key turning in the door. It came as something of a surprise as she had certainly not heard any footsteps. She stepped back as the door swung open, prepared to meet the old man who had let them in.

Instead a tall figure stood before her, a man who could have been anything between thirty and sixty, so few markers of age were on his face. Johanna had been about to remonstrate angrily about having been locked in, but something about the man's grave manner prevented her. Instead she acknowledged his presence with a terse small nod and said, 'Who are you?'

The man ignored the question. 'I will open the door for your companion, my lady, and then conduct you to your breakfast,' he said. Then he turned and selecting a key from a jingling ring he opened the door immediately opposite. The door swung inwards, and there stood Hugh Cassin.

Hugh gave a quick relieved glance at Johanna then hurried to her side. Their jailer seemed completely incurious. Without expression he murmured, 'Follow me,' and turned on his heel.

Who is he? Johanna asked herself as she followed his long strides. He was wearing a dark cloak made even darker in the gloomy passage. They left the corridor and entered a small gallery and the man ushered them in to a large chamber opening on to it. This seemed to be some sort of refectory although it was deserted. There were four long tables with forms on either side.

'Sit down,' said the man.

Johanna looked around. The room was simply furnished, monastic, she imagined. Presumably this was where they were to be served breakfast.

But where was Tobias? She remembered the previous night that Tobias had not been escorted to bed as she and her uncle had. A pang of anxiety caused her to forget her caution and demand of their escort, 'Where is my brother?'

The man turned to her and raised his eyebrows as if perplexed by the question. 'Your brother, my lady?'

Johanna felt a growing apprehension. Why had they been separated? Why had she and her uncle been locked in their rooms? Why was this strange silent figure feigning, she was sure he was feigning, such ignorance? She quickly looked at Hugh. He, too, was looking at the man, worry lining his face.

'My brother, Tobias Swallow. Tobias Swallow of Blackfell.'

The man shrugged. 'I have no idea, my lady. If you have a brother,' and he seemed to imply there was some doubt about the matter, 'he may be with the Master. However, I have not been informed.'

Johanna bit her lip with vexation. This was an annoying and frustrating complication.

'Sit down,' their dark escort repeated. 'I will go and arrange some food for you.' Then without either another word or another glance he turned and left them, pulling the door shut behind him.

Johanna waited for a moment or two and then slipped towards the door, twisted the handle and pushed. This time, however, the door opened. She shook her head and pulled the door shut once more. 'At least we're not locked in again, Uncle,' she said.

Hugh looked at her. 'What do we do?' he asked.

'I don't know,' Johanna said. 'Perhaps Master Grim really doesn't know anything about Tobias. Perhaps he'll go and find out.'

Hugh nodded, but he did not feel that it was very likely.

'It's so annoying,' said Johanna. 'Aunt Posy Beet will be worrying. We should be on our way, but we can't go without Tobias.'

'Of course not,' said Hugh. 'But he'll be somewhere. No doubt he'll...'

'I'm going to find that old man and ask him what's happening.'

'Yes,' said Hugh. 'Of course, of course. But let's not be too hasty, my dear. Remember, it was good of him to offer us shelter last night. And it was awkward for him. The watch, you know.'

Johanna looked about her and shivered a little. 'That's very true, Uncle. But I'm just beginning to wonder whether this house was the best house to seek shelter in.' She turned to him. 'You know what they say about frying pans and fires.'

'True,' said Hugh quietly. 'But don't forget, we had no choice.'

'I know that. I know that,' said Johanna. 'All the same, this place does not feel right to me. There's something about it.'

Hugh nodded.

Johanna gave him a quick smile. 'In fact, Uncle, if it weren't for your being here, I think I'd be feeling a little frightened.'

Hugh smiled in return and nodded. He felt exactly the same. Without Johanna he would have been feeling most fearful.

Chapter Five
DELAY

After leaving the two guests, Brother Sheldrake, for that was their grim escort's name, made his way across the gallery to a large kitchen across the way. The room was warm from the heat of a large iron wood stove and filled with an aromatic steam mingled with a nutty yeasty fragrance of freshly baked bread.

'I have taken the maid and the musician to the refectory, Brother Gull,' he announced to a tall and somewhat cadaverous older man who was bent over the stove as he sniffed at a steaming tureen of gruel. 'Has the Master given any further instructions?'

The old man did not even glance over his shoulder. 'He has, Brother. He has…'

Brother Sheldrake waited patiently. Brother Gull was ever deliberate, ponderous, mysterious even, especially when he had something of importance to impart. And an instruction from the Master was important. A faint smile came to Brother Sheldrake's face as Brother Gull delayed any announcement still further by dipping into the tureen with a large copper spoon and bringing it forth to drip over the bench. This instruction must be particularly serious.

'You are to take them their breakfast. Two bowls of this excellent potage.'

Brother Sheldrake nodded. He understood this already, but from Brother Gull's manner there was surely more. However, whatever it was would have to wait, for at that point an old woman entered the kitchen from an anteroom pantry. She was carrying a wooden tray with two empty bowls.

'The bowls, Brother,' she said to Gull, giving Brother Sheldrake a stiff little nod as she saw him standing there.

'Thank you. Place them there.'

After the tray had been laid down on the bench near the stove, Brother

Gull carefully spooned gruel from the tureen to the bowls. Despite his care, however, a slight tremor at his wrist meant that much of the liquid went elsewhere: the tray, the bench, the well-swept flagstones. The old lady pursed her lips with resentment but said not a word. Neither did Sheldrake.

At length the bowls each held a generous serving and the old man nodded. Brother Sheldrake, eyebrows lifted in some surprise, stepped forward.

A quivering finger stopped him. 'Wait!'

Brother Sheldrake nodded. Gull, the dramatist, had waited for his moment.

'The Master did think it would be a good idea if our guests enjoyed a rather protracted sleep after their repast.'

At that, he reached into his cloak and from a pocket he withdrew a small phial of blue glass. He pulled off the cork stopper and emptied several drops of a colourless liquid into each bowl. 'I believe that should suffice. Thank you, Brother Sheldrake. You may now take our guests their meals.'

Tobias felt a great weariness. He had no idea of the hour. The small chamber was heavily curtained and the flickering light from the oil lamp caused the shadows to dance about erratically. Before him on the table sat the jeroboam and its whitened prisoner, the frozen snake, and behind these sat the figure of Manfred Bufo, his eyes not the least weary but sharp and attentive, glittering in the gloom.

'You would have power,' he murmured.

It was not a question. It was not even a suggestion. It was simply a statement of scientific observation.

Tobias nodded.

'There will, of course, be a price.'

Again Tobias nodded.

Since their return to this small chamber they had talked long and deeply. Or rather, Tobias had talked. Bufo had spoken scarcely at all; a comment here, a suggestion there, but all the while in complete control, as a master-sailor, merely by slightly adjusting the tiller this way, can navigate with ease through perilous seas. Tobias had found himself telling the old man his life's story and the story of his family: the once-powerful but still fiercely proud Swallows, and the ever-dreamy Cassins with that suggestion of ancient magic in their bones. This despite the fact that the only magic evident today was in the magic wrought by his uncle when he charmed listeners with the beauty of his music. Tobias had told Bufo how his father had been killed while hunting, and how his grandfather, old Titus, had placed a hand on his shoulder and told him it would now be his task to restore the family's fortune and reputation, not just in Blackfell but throughout the hills and valleys of all the land, even across the seas as far as Aser and beyond.

'And?'

There had been an edge of mockery in the unasked question, and Tobias's eyes had flashed with annoyance. 'I will be a physician,' he'd said. 'I will wear a black gown. They think I show promise in Aser.'

'You will be a common leech,' Bufo had observed mildly. 'A bone setter and a dispenser of herbs. But you could be more. Much, much more...'

Tobias had fallen silent. As much as he resented Bufo's demeaning judgment, he was beginning to feel there might be some justification in it, and that the man could provide him with something far beyond the possibilities offered by the University at Aser. He remembered his furious sense of impotence as Twyll's thugs chased him along the lanes of Gleam. Not even a doctor's long black gown would have prevented that.

'You will need courage,' said Bufo after a long silence.

Roused by the comment, Tobias raised his drooping head, flushing with unspoken indignation. He had courage. He knew that. He was always the daring one, the one who cocked his snoot at authority whether his mother's, his teachers' or even that of the venerable Master Portcullis himself.

Manfred Bufo stood up and came around to Tobias's side of the table. Tobias glanced up at him, but Bufo neither looked at him nor made any attempt to sit down. Instead he stood impassively, staring at the jeroboam.

Within it, the bleached snake stood from its coils staring with frozen anger. Its mouth was unhinged as widely as possible and its venomous fangs curved long and sharp with a deadly promise it could never deliver. Tobias was glad of it. Shuddering at the grotesque horror of the serpent's mock challenge, he looked away.

'Look at the snake!' Bufo's voice was sharp, insistent.

Tobias shrugged and obeyed. It was both horrifying and fascinating. He felt that vertiginous feeling he had experienced occasionally at the very edge of some precipitous cliff, that empty-stomach feeling, that wild temptation to jump and be done with it, and the accompanying fear that some madness might impel him to give in to the temptation.

'Look!'

Suddenly, Tobias felt a sickening jolt, a jolt causing the hair to prickle on the back of his head and his fists to clench, his nails squeezing into his suddenly sweating palms. The snake had moved. Almost certainly. He would swear to it. The head had shifted sideways and back again. The narrow lines of the eyes had widened and closed again.

Bufo hadn't moved. He was staring at the snake intently, eyes not deviating for a second.

Tobias's throat was dry. Surely he must have imagined it. They had drunk that wine. The snake was dead. Pickled. He licked his lips nervously. And then, as if in a mocking response, the snake's long black thread of a tongue slipped quickly out of its mouth and slithered equally quickly back. Tobias gasped in horror as the unmistakable inverted Y of the tongue emerged once again. And then, as if waking from the grip of a nightmare, the snake shook its head quite undeniably and thrust itself upwards and through the wide neck of the uncorked jeroboam until it swayed malevolently before them in the open air, the eyes narrowed in hate, the tongue flicking hypnotically in and out of the now closed mouth.

'Oh, my god,' whispered Tobias. 'How…'

In one long movement the snake then gathered itself and flowed out of the bottle and on to the table. Then it rose out of itself again and arched before them, ghostly white, head rearing backwards and ready to strike, the sibilant menace of its faint hissing suddenly loud in the charged silence of the chamber.

'No,' moaned Tobias. 'It…'

'Look at it!' whispered Bufo sharply.

Tobias had no choice. It was clear that the snake had selected him as its victim. He was transfixed, mesmerised by the swaying head, the glittering eyes and the slithering tongue. At any moment, he knew, the strike would come and he would have to jump, but he knew he couldn't, wouldn't.

And then the strike came. Instinct won and Tobias leapt back with an involuntary gasp of terror. He knew it was a paltry and ineffective defence against the inevitable bite and injection of venom. In jumping he must have closed his eyes and when he opened them he found Bufo must have also leapt for he was now some feet away. More astonishing, however, Bufo was gripping the snake securely just below the head. The serpent's mouth was stretched wide open, fangs bared. Tobias noted with a sickening certainty that they were dripping milky white drops of venom.

Tobias closed his eyes yet again and opened them once more.

Bufo stood there staring at him. The snake's long tail – and Tobias now realised that the snake was at least as long as Bufo was tall – was threshing from side to side like a furious whip.

'How did you do that?' Tobias gasped, nauseous with relief.

'I have the power,' said Bufo matter-of-factly.

'Put it back,' muttered Tobias. 'Put it back in the bottle.'

For a long moment the two men gazed at each other. Bufo appeared to be considering Tobias's request. 'I think,' he murmured at length, 'I'd prefer you to do that.'

And at that he drew his arm back and flung the whipping snake at Tobias who, in the shock of it, instinctively caught the snake by the neck, and found himself in the position of Bufo only moments before. The snake was now considerably angry. Its head writhed and thrashed about as it tried to find an angle from which to sink its fangs into Tobias's flesh. Its tail wriggled and swung. The air was filled with a vicious hissing.

Tobias looked helplessly at the grimly smiling Bufo. 'What can I do?' he demanded, the rising pitch of his voice querulous with fear.

'Put it back in the bottle,' said Bufo simply.

Tobias didn't respond. He couldn't even look at Bufo, so intent was he on trying to avoid the murderous designs of the serpent. The snake was ivory white, the tessellations of its skin seeming to have been etched with a fine steel tool, but its eyes were black and glittering and the flicking tongue was black too with a suggestion of fiery red. Tobias's arm was outstretched so that the tail, if it were prehensile, couldn't grip anything. Beyond him sat the jeroboam squat and waiting. The neck was short and the opening looked suddenly far too narrow for the unhinged head. Tobias ached to lurch towards the bottle but dared not. Instead he tried to will the snake to calm. Beneath his grip he could sense the firm flesh, the architecture of bones. The skin, despite its long tenure in the golden wine, was dry and surprisingly warm.

Tobias's terror subsided somewhat as he realised that the snake was for the moment as helpless as he was. His grip happened to be strategically placed so that there was no way the snake could attack with his fangs, and Tobias's reach was preventing the tail from gaining purchase. He glanced quickly at Bufo, who was watching him impassively. This, he realised, was another test. However, it seemed a stalemate. As helpless as the snake was, a moment's inattention, a momentary relaxation of the grip and the snake could strike. The snake appeared to realise this as well. Gradually, the wild thrashing slowed, then stopped altogether. The strike position of the fangs was abandoned and the slithery tongue began to flicker in and out again. The snake's eyes, however, never left Tobias, never lost their intense hatred.

Tobias waited. He did not allow his grip to change. Slowly, he began to feel he was gaining ascendancy. He inched closer to the table. The jeroboam sat there. The infuriatingly tiny bottle-mouth waited. How could the snake possibly be returned to the bottle?

Eventually, Tobias was close enough to the bottle. He bent his knees and imperceptibly lowered himself. The snake's body hung almost limply, twitching only occasionally. The tongue slithered swiftly in and out. The hissing had stopped.

Tobias waited. He could feel the cold as the sweat on his forehead evaporated. There would only be one chance. He knew that. There could be no mistake. No second opportunity. By now the neck of the bottle and the neck of the snake were almost side by side. As long as the snake's mouth was closed there might be a chance he could contrive a way to get the head into the neck of the bottle. It would be like trying to fit a living and reluctant key into a resistant lock. He would have to move more quickly than the snake's reflexes could respond. He would have to invert the body and thrust, squeezing the head into the neck of the bottle before the snake could realise what was happening. Impossible. He waited patiently. The bones beneath the snake's flesh were firm. The eyes glittered with hate. The tongue flickered.

Tobias forced himself to calm. If he were calm, surely the serpent would sense this, and become calmer as well. Tobias slowed his breathing. He breathed in deeply and slowly, evenly exhaled. Deeper. Slower. His grip, however, he kept steady and unrelenting. The light flickered. The shadows moved about. The eye of the snake glittered.

When Tobias eventually moved, he moved with such swiftness he almost surprised himself. He suddenly swung the snake upside down and thrust the head into the bottle. The long tail immediately lashed and slashed left and right, but Tobias did not hesitate. Furiously, hand over had, as if threading a thick and angry writhing thread through the eye of an impossibly large needle, he forced the snake's body back into the jeroboam. The snake thrashed around in the wine, stirring up the lees so that the liquid became cloudy, swampy.

Blindly, Tobias continued to feed the ivory body through the neck until there was only the tip of the tail remaining. He freed one hand and reached for the cork stopper and used it to tamp the last of the snake down and then, with a liberating sense of success, he pressed the cork home. He found himself panting once more as he leaned over, his arms rigid on the table, his shoulders shaking with relief.

'Oh, god,' he muttered. 'Oh my dear god.'

Finally, he felt sufficiently recovered to turn and face Manfred Bufo, who had not said a word throughout the entire operation. If he were expecting praise, or at least a small smile of commendation, he was to be disappointed. Bufo stood there, quite expressionless.

'Well?' demanded Tobias.

'I beg your pardon?' said Bufo.

'You see, I did it. I did do it,' said Tobias, more in wonderment than pride.

'What did you do?' asked Bufo.

Tobias looked at him in astonishment. 'I put the snake back in the bottle. You saw me,' he said.

'Did you?' asked Bufo innocently. 'Did you? Look at the bottle.'

Confused, Tobias wheeled around to gaze at the jeroboam. What game was the man playing now? Had he let the snake out of the bottle again? Was the nightmare to be repeated? To his amazement what he saw was stranger than any nightmare. Once again, the snake rose through the clear golden liquid from its coiled tail. Its neck was drawn back and its mouth was open, fangs bared, in the frozen act of striking. It was in the exact pose it had been when they returned to the room.

'You see,' said Bufo. 'Clearly, the snake never left the bottle. How then could you have put it back in?'

Tobias looked wildly between the bottle and the old man.

'How did you do that?' he whispered.

'You will not learn such things from Master Mountebank Portcullis,' said Manfred Bufo.

Tobias shook his head slowly. Indeed not. He had held the snake in his own hands as it writhed and twisted. He had seen its arching back, its bared venomous fangs, heard its angry hissing. He had felt the structure of its bones, its soft but firm skin.

'But how?'

'I could not tell you,' said Bufo. 'It is for you to learn. Suffice it to say that the snake is an agent of death. But we are masters of death and it must needs forever be our servant.'

Tobias was not quite sure he understood what the old man meant. He was not, at that moment, sure of anything. His mind was still in troubled disarray as he turned back to the frozen white snake in the bottle. Its fangs seemed bared in a mocking and grotesque silent laugh.

'I think,' said Bufo, 'it is time for us to partake of a little more wine. And then, perhaps, you should have some sleep. We will, of course, talk of these things later.'

Brother Sheldrake lay Johanna's limp body down upon the cot in the chamber he had led her from just an hour or so previously.

'Sleep, maiden,' he whispered. 'There are things in this house 'twere best you did not know about. The Master has business with your brother and it could take some time. 'Twere best you spent that time dreaming.'

He drew the meagre blanket up over Johanna's long green cloak. Her long eyelashes did not so much as flutter; her breath was deep and even. Brother Sheldrake straightened and quietly left the room, drawing the large door closed behind him. Taking a heavy key from the ring at his belt, he locked the door and returned down the corridor to collect the unconscious Hugh Cassin, still slumped over the table in the refectory.

Despite his great weariness, Tobias's whirling mind would not allow him to sleep. He and Manfred Bufo had shared another goblet of the fiery serpent wine, and then Bufo had excused himself suggesting that the young man should take the opportunity for some rest. It had been a long and disconcerting night. Now stretched out on a form in the small chamber, Tobias relived the sequence of strange and shattering events he had witnessed and experienced. Somehow, the solid earth he had thought he had been standing on had turned to jelly. He realised now that his grandiose schemes of returning to Blackfell as a black-cloaked physician were not grandiose at all. Now they seemed paltry things. Instead, he had been given a glimpse of something far more powerful, compelling. Here was knowledge of things deeper and darker than anything the University at Aser could offer. This House had a library beyond anything he had seen before. More significantly, this House seemed to have keys to the mysteries of existence itself. What had the old man said? 'Death is our servant.'

Masters of Death. What could you do, Tobias marvelled, if you could transcend death? If you could command death the way Bufo miraculously, frighteningly commanded the dead serpent to do his bidding? For a short and horrifying time the serpent had lived again. It had been real, undeniably, palpably real. Tobias had touched it, gripped its writhing body, heard its hiss of hatred and rage, and he had conquered it. That was something. But nothing to what Bufo had done, Bufo who had conjured the snake to live. How had he done that? To Bufo himself it had seemed a little thing. What else could he do?

Bufo understood him. Bufo understood how humiliated he had been by having to run from the oafish helots of the Markgrave's watch. What would Master Bufo have done? He would not have flown in terror. He would have stopped, turned and frozen the guards into such a terror they would have turned white from fright, ivory white and frozen like the serpent in the bottle. Or perhaps with a flick of his finger he would have summoned fire so that they would have been incinerated on the spot, leaving only blackened and charred remains to smudge the cobblestones. It was inconceivable, thought Tobias, that Bufo was afraid of anything. Nothing living, nothing dead. Not even Death itself.

He was being courted; he understood that. Bufo was giving him special treatment. The old man hadn't bothered with Johanna. He hadn't bothered with gentle Hugh. At the thought of his sister and uncle, Tobias had a momentary concern. Where were they? However, he brushed the thought aside, secure in the knowledge that, whatever else, they would be safe in this house. The Markgrave of Gleam wielded terrible power in the city and province but Tobias was beginning to feel that this House of the Toad held a power older and deeper than anything the Markgrave could wield.

He was being courted. He could be part of that power. He could wield it. Perhaps conjure life out of death.

But Bufo had said there would be a cost. What cost? What cost could possibly override the possession of the power over the serpent, the power over death? He would have to give up his studies at Aser. He understood that. His grandfather would be grieved. His mother would be disappointed. And Johanna? She would be cross with him for upsetting their grandfather and their mother, and see any change as simply evidence of his instability and unreliability. But Johanna could not understand. She had not tasted serpent wine. She had not held the serpent in her hands.

What did it matter if he gave up on the pompous old Jonah Portcullis? He already sensed the contempt for the man Dr Bufo felt. In his heart, he agreed. And his teachers? What of them? Dry bones and sawdust. Parrots of books they barely understood. Not one of them had the authority and magic of Manfred Bufo. To be an acolyte of such a man would be something indeed. Something worth living for. Something worth the cost.

Johanna woke to a gentle shaking. Her sleep had been full of strange frightening dreams. She had been charged by her grandfather Titus Swallow to look after Tobias. This had not seemed strange at all. They were leaving on a perilous journey and the old man had given them saddle bags of brown nougat and white marzipan, which they had slung over the backs of the two quiet white ponies who were to lead them through a dark forest of fir trees. The old man had been vague about the purpose of their journey, but Johanna understood somehow that it was to rescue their father who had been lost on a hunting trip.

The trees were narrow and tall, but through their corridors shafts of dusty sunlight occasionally reached small glades where on a blanket of green grass they would pause. The horses would crop the grass gently while little Tobias and Johanna would nibble the soft confectionary.

The warmth of the sun, the sweetness of the food and the gentleness of the ponies had lulled Johanna into a feeling of false security. The forest was not dangerous at all. They had experienced nothing more threatening than a strange bird call or two, the thumping of a jack rabbit as it fled before them on the needle-littered trail.

Then they came to a narrow gorge and a swift-flowing river. Slung high across the waters which crashed over a tumble of large rocks was a swing bridge, an intricate construction of ropes and timbers which looked as though it may have been put together by an ill-educated spider. It also looked weathered and very old.

Johanna approached the bridge apprehensively. Their path lay that way. They must cross the river somehow. The walls of the gorge were steep and the river below treacherous. The bridge was their only option. Little Tobias looked at her mischievously.

'Frightened, sister?' he asked.

Johanna shook her head indignantly. 'Not at all,' she said. 'It's just that Grandfather insisted that we take good care.'

Tobias laughed. 'I don't believe you, sister. It looks like fun to me. It's just the way you look at things. I see the bridge. You see the water and the rocks.'

'Don't be silly!' snapped Johanna. Why did Tobias have to turn everything into a competition, a race, a test?

'It's just good sense to see both,' she said tartly.

She reached out and touched the nearest rope serving as a hand-rail. The bridge itself was suspended from thick hawsers, which arched down from two rickety wooden towers on either side of the gorge. No sooner had she gripped the rope, than the bridge gave a perceptible shiver and began to sway slightly from side to side. Instinctively, Johanna stepped back and Tobias laughed again.

Johanna flushed with irritation. 'Stop that,' she said.

Perhaps sensing the growing tension Johanna's pony lifted her head and stepped forward and on to the wooden slats that, roped together, formed the bridge. Surely, daintily, she stepped along the slats, rolling slightly with the now much more obvious sway of the bridge. She proceeded steadily down the swinging slope and up the other side and then, with a slight canter, the pony hurried the last few steps and made it to the other side. 'See. It's easy,' the pony seemed to be saying. She was followed by the second pony, equally sure-footed. Johanna sighed with relief, chiding herself for her worry. She glanced at Tobias. 'You next,' she said. 'I'll come across as soon as you're on the other side.'

Tobias nodded and, with a laugh, skipped and scampered across the bridge, pulling excitedly at the hand-ropes to make the bridge sway as violently as possible. The wooden towers creaked as the tension came and went.

'Tobias!' cried Johanna. 'Don't be foolish!'

However, her voice was lost in the roar of the river and, anyway, Tobias had reached the other side. Johanna paused until the bridge's wild swinging calmed down. She realised, too late, that while she was waiting, Tobias had taken out a large knife and was hacking at the ropes, laughing as he did so.

'Stop that!' cried Johanna.

Tobias seemed possessed. He worked feverishly with the knife which must have been razor-sharp. Within seconds, it seemed, the bridge fell away down, down into the roaring chasm and the furious water before swinging back towards Johanna like a massive rope ladder.

'Tobias!'

Tobias stood on the other side, laughing and gesticulating. He was made brighter by a shaft of sunlight. Behind him the white horses were already moving along the path into the darkness of the far forest.

And then the sun was swallowed by a cloud. There was another deeper darker roar above the tumult of the river. Thunder.

'Tobias!'

As he stood there laughing with a madness Johanna had never known, billowing shadows flowed out between the trees and swept towards him. All at once he was engulfed by blackness and Johanna could see him no more.

She was still muttering his name when she became aware that the roaring and the forest had vanished and she was lying on a narrow cot in a strange room. She looked up, disoriented. Standing above her was a gaunt, vaguely familiar figure. He was dressed in a black cloak beneath which she could make out a leather jerkin, belt and leggings.

'What?'

'You've been asleep, my lady,' said the man. 'We thought it best to wake you, for it will be time soon to leave this house and continue your journey.'

'This house?'

Johanna pulled herself to a sitting position and the thin rug fell from her. Her head felt thick, her mind doughy. She was aware that she had no idea of the hour and only a vague recollection of where she was. This man before her: she had seen him somewhere, surely; but she could not remember the circumstances. Briefly the dream returned, or rather the last scattered pictures of the dream and the feelings they had induced.

'Tobias?' she asked.

The monkish man looked at her. 'My lady?'

'Where is my brother?'

Somehow she remembered asking this question before.

'Your brother will be waiting for you, I understand,' said Brother Sheldrake, permitting himself a frosty smile.

Throughout the previous day, while his uncle and sister had slept their long and unknowing sleep, Manfred Bufo had allowed Tobias to glimpse some of the mysteries of the House of the Toad. Following another visit to the library, Bufo had opened other rooms up to him, rooms filled with flasks, bottles, vials. Liquids clear and cloudy, thin and viscous; powders of all colours, pastes and unguents; apparatus and implements; retorts, callipers and crucibles. Rooms filled with drawers of dried herbs, barks, insects and fungus, all their pungent aromas, colours and flavours mixed together like some devil's salad. Shadowy figures had moved through these rooms but had greeted neither Bufo nor his visitor. At times they had returned to the small chamber where, mysteriously, simple meals had been laid out. How this food appeared and how the dishes and goblets disappeared after they had completed their repasts, Master Bufo did not explain, nor did Tobias feel it appropriate to ask.

In the evening they had returned to Bufo's chamber and had acknowledged their as yet unspoken agreement with a further goblet of serpent wine. The power of the wine was undeniable and Tobias sighed, staring at the bottle, realising where that power came from, realising what the bleached snake meant – how its life and colour had leached into the wine and how this was in turn absorbed by those who drank it, just as surely as if those frozen fangs had whipped from the jeroboam and punctured flesh.

'You would want power,' said Bufo at one point, as if reading his mind. 'But do you know where to find it?'

This seemed to be some sort of catechism. The answer was clearly not in the jeroboam. Tobias was tempted to answer, 'Here, in this House,' but that seemed too glib, and also seemed to beg the question. He was tempted to say, pointing to himself, 'Here, within,' but that seemed too obvious, too sententious. He played safe, playing innocent.

'Where do you find power?'

'It's a matter of perspective,' said Bufo. 'And of altering perspectives.'

Tobias was puzzled. 'What do you mean?' he asked.

'Look you, for example,' said Manfred Bufo, 'at this ant.' He pointed to a small black ant which was negotiating its way across the table towards a small puddle of crystallising wine.

Tobias glanced at the tiny creature making its determined journey. 'I see it,' he said.

'It is not something, I imagine, that strikes terror into your heart,' observed Bufo, adding drily, 'unless of course, you are one of those with an unreasonable terror of such tiny things.'

'I am not,' said Tobias.

'So,' said Bufo, 'you probably imagine that you have considerably more power than this little creature?'

'I would say so,' smiled Tobias. 'If it were my wont, I could dispose of it with my thumb.'

'Could you?' mused Bufo.

He studied the ant for some moments and then turned back to Tobias. 'Could you?' he repeated.

Tobias could not really understand where any of this was leading. 'Of course,' he said.

'Look at the ant,' said Bufo softly.

Tobias turned to it again. It had almost reached the puddle. However something was happening to it. It took Tobias some moments to realise what it was. The ant was growing. Steadily, inexorably it was increasing in size. The abdomen was stretching, distending, growing first into a bean then into a black shiny marrow with a leathery texture; the legs at first thin as hairs had fattened and stretched into black straws then small branches; by the time the ant had stopped and turned and altered direction so that it was facing Tobias the strange compound eyes at first growing into something resembling blackened sunflower heads had grown further so that they looked like large menacing platters over which the antennae, now the size of human arms, investigated the atmosphere in great sweeping movements as if able to sense the slightest current of air caused by a moving object. A moving object, for instance, like Manfred Bufo, who had risen discreetly from his chair and backed away from the table to a far corner where he stood silently.

With far less decorum, Tobias fell back, half scrambling in retreat. His chair fell behind him with a great clatter. The ant was now the size of a stretched mastiff and looked twice as brutal. Particularly horrible were its two great mandibles which opened and shut like steel pincers with an audible clacking sound. The creature, already too big for the table, half rose, its front two legs pawing the air as it lunged forward. To Tobias, in a state of complete horror, the monster seemed to be reaching for him, as a child might reach for a plum, in order to crunch his head between those two ominously clacking jaws.

He wanted to shriek, 'Oh my god!' But his throat was dry, constricted with terror. Then trying to back further away he stumbled over his overturned chair and fell onto his back. With a thump of legs and a flurry of antennae the ant pursued him and crashed from the table towards his kicking helpless body.

It was only then that Manfred Bufo clicked his fingers.

All at once the ant vanished.

Tobias, opening his eyes to silence and absence, scrambled to his feet. 'What happened?'

'What do you mean?' asked Bufo, returning to his chair and sitting down once more, as if nothing untoward had taken place.

'The ant,' gasped Tobias.

Bufo pointed. There, head down in the puddle, the tiny creature seemed to be lapping at the slight residue of wine.

'We were talking about perspective,' said Bufo, 'and of altering it. Once your perspective of the ant had altered it became terrifying.'

Tobias stared at him.

'The power you seek does lie in this Brotherhood,' continued Bufo. 'But only because we have altered perspectives. We have been able to magnify ourselves in various ways. It is these ways you will learn with us.'

Tobias was not sure he understood.

'But there will be a price,' added Manfred Bufo.

Tobias nodded. It was the second time Bufo had mentioned the price to be paid.

Early the next morning Tobias, his mind still tumbling with the excitements of the previous nights and day, had been a little surprised to hear a sharp knock at the door of the chamber. He opened it to a tall gaunt figure, who bowed his head stiffly in greeting, and asked to come in.

'I am Brother Sheldrake,' he announced. 'The Master asked me to inquire whether you had any needs and to tell you he would request another interview later this morning.'

Tobias thought quickly. He had no desire for food or drink, but his head was filled with unanswered questions. Manfred Bufo, despite the temptations he was offering, had been mysterious and tantalising. Perhaps this man, the only other inhabitant of the House of Toad Tobias had so far seen, could answer some of those questions.

'I'm not hungry,' he said. 'But if you are of this House I would talk with you.'

Brother Sheldrake looked at Tobias keenly. 'I am of this House,' he said. 'What would you know?'

Suddenly faced with what might have been an open book, Tobias did not quite know where to start. What would he have asked Bufo?

'The Master has spoken with me,' Tobias began. 'We drank the wine. He was able to do things. Conjure things. The snake, later an ant…'

'Yes?' asked the Brother.

'I mean, is it possible? If I were to…'

'Do such things?' Brother Sheldrake completed his question for him. He paused for some time, as if unsure whether he should proceed. 'To join the Brotherhood is something not to be undertaken lightly. And certainly not for the sake of learning how to conjure snakes out of bottles. Our arts are far deeper than that and require great discipline, great fortitude. I myself have been a Brother for many years, and yet I feel I have barely scratched the surface of the knowledge that is possible.' Again he levelled his stare at Tobias, this time with such penetration that Tobias flinched and turned away. 'It is not,' Brother Sheldrake added, almost scathingly, 'for the sake of parlour tricks.'

Tobias felt chastened.

'Of course,' said Brother Sheldrake, 'one learns these little manipulations. But these are not the real thing.'

Tobias turned back to him, picking up on the phrase. 'What is the real thing?' he asked, subdued.

'Power,' said Brother Sheldrake simply. 'Power. Not the power of an individual. But the power of the Brotherhood – and the power of the Brotherhood, greater than the sum of its parts, demands complete allegiance, complete submission. That is a paradox, but not a difficult one to unravel.'

Tobias nodded.

'You do not join the Brotherhood. The Brotherhood takes you.'

Tobias thought about this. The way this man was talking, the stone walls of the House of Toad began to feel heavier, greyer.

Brother Sheldrake looked at him steadily once more and Tobias found himself looking back at the man's grave and suddenly wise face. His eyes were dark and sombre. 'Be careful, Tobias Swallow,' he murmured. 'Be careful what you wish for. We are sometimes cursed with our wishes coming true.'

Somewhat startled that the man knew his name despite his not having given it, Tobias could not think of an appropriate reply to this last somewhat cryptic utterance.

'I will return later and conduct you to Master Bufo,' the tall Brother said easily. And he turned on his heel and abruptly left the room.

'You have made a decision?' Manfred Bufo asked.

Tobias nodded.

A soft emerald light was stealing through the narrow windows. Two full moons shone through a cowl of mist; it was still too early for the grey of dawn. Tobias was aware that he was about to embark on a momentous journey. Again the fear and excitement twined together around his gut, and his tongue was heavy and dry in his mouth.

'You know I must see my sister safely to my aunt's,' whispered Tobias.

Manfred Bufo nodded gravely. 'Of course. There is no urgency. Although I fear there may be difficulties. You were foolish to run from the watch,' he said. 'You could well have been seen entering here.'

'I know,' said Tobias. 'I was stupid. In the tavern there were so many…'

They considered the problem. Then Bufo, seemingly having made a decision, said abruptly, 'Roll up your sleeve. I can do something that will probably help.'

He stood up and crossed the room to a sideboard and pulled open a deep drawer. He returned to the table with two boxes. He opened these in turn and placed their contents on the table as Tobias watched, curious. One box contained a variety of styluses, and the other a number of small bottles of black and coloured inks.

'Hold out your arm,' Bufo ordered, 'and lay it flat on the table.'

As Tobias did so, Bufo brought a candle closer the better to illuminate Tobias's arm. He took the bottles out one by one and unstoppered them. 'Hold still,' he said, fitting a sharp steel nib into a holder.

Tobias watched, fascinated, as the old man assuredly drew the outline of a crouching toad on his arm at a spot midpoint between the wrist and the elbow. The nib scratched slightly but did not break the skin and Tobias did not flinch. Bufo worked swiftly and smoothly. The bumps, the bulges, the dripping dew-lapped throat and the bulbous eyes with their all-wise pupil-slits. Finally he inked in a brilliant scarlet asterisk on the bump on the top of the head. The toadstone site. When Manfred Bufo at length drew back and recorked the small bottles, Tobias could see that on his arm was an image of a toad identical in every detail to that he had glimpsed on Bufo's arm.

'Very handsome,' he said admiringly. The old man was a surprisingly good artist.

'There will be a time for something more permanent later,' murmured Bufo. 'This will suffice in the meantime.'

'Suffice for what?' Tobias asked.

'Should there be any difficulties,' Bufo explained, snapping the boxes shut and standing up.

Chapter Six
GATEHOUSE

When dawn did finally arrive, Johanna and Hugh Cassin were already assembled in the lobby of the House of the Stone Toad. Brother Sheldrake had delivered them there earlier and they had found their bundles waiting. Still a little groggy from their sleep, neither had any idea that Brother Gull's blue phial had robbed them of twenty-four hours of their lives. Some time later Manfred Bufo and Tobias joined them.

'You should make for the eastern gatehouse while the streets are still quite empty,' Manfred Bufo said. 'The fewer eyes; the fewer mouths…'

Hugh Cassin nodded. I can understand that, he thought. He doesn't want us to be seen near here. We've probably caused him more trouble already than our welcome was worth.

It was probably his imagination, Hugh thought, but the old scholar seemed slightly less distant this morning. Not quite human, but almost like. He then glanced at his niece. How pale and apprehensive her face was, what dark circles under her eyes. Though even with the ravages of a sleepless night and the fear of danger printed on her, he thought proudly, she already had a great beauty, all the greater for not being aware of her own loveliness. And then he looked at Tobias. Odd, despite the chill of the morning Tobias looked flushed and animated, his eyes shone with an inner excitement, and his movements were quick and agitated. I do hope, thought Hugh, that the boy isn't feverish. By all that's just, he thought, self-righteously, the boy should be waist-deep in the sludge of a hangover. His own head, he realised, was heavy and he felt dull, cold and lifeless. It was not fair that Tobias should appear so willing to climb steeples and towers.

Manfred Bufo opened the great door. 'Goodbye,' he said without warmth. 'The east gate, mind you.'

The esplanade was deserted. Beyond the sea wall on the other side of the road, a bleak grey sea pushed and rolled. A keen wind pulled at Johanna's green cape and she gathered it closer under her chin. Hugh turned to thank their host, but had only time to catch a glimpse of the white hair, the blue cap and gown before the heavy door swung fast against them leaving them to the sea, the wet cobbles and the morning. A strange man, thought Hugh. A very strange man. He had little time to pursue this thought, however, for already Tobias was striding off with a hunched intensity and Hugh and Johanna were forced to hurry after him.

Hugh did not mind having to do this. The hurrying seemed to purge the dreadful events of previous hours and the claustrophobic feeling of the house of the old scholar. In a way, he felt suddenly freed, uncontaminated, rinsed clean by the sea wind.

Had Hugh known that his fears during the night were justified, however, he may not have felt so pleased to be on his way. The watchtowers and gatehouses of Gleam had already been warned to watch out for the three fugitives. The publican Tobit Mulbert's description, especially of Hugh and Tobias, had been dispatched to all quarters. Martin Sculldung was not a man to waste time.

Tobias, meanwhile, had not slackened his pace. It was as if he were driven, and his mind too was racing. All that had happened in the House of the Toad whirled about his head in a confusion of dark and telling images. The leather books. The snake in the bottle and his crazed struggle with it. The ant. The stone crucibles.

Along the cobbled esplanade he strode as the sky gradually lightened and the dark-faced buildings came more sharply into focus. By the time they reached the small market square before the forbidding bulk of the east gate-tower the first hawkers were already setting up their stalls, trestles and charcoal braziers. Soon the cold morning air would become sweet and smoky with the flavour of cooking griddlecakes and fried dough. Here among the wagons and striped awnings Tobias, for the first time, paused and waited for his panting companions to catch up.

'Ready?' he asked.

Together they glanced at the square crenellated tower of dark granite; a tower designed, it seemed, to shut the world out and themselves in Gleam forever. 'Wait, Tobias,' gasped Hugh Cassin. His nephew had set such an exhausting pace he could feel the return of his stitch. Urgently, Hugh whispered his fears of the night before. 'We should try to pass through the gate separately,' he said. 'Johanna first. You and I can follow later. They're bound to be on the watch for a woman and two men travelling together.'

Tobias nodded. It was well thought. 'What do you think, sister?' he asked.

'Would you go through the gate alone?'

They were standing less than fifty yards from the tower but were partly hidden by a wagon loaded with vegetables. The iron rails of the gates were topped with sharp spikes that reinforced their impression of being caged within. Guarding the gate stood two watchmen, each wearing an iron breastplate and carrying a long pike. These men were liveried in the deep scarlet of the House of Twyll. Already they were waving into the city the first farmers and merchants with their wagons and drays of produce for the fair.

Johanna nodded. 'If you think it best,' she whispered.

Hugh Cassin took hold of her hand and squeezed it encouragingly. 'You're sure to be quite safe, Johanna,' he murmured. 'You, at least, had the good sense not to draw attention to yourself in the tavern. I doubt anybody would have noticed you.' He looked at Tobias with a rueful expression which the young man acknowledged with an embarrassed little grin.

The two men waited out of sight as Johanna whispered her farewells and took her leave. Hugh was relieved and slightly surprised to see how, despite the danger she must have felt herself to be in, Johanna walked confidently and easily, her head held high, with her cape around her shoulders and her long fair hair flowing free. Peering round the wagon, Hugh watched her approach the first of the watchmen and was relieved to see enacted one of the oldest stories: at the sight of the beautiful young woman, the watchman's face creased into a smile and he bowed attentively towards her while Johanna explained her business. Then she bobbed her head and, Hugh guessed, smiled in return. The watchman took her arm briefly, and waved her through the archway with another broad smile and a flourish of his pikestaff. Johanna passed beneath the arch and, without looking back, disappeared from sight.

'Well, that was simple enough,' whispered Hugh, beginning to think his fears had perhaps been misplaced. Tobias nodded, and Hugh noticed how bright his eyes were, how he seemed on edge, as alert as a hunting cat.

'Shall I go next?' asked Hugh after a time. Tobias nodded again, and Hugh stepped out. The market square was a little busier already. It was clearly fair day. He looked about him. Trestles were being set up and goods laid out: turnips, pumpkins and sacks of grain. Over his shoulder he could see the dark fretwork of the citadel's tower glinting in the first licks of the sun. It was a sudden spur. 'Enough,' thought Hugh. 'Let's get this over with.'

He set his chin forward and strode more purposefully than he felt towards the iron gates and the figures of the two watchmen. Hugh Cassin was not a beautiful young woman so there was no smile of welcome for him. The first gatekeeper was large and severe with a moustache that covered his mouth. His heavy breastplate gave him the appearance of a barrel.

'State your name and your business, stranger,' the gatekeeper demanded, staring suspiciously at Hugh.

'I'm a musician,' explained Hugh. He felt quite intimidated by the man's manner and bulk. 'I'm just passing through the city on my way from Blackfell to Lamaria.' The gatekeeper waited. 'Abel Larch is making me a new lute,' added Hugh. He'd thought it best not to mention Posy Beet and Flintside, as Johanna had probably done so already.

'Your name?' the gatekeeper repeated flatly.

'Hugh Cassin. Hugh Cassin of Blackfell. I'm…' He was feeling confused and now somewhat panicked by the man.

'Master Cassin, is it?' asked the guard, and Hugh nodded unhappily. He was examined carefully once more, and then the guard asked, 'Master Cassin of Blackfell, you wouldn't have been drinking, by any chance, in the Gut and Cuttle tavern a couple of evenings ago, would you?'

Hugh stared at him, unable to speak. His head rang. His worst fears had been realised.

As he shifted the lethal-looking pike from one hand to the other, the guard's malevolent eyes never left Hugh's.

'I…' began Hugh, conscious of his silver hair, his silver beard. How conspicuous he must look. 'Not a couple of evenings ago,' he said. He did not understand. Why did they think it was two nights ago? Surely they must have known it was only the night before.

'With a young man wearing the cape of a student? A young man with fair hair and a loud voice?' continued the gatekeeper, warming to his theme.

Hugh, still unable to find any words, looked about him in alarm. The gatekeeper called to his companion, clearly a subordinate. 'Seize him!' And suddenly Hugh felt his upper arms gripped firmly and painfully. Before he knew what was happening he was being frog-marched towards the gatehouse itself.

'Don't look back!' Johanna told herself. 'Don't look back!'

Do nothing to encourage him or raise his suspicions.

Don't look back.

It had been so difficult to smile brightly at the leering guard, to suffer his fingers paddling at her upper arm as he began to escort her through the stone arch, past the spiked bars and into the watery sunrise on the other side. It had seemed so easy. To be free of Gleam just like that. One step, two steps, and then a dusty road with sun shining through dancing motes and all the danger and darkness of Gleam behind her.

She would walk for a hundred yards or so she decided. Perhaps a little further. Once well out of sight of the gatehouse, around a safe corner where she could have the wind in the trees and the breeze off the sea for company, she would rest on a bank by the wayside and wait for her uncle and brother.

Tobias watched his uncle's progress closely. He liked his uncle. When he was younger he had enjoyed a certain pride in being the nephew of one of the Mastersingers of the province. He liked him for his gentle, dreamy ways rather than in spite of them. Whenever Tobias thought about it, Hugh Cassin had been associated with some of his happiest times; he would always connect family occasions with firelight, warmth, the smell of cooked food, and, above all, his uncle's lilting voice singing tales and magical stories of long ago, his long fingers weaving figures of exquisite beauty on the strings of his lute.

Now he saw his uncle pause and gaze about him as if experiencing a morning for the very first time, breathing in the market square, then moving towards the gatehouse. Tobias saw Hugh approach the guard and could see that there was an exchange of words. The guard looked somehow threatening, and Hugh's slighter figure was defensive. Suddenly Hugh stepped back and, as he did so, the other guard came rushing up, grabbing him from behind. Horrified, Tobias could see his uncle being pushed and shoved towards the guardhouse.

He did not stop to think. With a half-shout of 'Stop! What do you think you're doing!' he leapt from behind the cover of the wagon and ran towards the gate. The other figures halted then turned and Tobias could see Hugh's frightened face and the expressions of surprise on the faces of the two huge gatekeepers, the light glinting off their helmets, and off the tips of their pikes.

'Let him go!' Tobias yelled as soon as he was within a few feet of them.

The violence of his running and shouting had attracted more than the attention of the guards. Already most of the few hawkers and street vendors were looking about grinning and beginning to follow him. There was the promise of excitement in the air. The guards, once their initial surprise was over, grinned too at the temerity of this youth daring to issue orders to those holding warrants from the Markgrave of Gleam. It was more than Hugh could cope with. He raised his eyes in supplication. What, in the name of God, had driven Tobias to this insanity? Now two geese were about to be cooked!

Tobias's face was pale with anger. 'Let him go! He's done nothing!'

The first guard quickly took in Tobias's appearance. The fair hair. The student's cape. He laughed. Apples falling from the bough right into his basket. 'Done nothing? That's for us to find out,' he said. 'And as for you, Master Cockdoodle, where did you happen to be a couple of evenings back? Drinking Tobit Mulbert's ale and crowing like a buck bantam, I'll be bound! Well, you just come along with us as well, Master Breakwind! We want to talk to you!'

And suddenly he swung his pike down level and jabbed it like a spear directly at Tobias's midriff. The young man stepped back quickly, but otherwise seemed unflustered by the gesture and the bullying words.

'Let my uncle go,' he repeated angrily, 'and I'll answer whatever you want!'

Unused to such vehement defiance, the guard holding Hugh did release him and stepped back. The first guard lowered his pike, and after shouting at the grinning spectators to scatter, said, 'Come with me!' He then led the way as the small party entered a cell-like room built into the wall beneath the gate tower.

'Over there!' ordered the first guard, pointing to a wooden bench. The second guard pushed Hugh violently in the back and he stumbled as he fell forward. Tobias turned towards the guard with a look of cold fury and said, 'Don't touch me!' Although the guard gave a short contemptuous laugh, some strength in Tobias's anger commanded enough respect for him to keep his hands to himself.

'Your name?' demanded the first guard.

Tobias, who had remained standing, replied, 'Tobias Swallow of Aser.'

'Business?'

'I am returning to my university from Blackfell. I am studying medicine. My uncle and I, we are freemen both. Why have you stopped us?'

The guard ignored his question. 'Two nights ago you were drinking in the Gut and Cuttle?

'I was.'

'And you ran from the watch?'

Tobias stared at the man. It was his turn to ignore the question. 'I entered a house on the waterfront.'

The second guard had backed off a little and had levelled his pike at the forlorn figure of Hugh Cassin who sat crouched into himself on the bench. Hugh could not understand what was possessing his nephew. Probably all these men needed were a show of complete subservience and a few silver coins. That was the way the world worked. To goad them, defy them and treat them like the filth they surely were would only invite trouble and pain. That was the way the world worked, too.

The first guard had been deflected from his line of questioning. He tried to reassert his ascendancy. 'What house?' he demanded sharply.

Tobias, as the gatekeeper's heavy face leered into his, had a fleeting vision of the House of the Toad. The dark study, the entwining serpent wine, the curling smoke from the guttering candle. He saw Manfred Bufo's impassive face as the stylus etched scratchily into his arm. And once again he saw the crouching toad and heard Bufo's whisper: 'This should suffice.'

'Well?' insisted the guard.

Tobias reached for the man's sleeve and pulled him back out into the light. Puzzled, the guard allowed this. Then Tobias drew back his own sleeve.

'This house,' he whispered, gazing at the image of the toad looking like a brilliant tattoo. The guard followed his gaze, and there was an involuntary intake of breath as he saw the toad, saw its eyes staring malevolently up, saw the scarlet asterisk. Quickly, smoothly, Tobias pulled the sleeve back. Nobody else could have noticed the transaction. But, something strange had taken place in the chemistry, as if the sky had changed colour, the buildings had shifted slightly, the people had been replaced. Suddenly the guard was a very different person. All aggression was gone. Instantly there was servile politeness. 'The waterfront, did you say, Master Swallow?' he asked hesitantly.

'I did,' said Tobias.

And the guard's being a different person changed Tobias. He felt taller, stronger and no longer angry. He felt in control. It was a feeling that gave him a rush of pleasure and he almost forgave the guard for his former obnoxious manner, rather as a visitor forgives a yapping aggressive lap dog when it begins to fawn and wag its tail.

Neither Hugh nor the other guard still in the stone cell knew any of this. When the guard and Tobias re-entered, Hugh looked up miserably. He could not understand why Tobias had insisted on behaving in such a high-handed manner. His fearful imagination was already swamping him with visions of rat-infested dungeons, the cold, the darkness, of chains and manacles, urine-filled buckets and the stench of captivity. He was astonished to discover that the previously belligerent officer was now curtly dismissing his colleague and courteously asking that he, Hugh Cassin, should stand.

'I'm sorry, Master Cassin,' he said. 'My fellow officer does get a little carried away. We didn't realise…'

As he slowly stood, Hugh looked at him in amazement; an amazement which grew as the guard flashed Tobias a fearful version of the smile he'd presented to Johanna and whispered. 'You will excuse us, Master Swallow. We didn't know. Really.'

Tobias laid a forgiving hand on the man's scarlet sleeve. 'No matter. No matter,' he murmured.

The guard nodded, dabbing through his moustache at his upper lip with his thick finger. 'I'll see you through the gate,' he said, and then with a bleak warning glare at his surprised fellow officer he escorted Tobias and Hugh to the other side.

'What happened back there?' asked Hugh Cassin wonderingly.

The two men had paused. Ahead of them, sitting patiently on a pine stump by the wayside, they could see Johanna. The sun had risen higher and was shining on a glittering sea now visible from the road. The ocean's surface was littered with whitecaps and the breeze was salty and bracing. Tobias breathed it in, allowing his chest to expand with it. Something had happened. He had never felt so filled with power. There was a drunkenness in the exhilaration of it.

All the same, he felt an instinctive need to protect the source of this power, to keep his sleeve down, just as he had been careful to ensure that the guard had been given only a glimpse of the toad. It had been enough. Manfred Bufo was right. It had been sufficient.

'Nothing really,' he said. 'Why?'

Hugh looked at him, startled. That something completely out of the ordinary had happened was perfectly clear. That Tobias knew about it was equally clear.

For his part, Tobias felt a momentary pang. He had never knowingly lied to his uncle. Tobias was not by nature a furtive double-dealing person, and Hugh was so open and generous of spirit it would have never occurred to him before to be deceitful to him. But, now, somehow he knew that deceit was the necessary dark side to the exhilaration. He had no choice. He was reminded, too, that even this walk to Posy Beet's with Hugh and Johanna was an act of deceit. That he had already decided on his betrayal. As soon as they were safely delivered he would make his way back. Not to Aser as planned, but to the House of the Toad.

He smiled innocently at his uncle, and lifted his eyebrows slightly. Topic closed. 'Let us join my sister,' he said. 'She must have been worried.'

Chapter Seven
FLINTSIDE

It was a merrier group who followed the dusty road to Flintside, although Hugh Cassin could not ease his bewilderment at the guard's inexplicable change of attitude. From time to time he glanced with increased respect at his nephew whose good spirits seemed to have returned with their escape. I have been underestimating the boy's powers of persuasion, he thought. Perhaps he should be studying to be a lawyer, rather than to be a physician.

A warm welcome awaited them in the small dwelling house by the river. Posy Beet was delighted to see her sister's children, keen to show off her little daughter and to hear news of Blackfell. It was wonderful to see Hugh again as well, and brother and sister embraced tenderly. Posy was the youngest by far of the three Cassins, and Hugh had always spoilt her. Looking at Johanna and Posy side by side he was struck how more like sisters they seemed than aunt and niece.

Gabriel Beet had been surprised to see them arrive so late, but he had been able to assure Posy that her family were arrived in Gleam. Besides, Tobit Mulbert's ale had put Gabriel in good spirits and he was quite without resentment at his fool's errand. He now shook their hands warmly and vented his astonishment at Johanna's beauty, Tobias's moustache and Hugh's silver hair.

That evening a large iron tureen bubbled on the hob and its savoury steam filled the little parlour. Gabriel Beet had caught a brace of rabbits and they were stewing in a broth flavoured with herbs and turnips. Already he'd broached a small keg of ale and the men's faces were flushed with warmth, beer and companionship.

As Posy sat with her baby at her breast in that quiet time before going to bed, she felt that life was suddenly better. Johanna was growing into a beautiful young woman, her nephew had a rich laugh and a quicksilver wit, and Hugh, dear Hugh, had sung the achingly sweet songs she'd known all her life of the hills and valleys of home. She even felt an affection for her feckless husband as he sang the choruses softly and whittled busily away at a little figure she guessed would be a present for Johanna. A little baby doll, perhaps, or a wooden kitten curled into sleep. It was hard to tell. Appearances were deceptive in the soft golden light and the deep brown shadows.

She was a little surprised later to see Gabriel pass the carving to Tobias and in the moment of passing she saw that it wasn't a baby or a sleeping kitten, it was something squatter, lumpier. Tobias seized it warmly with a glance of thanks, stroking it as if to cement his ownership, before slipping it inside his jerkin. Some whisper passed between the two men, but Posy couldn't hear it.

With the dawn however things had changed. The feeling of well-being had dissipated in the chill of the morning. And in the chill of the morning it became clear that Tobias had gone. Somehow he'd slipped away in the night or in the very early morning long before dawn. The River Flint rippled over its flat stones as Posy opened the door. The wind sighed and shifted the leaves of the aspen poplars so that they wantonly flashed their white under-leaves. And Tobias was gone.

'How could he go without saying goodbye?' asked Posy.

Hugh Cassin, who had already been out onto the roadside, shook his head. 'No sign of him,' he said. 'I don't understand it.'

Johanna looked troubled. 'Something has happened,' she whispered. 'He was not himself yesterday, was he Uncle?'

Hugh recalled the Tobias of the previous day. The striding ahead. The silence. The smouldering anger and the determination when they'd been arrested by the gatekeepers. Hugh remembered his perplexity at Tobias's odd behaviour that had seemed calculated to land them deep in trouble. He had done everything wrong, and yet… Suddenly Hugh saw the face of the gatekeeper, no longer bullying, but somehow compliant and somehow frightened. How had Tobias Swallow, medical student, overwrought youth, managed to put such fear into a hardened guardian of Gleam? And afterwards? Afterwards Tobias had such a sense of elation that his moodiness had given way to a light-headedness that was quite infectious. Hugh had thought it had something to do with their escape, but now he wondered.

'Would he be joining his boat?' asked Johanna.

'He would not have to leave so early,' murmured Hugh. 'His boat does not sail until much later. He was to stay here for some days.'

'He'll not be catching any boat,' said Gabriel Beet. 'He's not going to Aser no more.'

'What?' asked Johanna, astonished.

'No, no,' grinned Gabriel, pleased to have had the intelligence to himself. 'Tobias, he's found another place to study.'

'Husband,' said Posy, 'what do you mean?'

Gabriel Beet shrugged. 'I mean he asked me to fashion a little wooden creature. He wanted to give a present to his new master.'

'New master?' demanded Johanna.

'What was it?' demanded Hugh Cassin. 'This wooden creature?'

'It was a toad,' said Gabriel. 'A crouching toad, just like the one on his arm.'

'On his arm?' said Johanna in bewilderment. 'But he hasn't got…'

Hugh gripped her hand. 'I don't understand this,' he said. 'But the toad – at least that tells us where he is. Before I go to Lamaria, I'll call in and see what I shall see.'

'Oh Uncle,' cried Johanna. 'Go now! You must go today!'

Hugh stared gravely at her troubled face. 'Yes,' he said. 'I suppose you're right. I'd better go today.'

Hugh Cassin looked across the cobbled street to the lowering porch and the heavy door within. The watery late afternoon sun highlighted the toad embossed in stone. Hugh gave a little shiver, not entirely caused by the cold wind off the sea, and then he crossed the street and approached the door.

After his frightening passage through the gatehouse the previous morning, he'd thought nothing would induce him to enter Gleam for months, if ever again. Necessity had, however, screwed his courage tight and he had approached the guard on the gate with as confident a front as he could muster. Without Tobias's bravado, though, he was unsure in his heart whether this feigned confidence would be enough.

He need not have worried. The guard had merely asked his name and business and then had grunted at him to enter. There had been no suspicious examination, no suggestion that he was anybody worthy of any pursuit. Somehow he no longer seemed to be a wanted man. It had been a huge relief.

Now that he had found the House of the Toad again that relief had dissipated. He had no real plan in mind, not having thought it through. As he'd walked the few miles back to Gleam his simple aim was to find Tobias, to talk to him, and, hopefully, to persuade him that he should continue his studies at Aser. Although Hugh did expect to find his nephew, he was less sure about being able to persuade him. Tobias was ever a stubborn, erratic boy. It was beyond Hugh's understanding why Tobias should have made the astonishing decision to stay in the house of Manfred Bufo. Hugh was grateful for Manfred Bufo's intercession, but still felt there was something cold, repellent about the man. He had been pleased to be out of his house.

He knocked at the door and listened for any footsteps. There was nothing. Again he knocked. This time louder, more urgently; but again nothing. Hugh looked about him helplessly. The porch did not allow access to the ground-floor windows, which in any case were set well behind protective iron railings. The fortress-like nature of the house was now quite apparent. The only way in was this heavily studded door and it was impenetrable, determinedly deaf to any knocking. Perhaps there was nobody at home. That was unlikely. Even were Bufo and Tobias not in, there would surely be a domestic of some kind. Hopelessly, he knocked again, barking his knuckles in an attempt to rouse those inside. Nothing. He put his ear to the door. Again, nothing.

Finally, reluctantly, Hugh accepted the inevitable. Tobias, famous as he was for being rash and headstrong, had surpassed himself. Already Hugh could see the bewilderment and pain on his sister's face when he came to report his nephew's latest folly. He felt a welling resentment against the young man for unnecessarily causing such pain to his mother, worry to his sister and aunt, and inconvenience to himself.

Backing away from the door, Hugh felt at a loss. He would come back, of course. After dark there might be a light. That might prove something. All the same, he knew in his heart that the door was not then, or any time, going to swing open in welcome. He began, aimlessly, to wander back along the waterfront, automatically retracing his steps towards the square that was the site of their folly. Then it occurred to him that he might discover something of the house if he asked the right questions. But where? He had no acquaintance in Gleam.

The sight of the tall masts of ships berthed at the quayside lifted his spirits somewhat. It was just possible that Tobias had boarded his ship after all. He would make inquiries there. The more he considered the idea, the more likely it seemed. Somehow he'd allowed the association of wooden toads, stone toads and studded doors to obsess him. Gabriel Beet was always one to add one and one and get five. Of course, Tobias would have slipped away to join the ship. With a lightening of his heart and a quickening of his step he headed towards the quay.

The port was small but busy. Many of the fishing boats had already returned and their nets were laid out to dry. Everywhere was the smell of fish and salt and kelp, the quarrelsome calling of gulls, and the shouts of fishermen echoing across the stretches of water as they exchanged tales and gossip. Moored against the stone quay was a larger vessel, the *Firefly*, bound in a few days time to cross the sea to Aser.

But when Hugh inquired of the first mate whether they'd taken on board a student bound for the University, the man had shaken his head before spitting accurately between the gunwale and the quay.

'No sign of the lad,' he said. 'Master Swallow, ye say? I'll keep a weather eye out. Where'll ye be?'

Hugh shrugged, disappointed. He hadn't thought about it. It would probably be necessary to find some lodging. Darkness was not far away. It would not be a good idea to try and return to Flintside that night.

'I don't know,' he said. 'I don't know. I'll come back in the morning.'

'Tell you what, Master…'

'Cassin,' said Hugh.

'Master Cassin. If ye've nowhere to stay there's a hammock for ye below decks if you fancy. It can get right cold in these parts. And if your friend turns up, ye'll be here to greet him.'

Hugh nodded, thanking the man. 'That's generous, friend. I'm very much obliged. There is another possibility I must check out first, but by your favour, I'll be back.'

The mate nodded amiably enough, and then spat again, the jet squirting unerringly down the narrow gap to thwack on to the surface of the water. Hugh saluted and turned, smiling. Years of practice, he thought. Years of practice.

He walked down the quay thoughtfully, hardly taking in the large crudely formed letters plastered on the sea wall. MAIDEN. The letters must have entered his consciousness, however, for suddenly the discussion in the tavern came back, and he could hear Tobias's excited voice as he held sway in the murky tavern.

Tobit Mulbert's eyes narrowed as the figure stepped from the light outside into the gloomy taproom. Then his squint widened in astonished recognition as he made out the silver hair and the silver beard. This could be a wonderfully profitable surprise.

'A drink, sir?'

Hugh Cassin nodded and took the frothing tankard gratefully when it was proffered. Tobit Mulbert watched him curiously as Hugh blew at the brown spume.

'Your companion not with ye today? The young fellow? What was his name?'

Hugh shook his head. He was disappointed the tavern was deserted. He'd hoped to see one or two of the more forthcoming drinkers of the other evening to ask about the House of the Toad. 'He hasn't been in here then?' he asked of the villainous-looking barman, but without much hope.

'Not today.'

The innkeeper watched Hugh with an ingratiating grin. This was a happy surprise. There could be money here. However, the musician seemed in no hurry to engage in conversation, and Mulbert, who was no talker himself, quickly became aware of the silence. 'Master Cassin, isn't it?' he asked finally.

Hugh lay down his tankard in surprise, looking at the face of his host. The thick pocked jowls with their coarse scatter of white whiskers, the narrow eyes forever closed against the smoke, and the studied grin devoid of humour. Hugh nodded. 'Yes, mister tapster, it is. But how did you know that?'

It would have been easy for Mulbert to have explained that Gabriel Beet had spoken of his relatives, but Mulbert was ever one to prefer intrigue to straightforwardness. Instead he rubbed his nose with a flat finger and winked. 'News travels hereabouts,' he said mysteriously.

Hugh stared at him, then shrugged. 'So it would seem,' he murmured. However, not trusting the man he did not pursue the matter, frustrating the landlord of the Gut and Cuttle even further. When it became apparent that the well of conversation had dried, Mulbert gave a curt nod and stomped out the back. There, scrubbing barrels with lye, he found a thin unwashed boy who gave him a frightened look. 'Here,' he whispered harshly, aiming an instinctive kick at the lad. 'Get you to the citadel! Tell the guard that Mulbert says there's a prize here for Officer Sculldung. Get you quick, mind! Any delay, and I'll have your hide!'

The boy understood that. As quick as a terrified flash, he jumped up and disappeared out of the rear door. Then, fashioning his face into a grotesque parody of good humour, Mulbert returned to the taproom.

'So you're staying with Mistress Beet, then?' he asked amiably.

Hugh nodded.

'Gabriel. He comes in here from time to time. A good man, Gabriel Beet.'

Hugh began to understand. It must have been Gabriel who had revealed their names and business.

'A good man to know,' continued Mulbert. 'Especially if you have a taste for game.'

Hugh nodded again. 'He did find a nice enough pair of coneys for us last night,' he admitted. Again he smelt the delicious rabbity herby stew in the warmth of the friendly parlour, saw Posy's contented face and Tobias's shiny cheeks and bright eyes. After the bleak wind, closed doors and disappointments of the day, that stew seemed a long time ago, a long way away.

'He's done the same for me, many a time,' said Mulbert. This was not true, but at least he'd provoked Hugh into conversation and he needed to keep it going. He reached for Hugh's tankard and refilled it, then filled another for himself. It looked as though it would be easier to keep the man here than he'd first thought…

Martin Sculldung received the message from the grubby boy with some misgivings. Tobit Mulbert was a useful man, but stupid and greedy. He guessed that the message meant that those whom the watch had pursued had returned. Mulbert had already claimed a couple of gold pieces for their names, but what Mulbert had not been told was that there was a possible connection with the Brotherhood. Not only had the fugitives undoubtedly gained admittance to the House of the Toad, but also they had left two days later. A report from the eastern gatehouse had confirmed that a party matching their descriptions had passed through and that, moreover, the young man, Swallow, had borne the Mark of the Toad on his arm. The last thing Sculldung wanted at this juncture was to offer some offence to the Brotherhood.

Accordingly, and with some urgency, Sculldung wrapped his long scarlet cloak of office about him and called his two most trusted lieutenants.

'We must to the Gut and Cuttle with much haste,' he said. 'Tobit Mulbert has sent word that he has a surprise for us, but I fear the surprise could well have a scorpion's sting.'

The men nodded, although they comprehended little of this. Sculldung was a notorious riddler. It was best just to nod and follow.

Shortly afterwards, the three figures strode through the gathering dusk, their long swords bouncing at their sides.

Chapter Eight
DAGONET

Inside the tavern it was growing increasingly gloomy. Tobit Mulbert busied himself with the lighting of a couple of meagre oil lamps, all the while throwing out gobbets of conversation which Hugh largely ignored. He was growing irritated by the man and anxious to leave. He still had not been able to ask anybody about the house on the waterfront, a house he needed to return to now that darkness was falling.

He drained his tankard and set it down with finality before his leering host. The man was odious. He seemed to be fawning over him. Hugh threw a generous quantity of coins on to the counter. 'No more,' he said, both to the ale and to the attention he couldn't seem to escape from.

'You must! You must!' cried Mulbert, seizing the tankard and turning towards the keg.

'No! I insist!' said Hugh sharply. All thought of asking this furtive creature about the house with the insignia of the toad had long vanished. Increasingly, all he wanted to do was to get out of the fug of this foul hole and away from its grotesque master. He desired above all to stand again in the relative freshness of the square outside, to breathe in the cold night air and gaze up to the glinting stars. Ignoring the man, Hugh turned on his heel and made for the door. There was a desperate clatter behind him and he turned to see the counter raised and the hunched figure of the innkeeper lurching through.

'Wait, Master Cassin, wait!' he cried.

The man was demented, thought Hugh, turning again.

'Wait! I told you a lie. Master Swallow did come in, not more than two hours ago.'

This intelligence stopped Hugh in his tracks. He turned to face the innkeeper who was shambling towards him.

'But why did you…?' he began.

'He asked me. He asked me not to mention his being here,' said the innkeeper craftily.

Now that he was standing looking up at him, Hugh guessed that the innkeeper must have been standing on a box behind the counter. He considered what the man had said. It did make sense, although Hugh guessed that Tobias had probably paid rather than begged the man to keep his mouth shut.

'Where was he going?' demanded Hugh.

Mulbert shook his head sorrowfully. 'Ah, that he didn't say,' he said. 'He just came in for a tankard or two of my fine ale. Best ale in Gleam,' he reckoned. He smiled his ingratiating smile, which shone in brilliant falseness.

Hugh stared at him, considering this. It did not make sense. Either the man was lying to protect Tobias, or he was simply lying. Hugh thought quickly. How to test the man?

'I don't know why he should have asked you not to tell me he'd been in,' he said. 'We had arranged to meet here at sundown. Did he not say?'

Mulbert's eyes slid uneasily past Hugh's and glanced at the door. Then they shifted back again and he swallowed. 'Well, yes, Master Cassin. Now that ye mention it he did say something about your coming in. Yes he did.'

'Well?' Hugh demanded. He glanced at the door himself. Was the man expecting somebody? Was that it? All this delay.

Mulbert licked his lips nervously. 'He said you were to wait here, sir. That he would return with cooked capon and some bread. For your supper. That was it.'

The lie was so clumsy that Hugh almost laughed. Then he felt a surge of anger at the innkeeper for his stupidity and the delay. 'Get back to your trough, man,' he muttered and turned once again for the door.

Mulbert had considered this emergency and was prepared for it. As he'd scrambled out from behind the counter he'd seized a long crock that was still half-filled with sack. Now he swung the crock back with all the force he could muster and, leaping after Hugh's departing back, he brought it crashing down on the back of the musician's head.

Hugh was only aware of the stunning impact. The glinting stars he had longed to see were suddenly before him in a whirling constellation of yellow in a red sky in a room tilting up and up as he tumbled to one side and crumpled to the straw covered floor.

Martin Sculldung pushed through the door of the Gut and Cuttle, followed by his two lieutenants. It took them some seconds to adjust to the smoky gloom of the room.

'There's nobody here,' muttered one of his men, peering about him.

'He'll not be far away,' murmured Sculldung. He crossed the room and banged on the counter with the flat of his hand. 'Mulbert!' he shouted. 'You have something for us?'

There was a scuffling sound and then Tobit Mulbert emerged from the back room. He was grinning proudly, and rubbing his hands together in front of his greasy jerkin.

'Officer Sculldung,' he said. 'What a pleasant surprise.'

'You were the one with the surprise, were you not?' said Sculldung shortly. He disliked games. 'Where are they?'

'They?'

'Get on with it, man!'

'There's only one. The older one. Cassin the musician.'

'Where has he gone?'

'Nowhere,' said Tobit Mulbert with satisfaction. He jerked his thumb across the room and the officers of the watch glanced that way. There slumped on the dirty straw in the dark shadows of the corner lay a still figure. Sculldung rushed over and knelt beside the body, touching it tentatively.

'What happened? Is he dead?'

As if in denial the figure twitched and made a low troubled grunt, like a pig dreaming. 'What happened?' insisted Martin Sculldung. There was a sharp edge to his voice, an edge a less self-congratulatory creature than the innkeeper would have noticed. He drew his fingers away from the back of Hugh Cassin's head. There was something warm on them, warm, slippery and sticky. Blood. He could now feel in the straw the broken shards of the crock that had smashed with the force of the blow. Rising slowly to his feet he turned to the squat figure still standing on his box behind the counter.

'He would have left,' explained the man. 'He would not stay. I was afraid…'

'You clumsy stupid fool,' whispered Sculldung furiously. 'You are so right. You will be afraid. You will know more fear than even the Markgrave can inflict if this man is who we think he is.'

'But…' protested Mulbert. 'I…'

'Seize him,' ordered Martin Sculldung coldly. 'He can enjoy the relative safety of the dungeons until his fate is decided. And this man,' he said, turning to the slumped shape on the floor, 'we must bring to the Citadel to treat his hurts.'

Hugh Cassin awoke to a throbbing head. He squeezed his eyes shut against the painful light and flashes of brilliant scarlet, yellow and green seemed to dart into his skull.

Gradually he accustomed himself to the onrush of consciousness and rode out the pain and the fireworks in his head. These came in such violent waves he thought he would be sick, but gradually the waves eased, softened and he was able to open his eyes and try to orient himself. He was in a small sun-splashed chamber and stretched out on a bed more comfortable than any he had ever known. He put his hand gingerly to his head and found it wrapped about with a fine bandage of lawn or soft linen. A coverlet of rich brocade and woollen blankets kept him warm, and his neck and shoulders rested on a velvet bolster so that he did not have to pull himself up. Glancing to one side he saw a wide silver goblet filled with water and a piece of linen. Clearly somebody had been caring for him.

He stared about with the strangeness of it and the stabbing pains and light show overcame him again. He straightened his head and closed his eyes, and fell once more into an aching slumber.

As the door clanged behind him Tobit Mulbert moaned helplessly. The pikemen had not been gentle as they'd pushed him down the narrow stone steps that seemed to climb down forever beneath the Citadel of Gleam. They had carried braziers that had thrown grotesque and crazy shadows before them, but Mulbert had been in front blindly feeling his away against the roughly hewn and dank stone walls. At times he'd stumbled and fallen against the walls, grazing and scratching himself. Far from assisting him, the pikemen had kicked him along, their heavy boots prodding him in the small of his back so that he would have fallen headlong into the darkness had he not kept clutching at the wall.

He could not understand what was happening. He could not comprehend by what strange magic the fugitive musician had become somebody significant, somebody not to be hurt. He had expected gold; instead he was given pain, ignominy, the possibility of death. Now in the chill blackness of the cell, in a cold and darkness deeper than any he had known, he tried to gather his terrified and wild thoughts together. 'You'll be safe here from the Brothers,' one of his tormentors had laughed as he'd kicked at the door to close it.

'If you're lucky,' the other had growled with grim humour as he'd slid the heavy iron bolts across the door.

With the door shut the darkness was complete and Mulbert crawled and felt his way to a corner and huddled there, hugging his knees in terror. There was a bitter smell in the air, of ancient urine and the dark secretions of the city of Gleam. All that was hideous must leach down into this small cell. This refuge.

Safe from the Brothers if you're lucky.

He began to tremble.

What in God's name had he done?

When Hugh Cassin opened his eyes for a second time, the pain seemed less intense; the blinding lights less brilliant. The throbbing was still there, but less insistent, more a dull pastel-coloured ache that came and went. He groaned and turned on to his side.

Suddenly he became aware that he was not alone. A shadow. A shape. A presence. He gingerly turned back again and opened his eyes, forcing himself to look about him.

'*Oh brother, brother not my brother other other outer brother... Brother's better?*'

Gibberish. He struggled to focus. There, across the room sitting cross-legged on a large fumed oak cabinet, was a boy dressed in a fantastical costume of crimson. Dyed kidskin, probably, with tassels and chains, and a strange hat with three short floppy red antlers. He carried a small scourge that he flicked about him as if swatting midges.

'*Brother better?*'

The voice was high-pitched and the delivery oddly singsong. Hugh Cassin grimaced and struggled even further up on to the bolster. On closer inspection the 'boy' was clearly older. A man, albeit a tiny man, of anything between forty and fifty.

'*Not better, brother?*'

'I'm a little better. What happened?'

'*Are you a brother, brother? Not my brother... Brothers' brother?*'

Suddenly the little figure leapt from the cabinet and landed in a bouncing squat on the floor, then he pranced up and danced towards the bed flicking his scourge. The movement was monkey-like and Hugh instinctively flinched back.

'I'm a brother, yes. If you mean I have sisters?'

The little figure, a jester obviously, perhaps the Markgrave's fool, shook his head wildly. Not what he meant, clearly.

'I have two sisters,' explained Hugh.

'*Once a king, once king. Fat king thin king... I'm thinking you're a once king.*'

The high-pitched singsong voice, the grinning face, but the serious eyes. Hugh shook his head, confused and annoyed. 'What do you mean? I'm not a king.'

'*Not a brother. Not a king. No. You're a once king, boyo!*'

Hugh tried to close his eyes against the intrusion. He could not cope with the mad falsetto, the flying tassels, and the flicking little whip.

'*You broke your crown! You broke your crown in half! But you're a rich boy, rich!*'

Rich? What did the prancing figure mean?

'*You've two half crowns*!'

'Go away.' Hugh closed his eyes once more.

'Who are you?' This time the voice was a whisper, not a screeching song. Hugh could feel the faint wind of garlic against his cheek. He realised the little man was leaning across his face. He opened one eye and saw he was being stared at gravely.

'Hugh Cassin from Blackfell.'

'Hugh Cassin the Mastersinger?'

Although it was painful, Hugh nodded, and the little man sighed. 'Not a Brother,' he murmured, almost to himself.

'Who are you?' asked Hugh in return, and the little man stared at him in surprise.

'Dagonet!' he exclaimed. 'Who else? Dagonet! Dagonet! Dagonet!' He spun away again in a sudden violent movement and pirouetted wildly, before leaping back to his position close to Hugh's face.

'Hugh Cassin the Mastersinger,' he whispered. 'Let them believe you're a Brother.'

'What?' asked Hugh. He was confused by the mad talk of brothers, by the crazed fluctuations in Dagonet the Fool's movements and behaviour.

'If you don't…' whispered Dagonet. He stepped back and drew his finger across his neck beneath the chin. The meaning of the gesture was unmistakable.

'But why?' asked Hugh desperately.

Dagonet did not reply for at that moment the door suddenly opened, and he leapt back up and on to the cabinet with an amazing agility and resumed his bizarre cross-legged station.

The figure who stepped into the room was wrapped about in a scarlet robe and carrying a bright lantern which he held up over Hugh. 'Is he awake?' he demanded of the little man.

'*Awake awake there'll be no wake, for he's awake for mercy's sake*!' cried the jester in the parrot voice he reserved for his doggerel.

'The devil take your prattle and nonsense,' said the voice sternly, and Dagonet was immediately silent.

Hugh looked up at the man holding the lantern. The face was dark with the light behind it. One keen eye gazed at him curiously, trying to measure him. The other socket was blank, closed into a wrinkled prune. Hugh felt his fingers instinctively clutch at the counterpane as he withstood the gaze.

He was staring into the face of the Markgrave of Gleam.

'Please be assured, Master Cassin,' said the Markgrave in a thin high voice, 'that the felon who brought you to this sorry pass has been apprehended and will live just long enough to curse the day he slithered from his mother's womb.'

Hugh Cassin nodded, sick at heart, his face expressionless. He was not to know that for the ruler of Gleam, who apologised to nobody, this was as near to an expression of grace as he was ever likely to receive.

The Markgrave glanced towards the sideboard. 'Dagonet, begone!' he ordered.

'*You would have me be two*?' demanded the fool.

The Markgrave paused.

'*Once, Dagonet, twice gone*!' Dagonet cried, leaping from the cabinet, and prancing towards the door.

'Twice gone!' insisted the Markgrave.

'*Then*,' cried Dagonet, '*I shall be three*.' As he leapt out of the door he called, '*Thrice nothing*,' and disappeared, tassels flying.

The Markgrave swept around and closed the door, then returned to the bedside. 'Master Cassin, I have reason to believe you are of a certain Brotherhood.' When Hugh did not reply, the Markgrave continued: 'I will grant you an audience in a day or so, when you have recovered from this treacherous blow. I believe there may be some matters of mutual interest to discuss.'

Hugh gripped the counterpane again. He could not imagine what he and the Markgrave of Gleam could possibly have to discuss, and he was bewildered again by the mention of brotherhood, remembering the fool Dagonet's bizarre ramblings. Seeing, but misinterpreting, his confusion, the Markgrave said, 'It concerns these murmurings of this Maiden, the end of the century and such talk. It is a matter of some concern to me.'

Hugh nodded, and closed his eyes involuntarily. It was as he had most feared. Tobias's rash and ill-considered arguments in the Gut and Cuttle had rebounded once again, this time entangling him like a helpless fly in the sticky web of the spider of Gleam. How he wished he'd never entered that smoky hole.

Seeing the musician's eyes droop, the spider himself whispered, 'I'll take my leave, Master Cassin. We will talk later.'

Hugh nodded, his eyes shut, and scarcely heard the soft footsteps as the Markgrave left the chamber.

Chapter Nine
FOOLSCAP

Hugh Cassin passed a restless day, sometimes quite alert although with an aching head, but more usually in and out of a fitful sleep in which he was visited by strange dreams and strange realities. The strangest of these was Dagonet. Often, he was aware, the jester would slip through his door to check on him. Sometimes he would slip out again so quickly and quietly that Hugh could never be sure whether the little man had really appeared or whether a shiver in the drapery had only suggested his presence. At other times Dagonet would silently take up his station on the cabinet across from the bed, staring quietly, as still as a china ornament.

Towards late afternoon Hugh felt a little better. A stolid uncommunicative woman brought him a bowl of thin gruel with slivers of chicken, and he sipped some of the warm liquid and felt strengthened by it. The ache was receding.

Dagonet, who was in attendance, slid to the floor and crossed to his bedside, where he sat cross-legged on the floor. He had, for the moment, given up his falsetto foolishness, and spoke in a soft whisper. Hugh had to lean towards him to catch his words. Now that he was able to focus more clearly he could see that the man was of middle years, his face already lined. He was clean-shaven except for a wispy moustache. Hugh had rarely seen a smaller more perfectly formed grown-up. Sitting on the floor gazing up as he was made him look like a helpless puppy, and Hugh had to suppress an urge to reach out and pat his head or chuck him under the chin, until he realised that this apparent helplessness was clearly the Fool's strategy, his means of protecting himself in a cruel and hostile world. His eyes gave him away. For they were serious, concerned and intelligent.

The eyes looked at him now. 'Tell me, Master Cassin have you any idea how you've come to be supping soup in a bed of the Markgrave of Gleam, and why he should be treating you with such uncharacteristic courtesy?'

'I fear I don't know,' confessed Hugh. 'I was struck down in a tavern called the Gut and Cuttle. I awoke and here I am.'

'You are right to fear, I fear,' said the jester softly. 'Tell me what you do know.'

Hugh Cassin told the jester everything. Of their journey to Gleam, of the episode in the Gut and Cuttle where Tobias had spoken unwisely of the Maiden, of their pursuit, and of their refuge in the large house on the waterfront, the house with the sign of the toad above the porch. As Hugh spoke of this house, the Fool nodded in sudden understanding. 'Go on,' he said.

'The morning we left, Tobias seemed strange,' explained Hugh. He then told his little listener of Tobias's oddly excited manner and how he had managed to persuade the gatekeepers to release them.

'How did he do this?' asked Dagonet, highly interested.

Hugh shrugged. 'I know not. He had some words with one of the guards and the man's manner changed completely. He was ever good with words, Tobias, and he has much charm.'

'It was more than charm,' said Dagonet softly.

Hugh shrugged again. 'Tobias was in good spirits after that. We joined my niece, Johanna, and reached my sister's place safely. Late that night, however, or very early next morning, Tobias disappeared, and Gabriel Beet said he had changed his plans, that he wouldn't be going to Aser, that he'd found somewhere else to study. I guessed Tobias would have returned to the House of the Toad, and left early to find him; but I couldn't gain admittance.'

When Hugh finished his story, Dagonet was silent for a time. Then he sighed deeply and murmured, 'Oh my giddy goodness. Why must good men be such fools?'

'Am I a good man?'

'You are an innocent and you are a fool. Here you have just revealed to me all I need to know to have you flung into the deepest dungeon like a sack of offal, a dungeon where you'd probably be racked and stretched for wasting people's time.'

Hugh looked at the jester in alarm. It had not occurred to him that Dagonet the Fool could be a spy.

Dagonet, seeing his sudden fear, murmured, 'Too late. Much too late, and I've been a faithful servant of the Markgrave for twenty-five years. I've survived. I must have been faithful.'

'Oh.' Hugh Cassin slumped back onto his bolster. 'What are you going to do?'

'It depends on whether *I* am a good man or not, doesn't it?' said Dagonet.

'Are you a good man?'

As if in reply Dagonet raised his three-antlered cap and twirled it around on his finger. 'I'm a fool,' he said simply.

'You said good men are fools,' said Hugh Cassin carefully. 'Does that mean that fools are good men?'

'*It means fools are fools*,' cried Dagonet, this time in his wild parrot voice, and he leapt back and jumped up on to the cabinet once more.

Much later, for it was very dark, Hugh Cassin opened his eyes. He had slept for a long time. A single candle flickered on the cabinet but, initially, Dagonet was nowhere to be seen. As he grew accustomed to the gloom, however, he was aware that the jester had pulled up a three-legged stool beside his bed and was waiting there for him to wake. He seemed strangely excitable.

'Master Cassin! Master Cassin!' he whispered urgently. 'I have made something.'

Hugh grunted.

'But you will not be able to see it,' whispered the jester.

'Why? Is it in the dark?' grumbled Hugh. He was in no mood for Dagonet's wild and wheeling riddles.

Dagonet ignored his question. Instead, he counted off his fingers, 'I have made something you cannot see, touch, taste...'

Hugh sat up and Dagonet handed him a goblet filled with sour wine. Hugh took a deep draught and grimaced. 'What are you talking about?' he asked. 'What have you made?'

'A decision!' said Dagonet simply, grabbing the goblet back and taking a drink himself.

'Oh,' murmured Hugh, disappointed. 'There's little alchemy in that.'

'Oh, but there is, there's much magic in it,' hissed the jester. Then he added, 'You do realise that you'll be discovered? The Markgrave will learn you're not a Brother. That you're just a harmless little musician?'

Hugh did not reply.

'His anger will be huge and black. It will blot you out!'

'But...'

'It will blot you out, Master Cassin. Your songs, your lute... Nothing but cold and darkness.'

Hugh considered the jester's agitated and worrying words. 'Why are you telling me this?' he whispered.

'It is not something I would like to see,' said Dagonet, 'and I have decided to help you escape. We must make our move quickly, before you are discovered.'

'Now?'

'How is your head?'

'Better, I think.'

'Right now, then. There will be safety in it. Magic in your sudden disappearance. Later you would not be able to withstand his questions. Nobody could. As long as he thinks you are a Brother there will be respect. Fear even.'

Hugh stared through the darkness in the direction of the rapid, disjointed whisper. The image of the Markgrave of Gleam, whose terrible scar he had now seen for himself, rose before him. The idea of such a man being frightened of anything on this earth, let alone Hugh Cassin, musician of Blackfell, was both novel and ludicrous. He wondered what possible authority this so-called Brotherhood possessed.

'If you stay and are found out he will be very angry. He will blame you for having fooled him and you will suffer.'

There was no relish in the jester's voice at these dire predictions, only a sorrowful certainty: the certainty of one who knows from long and personal experience. Hugh trembled and took another draught of wine.

'You know him well?'

'Aye,' whispered Dagonet. 'And I knew his accursed father.'

'I must escape then?'

'Yes.'

'How?

'Leave that to me. You do not have your lute with you?'

Hugh shook his head. 'I was going to Lamaria. Abel Larch has been making me a new lute. Why?'

'Later, I will explain later.'

'But we will be pursued.'

Dagonet gripped his sleeve. 'You still do not understand. He thinks you may be a Brother. A Brother! If you disappear before he discovers you are not of the Brotherhood it will be an act of great mystery and power. It will convince him of your status and he will be troubled, so troubled he will not pursue you for fear of adding to his offence.'

Hugh nodded, although he could not begin to understand the jester's words. 'What must I do?'

'I will lead you.' Dagonet paused. 'If we get out, you must leave Gleam immediately.'

Hugh scarcely noticed the pause, and the jester's use of 'if' instead of 'when'. 'But my nephew…' he protested.

'Your nephew,' Dagonet murmured gently, 'I fear is lost to this world, and I fear even more for his soul in the next. You must forget him.'

Hugh felt a coldness grip his heart. 'But…'

'Forget him,' said the jester sharply. 'Wait, now. I will fetch you a lute. It may be your only hope.'

'This way!' hissed Dagonet.

They had been moving furtively, through dark empty halls, deserted corridors, heavy forbidding doors, and always downwards. They had paused at the end of a long corridor. It seemed to Hugh that they were deep below the Citadel. At this level the stone walls, damp with seepage, were shining in the flickering lamplight and the air was as cold as a crypt.

Shivering a little, Hugh whispered, 'How much further?' he still felt far from well. His bag was heavy in his hand and the lute, slung over his back, swung awkwardly from side to side whenever he lurched, which was often in the darkness.

'We have to pass by the dungeons,' whispered Dagonet, 'and then it's just one more flight of steps.'

Not more steps, thought Hugh wearily. The backs of his legs had begun to ache from the number of steep steps he'd descended. Always, there'd been the danger of slipping because of the deep darkness, the treacherous surfaces and the uneven levels. More than once he'd stumbled and discovered that hand rails were few and often broken.

'And then we only have to deal with Garth the Simple,' added Dagonet.

'Deal with Garth the Simple?' asked Hugh anxiously. He did not like the sound of that 'deal with' – the jester's voice had been grim.

'The gatekeeper,' murmured Dagonet, pushing open a heavy iron-studded door. 'The dungeon master.'

They were now in a broader corridor lined with doors, many of which had barred windows. Cells, clearly. There was a gloomy yellow light in this section as a number of cressets had been affixed to the walls, and some were burning with a smoky glow. More than anything else, though, Hugh was assailed by the smell of the place, a stench compounded of dankness, urine and waste, of reeking fear-filled filth-crusted humanity.

Hugh stopped, his eyes wide with disgust and momentary panic. Instinctively, he put his hand to his nose, trying to suppress a cough.

'Come on,' insisted Dagonet, moving ahead. Hugh followed, shuddering, finding himself maintaining a middle path, keeping each barred door as far away as possible, as if he were negotiating a dangerous tightrope and could fall off and plunge into hideous confinement at any false step. The silence was intense, palpable. Although he was walking as stealthily as possible, Hugh wondered why the sound of their steps, which seemed to reverberate among these subterranean chambers, had not wakened the inmates.

'Are there…?' he asked, catching at the jester's sleeve. 'I mean, is there anybody in these cells?'

Dagonet glanced over his shoulder and up at Hugh. 'Oh, yes,' he said.

'But Garth doesn't like his guests to draw attention to themselves and they very soon learn not to. Your friend Tobit Mulbert'll be rotting down here somewhere, if he hasn't putrefied away already!'

Then Dagonet turned and walked quickly on once more. There had been a brutality in the jester's tone that had taken Hugh aback. He did not reply, needing the tiny man's protection in the hostile silence.

Chapter Ten
GARTH THE SIMPLE

Manfred Bufo stared speculatively at Tobias. The young man had been recounting not only how the guard at the gatehouse had become so servile at the sight of the painted toad, but how that servility had in turn been strangely exciting to Tobias, how it had given him such a sense of power and confidence. Manfred Bufo nodded appreciatively at the story.

'It is good,' he said. 'The toad should be respected.'

'But how can a drawing of a toad do that?' asked Tobias.

'It is not the toad,' said Manfred Bufo drily, 'but what the toad represents.'

'And what does it represent?'

They were in the library. Bufo was seated before a low refectory table, a quill and notepaper beside him and a small book in his hand. Tobias, who had been sitting on the other side of the table, studying the anatomical illustrations in a beautiful edition of Mercutio Aubutilon, had, in the excitement of recollection, pushed his chair back and stood up, and was now pacing the floor slowly.

Bufo did not immediately reply. Instead he put his book down and reached for a square of paper. He picked up the quill and dipped it in a small well of black ink. Carefully he drew a circle. Then around the circle he drew a series of short radiating lines. He pushed the simple image towards Tobias.

Tobias looked at him. 'The sun,' he said.

'And what does this little picture represent?' Bufo asked sharply.

Tobias nodded. He thought of the sun in the sky and all it represented. Heat beyond imagining, light inexhaustible, the life and death of the world on which they lived.

But the toad was not the sun. Bufo had intimated *how* the picture could represent something far beyond its crude outline, but he had not told him *what* it represented.

Tobias stopped pacing and turned to stare in fascinated excitement at the old man. 'There was power there,' he said. 'I could feel it. That power felt – oh, I don't know what it was. But it wilted the power of the guard.'

Bufo gave a bleak smile. 'It would. The guard's power was sullied, muddied. It derives simply from the man in the tower's desperate need to stay the man in the tower. The power the toad represents is pure, unsullied. It is disinterested. It derives from knowledge of the farthest places, the deepest places, the darkest places.'

Tobias turned towards the old man. Such talk entranced him. Dr Portcullis never talked this way, never hinted at the knowledge beyond, or of the power that was obtainable there. He felt affirmed in his decision, and gave Bufo a small appreciative nod, which the old man did not acknowledge, having returned to his book.

'What is the Brotherhood?' asked Tobias.

Bufo looked up once more, but did not answer for some seconds. Finally he said, 'There will be a time to tell you of the Brotherhood. And even, perhaps, a time to admit you into the Brotherhood. But those times are to come. It is too soon.'

Tobias looked chastened. He had been given a taste and a warning. It was both exciting and dissatisfying.

'I would perhaps say this,' said Bufo. 'You have met the serpent in the bottle. Among the common people of the land it comes from it is known as a love snake. And it is deadly in the extreme.'

'Love snake?'

'The reason it has been given that curious name is that it is thought that should you inadvertently kill one, its partner will not rest until it has gained vengeance. Those who kill a love snake are, it is believed, doomed. Sooner or later the surviving serpent will wait its chance, wait with the patience of the obsessed, and strike. There will be no mercy, no questions, no hesitation.'

Tobias stared at him.

'The people in that land,' said Bufo drily, 'do not harm love snakes.'

'So…' said Tobias.

But once again Bufo had turned to his book, a gesture dismissing Tobias, and at the same time filling him with urgent anticipation.

The little jester tugged at Hugh's sleeve with one hand and pointed with the other. There had been no need to do this, however, as Hugh had already stopped in astonishment at the sight just ahead.

'Pray to God he likes the way you pluck your strings, otherwise you'll not like the way he'll pluck yours,' muttered Dagonet.

Garth the Simple must have been the largest man Hugh had ever seen. Hugh and Dagonet had entered a short chamber, more a sort of hallway in reality, and more brightly lit than the other passages they had passed through, although the light was still an oily yellow of flickering shadows. The hall ended in a large studded door in front of which, flopped over a three-legged stool, squatted a monstrously fat figure. He was a creature of leather, grime and grease: a shiny bald head as squat as a turnip, a huge flowing jerkin, a vast leather apron, and outsize boots. Littered about him on the stone floor was a scatter of bones piled in places like driftwood: chicken bones, pork ribs, ox tails, chewed, sucked, split and discarded. A flat sour smell permeated the chamber, a smell of sweat and fart all overlaid with the fox-like stench of a carnivore in its lair.

The giant was immediately aware of their presence.

Hugh suddenly realised he was being stared at. The wide foolish grin on Garth the Simple's face faltered as he struggled then failed to recognise him. Garth then glanced down at Dagonet and the grin returned and he nodded happily. This was a familiar figure. Hugh had a sudden image of Posy Beet's little baby gurgling contentedly in her crib.

'Dagonet!' cried Garth, chortling with the surprise of it.

'Garth likes meat and Garth likes music,' whispered Dagonet.

'Likes music!' came the chortling echo.

Dagonet delved into his bag and pulled out an oilskin package that he unrolled. There was a cooked chicken inside which he handed solemnly to the squatting giant, who in turn seized it like a dog and began tearing it apart. Hugh had to look aside as the chicken was devoured without ceremony; greasy fingers shoving legs, wings, and breast indiscriminately into the working maw of a wide open mouth. It was not a pretty sight, but eating did engage the giant's full attention and this allowed the two men to exchange a hurried few words.

'Garth has only one task to do in this world,' whispered Dagonet.

Hugh leaned his ear forward for the jester to continue.

'To prevent people getting out through that door.'

'How does he do that?' asked Hugh.

'He kills them,' Dagonet said simply.

Johanna, holding the baby Ellen, stood by the strong figure of her aunt as she pounded dirty linen in a small pool of the River Flint. The younger woman was rocking from side to side and crooning wordlessly, trying to nudge the little one gently into sleep. Posy Beet sighed, and looked up. Johanna's troubled face was directed southwards towards Gleam. It had been some days since her uncle had hurried off to seek out Tobias, and in that time there had been no word from either.

Aunt Posy had sent Gabriel Beet back to Gleam for any news, but he had returned several hours later full of ale but empty of information, except the irrelevancy that the Gut and Cuttle was deserted and the landlord apparently arrested.

'I'm not interested in your tavern tales,' Posy had said irritably. 'Did you learn nothing of Hugh? Nothing of Tobias?'

Gabriel Beet had shaken his head, smiling foolishly. 'The gatekeeper took a shilling off me to tell me he couldn't remember a thing,' he'd confessed. This confession had been a lie. Gabriel's shilling had been invested in dark Gleam ale.

Now Posy could see the worry in Johanna's face. 'You're thinking, child?' she prompted.

'I'm thinking,' replied Johanna, grateful for her aunt's sympathy, 'I ought to go into Gleam. Tobias could still be at that house where we sought shelter. My uncle could be there too.'

'You'll not go on your own,' said Posy Beet, returning to her washing. 'And my man is not much of a protector.'

Johanna nodded, and pulled her shawl closer around both her shoulders and the baby. There was a cool breeze blowing off the stream. 'She's gone to sleep,' she said, smiling.

Posy Beet stopped pounding once more and straightened, wincing as, arm akimbo, she supported an aching hip. 'We'll put her in her crib,' she said. Reaching up, she took Johanna's free hand and was pulled up the bank. 'And leave it awhile. The trip to Gleam, I mean,' she advised, taking baby Ellen. 'Perhaps if something does not turn up soon, then will be the time to…'

She was reluctant to suggest accompanying Johanna herself, although that was what she had decided to do; just as she was reluctant to give voice to her deepest fears regarding Hugh's possible fate: that he had been set upon by cutpurses and left, stripped, in some ditch or dark alley, or that he had somehow incurred the wrath of the citadel and been dragged to a dungeon, beaten and chained to a wall of stone.

Her fears for Tobias were equally deep, but less graphic. The fact that Gabriel Beet had carved a small wooden toad for Tobias's new master troubled her with a vague memory of old dark tales, of murky rumours and suggestions. Something of violence, something of danger was there, she recalled. Stories of death-dealing, of ancient lore, of secret societies. She glanced again at her beautiful young niece. It would not do to alarm her unnecessarily. For the moment she would keep her counsel.

Hugh Cassin, at Dagonet the Fool's prompting, edged closer to Garth the Simple as soon as the huge man had finished demolishing the chicken. 'Something soft and sweet,' Dagonet had whispered. Garth's blubbery smeary face stared up at him expectantly as Hugh slung the lute from his neck, feeling uncomfortably like the second course. The litter of broken bones did not make him feel any more secure.

He tuned the instrument quickly, expertly, and then his fingers found the strings and he plucked at the beginnings of a melody he had first heard from Alissa of Lamaria, a lilting song of the tall peaks, deep valleys, and rushing streams of that beautiful region.

The giant nodded happily. 'Music,' he said.

Hugh Cassin had a fine sweet tenor voice:

The geese fly
High in the sky
Their far-off voices cry
Mountains
Mountains

Behind him, Dagonet smiled nervously. 'Ideal,' he whispered. 'Ideal.'

The gentian glows
Deep in the snow
Murmuring soft and low
Moonlight
Moonlight

My love lies
Beneath the birch
Above the earth and sighs
Yesterday
Yesterday

Between each verse Hugh let his fingers linger on the strings in soft arpeggios summoning in turn the blue of tall mountains, the emerald of moonlight and the sadness of yesterday. Garth the Simple swayed to the music, his eyes closed with the rapture of it, and as the melody rippled on like a mountain stream, his breathing grew deeper and his head slumped.

'Sing it again,' whispered Dagonet. 'And again and again if necessary.'

Nodding, but without pausing, Hugh carried on. He now realised what the fool's plan was and he sang ever more sweetly and plaintively, not just for the slumbering giant, but for the great studded door with its small vented peep-hole behind him.

Finally the giant's chin fell to his chest, which heaved in the ebb and flow of sleep. 'Play on, sing on,' whispered Dagonet, slipping past Hugh and going right up to the sleeping figure. Even at his full height Dagonet was barely as tall as the slumped, seated Garth. Foraging in his bag once more. Dagonet withdrew a small vial and a kerchief, and, unstopping the vial, he poured some of the contents onto the fine linen. Gently he brought the sodden cloth to the giant's face and draped it over his eyes and nose, as if it were a tiny counterpane over a bumpy mattress. He turned and gestured with his arms for Hugh to continue singing and playing and then he stepped back, waiting thoughtfully.

At Garth's waist, from a leather thong as thin as a bootlace, hung a large brass key. After waiting some minutes, and with the giant seemingly deeper in sleep than before, Dagonet crept right up to him once more. Slipping his hand into his jerkin, he took out a thin sharp dagger whose blade glittered in the yellow light. Hugh's eyes widened in horror, his first thought being that the jester was about to plunge the knife deep into the sleeping flesh.

Dagonet, however, instead took careful hold of the key and then swiftly slashed at the thong. The knife must have been razor sharp for the thong parted and Dagonet turned, eyes shining, holding the key aloft. Crooking his finger, he signalled to follow as leaning past the giant he worked the large key into the keyhole.

'Move quickly,' Dagonet whispered. 'This will be difficult.'

Hugh nodded, understanding. He left off playing, slung the lute over his back once more and, picking up his bag, hurried as quietly as possible towards the door against which Garth was still slumped. Now that they were so close, he paused in astonishment at the huge bulk of the man. How could they possibly pull the door open against that dead weight?

As if he knew what Hugh was thinking, Dagonet, with a tight little smile, pointed and whispered, 'The stool!'

Hugh looked again and saw what Dagonet meant. The stool had tilted back and was pivoted on a single leg. If they could only start the giant moving the stool would tilt forward, and if they were able to generate some momentum the giant could probably be pitched forward and clear of the door.

Hugh nodded. The plan could work.

There was only one problem: once pitched forward Garth the Simple would certainly be awakened violently. That was not at all a pleasant thought. Again Hugh had a vision of the greasy-faced grin as the chicken was torn asunder.

'Help me,' whispered Dagonet.

Their only hope would be to squeeze through the door and make their escape before the huge man came to his senses. But how? What was on the other side of the door? What could be seen through that peephole? They must be deep within the bowels of the Citadel. Hugh had lost count of how many stairs they had descended. Surely escape lay in climbing stairs, not by descending ever deeper into the dungeons of Gleam.

'Help me!' repeated Dagonet impatiently, glancing nervously at the handkerchief as it slowly rose and fell.

It was too late to worry about consequences now. Hugh nodded and took a firm hold of the large iron ring that served as a door handle.

There was a pause as they steadied themselves, then at Dagonet's urgent nod they strained at the door. At first nothing happened. It was like pulling at a dry stone wall. Hugh was about to ease up when he saw the veins bulging in the little jester's temple and, shamed, heaved again with fierce determination. This time there was a faint giving, a slight spongy movement, then more, and then momentum was gained and Garth the Simple was lifted slightly as the stool leaned forward just a little.

Aware that any loss of effort now could send the door slamming shut again, Hugh made one final superhuman effort, grunting with the exertion of it. It had been like pulling a mill wheel up a hill. Now, as if that mill wheel was teetering on the balance before plunging down the other side, the stool hung for a moment and then fell on all three legs. With the sudden jerk, Garth was pitched forward and sprawled headlong onto the floor. More important, the door was wide open.

'Run!' screamed Dagonet, all need for silence gone.

Hugh needed no prompting, and flung himself after the little man out into a wider enveloping darkness.

In that darkness Hugh heard Dagonet's wild cry of 'Run!' again, and he stumbled after the direction of the voice. He swung his head from side to side, trying to work out where he was. Behind him an oblong of brightness was momentarily blotted out by the huge shape of Garth the Simple as his howl of anger echoed in the surrounding blackness.

As Dagonet and Hugh hurled themselves headlong away from that doorway and its howling occupant, their footsteps rang in the cold night air. To his utter astonishment, Hugh suddenly became aware that there seemed to be cobblestones rather than flagstones beneath his feet, and as he lifted his head to suck in precious air he saw, to his further amazement, a sky filled with stars. For all that, he did not pause, and his longer strides soon caught up with the little jester. He grabbed at his shoulder and pulled him into a doorway.

'Where are we?' he hissed. 'How in God's name did we get outside?'

'Shh,' panted Dagonet, 'and you'll hear no lies!'

'No more of your games!' whispered Hugh. 'Where are we?'

'Shh,' repeated Dagonet.

They were both as silent as their panting breathing would allow for a few moments. There was, however, no sound of pursuit.

'It is good,' whispered Dagonet, catching his breath. 'Garth will not leave his post. *Duty bound I'll be bound while we bound away!*'

'We?' asked Hugh.

'*The door was left right left right open, so we can march left right away. Hey!*' cried the jester in the singsong falsetto.

'We?' repeated Hugh.

'*We*,' said Dagonet, gripping Hugh by the hand. There was a smugness in his voice, a hint of crowing satisfaction. 'I am coming with you, Master Cassin!'

Hugh stared at the voice in the darkness.

Then Dagonet released Hugh's arm and jigged away, singing:

'*You were my foreman, man of four!*
You were my keyhole, you were my key,
You were my handle, you were my door!'

Hugh felt a sudden slap on his face as Dagonet flicked at him with his scourge, and began to understand that the jester's assistance was not entirely without self-interest.

'Where are we? You never said.'

The jester pulled Hugh back out into the street and now that his eyes were more accustomed to the darkness he was able to follow Dagonet's pointing finger. Far in the distance now he could see the small oblong of light that must have been the door through which they'd escaped. Above it was a rising bank of black, a deeper darkness, and up, up it Hugh's eyes travelled until he could make out the crenellations of the top of the citadel. Beyond the crenellations he could pick out the black eminence of the tower of Gleam.

'It comes right down to this street?' he asked, surprised.

The jester nodded. 'It is the rear of the citadel,' he said. 'The rocks fall away behind and the dungeons form the basement.'

Hugh nodded. It did make sense. But knowing that they were behind the Citadel did not make things any easier. He was still hopelessly lost in the warren of back alleys on the wrong side of Gleam. They needed to find shelter, and quickly. There would be no gates open at this hour and no passage through even if there were. No doubt there would be a search party. His one faint hope would be to get to the harbour and pray that the *Firefly* had not left port.

He turned desperately to the jester. 'How do we get to the port from here?' he demanded.

Dagonet shrugged. 'I do not know. I have not been out of the citadel for thirty years.'

Chapter Eleven
AUDIENCE

Among the inhabitants of the House of the Toad were a grim-faced old woman who worked in the kitchen preparing simple but solid meals, and a tall shambling figure who became known to Tobias simply as Master Gull, and who may have been a house-servant or may have been a Brother – it was hard to tell – for Manfred Bufo offered no explanation. Other, perhaps younger people came and went. Tobias would occasionally catch a glimpse of a hooded back moving down a corridor, or a door opening and closing. But, for some reason, Tobias was kept apart from these. He was aware, too, that at times people arrived and left the house, often at strange late hours, but again these visitors remained mysterious.

Master Gull was old, older even than Bufo, Tobias guessed, but he deferred to the master of the house so reverentially that Tobias took him for a valet or butler. And yet at times Gull dined with them on the ample beef stews or pies prepared by Mistress Quail. Only rarely on those occasions did Gull say anything, and then only in response to a question or a comment from Manfred Bufo. To Tobias he said nothing, and nor did he respond to anything Tobias said. The young man might not have existed.

One afternoon, some days after Hugh and Dagonet's flight from the Citadel, Gull shuffled into the library and approached Manfred Bufo.

'Master Bufo,' he croaked in his raven's voice, 'there is a personage to see you.'

Tobias looked up. This was something new.

'A personage?'

'A man, sir,' croaked Gull. 'From the Citadel.'

Tobias looked quickly at Bufo. Would this have anything to do with him? It might not be politic for him to be seen, even though he felt somehow secure in the House of the Toad. Would he be sent away?

'Name of Sculldung, sir. Martin Sculldung, an officer of the Guard.'

'I will see him,' Bufo said after a moment's consideration. It was as if he had a choice, Tobias thought, and wondered at the authority of a man who could decide whether or not to see a representative of the Markgrave of Gleam, who could make such a decision even when living within the walls of Gleam itself. Moreover, he gave no indication that he thought Tobias should go.

Gull inclined his craggy head, and silently withdrew.

'Should I leave?' asked Tobias. Bufo shook his head, saying nothing, merely making a cathedral of his fingers above the polished wood of the refectory table.

Some minutes later they heard footsteps approaching and the door opened. Martin Sculldung was ushered in.

Tobias had concluded that the officer was still pursuing the revellers of the previous week, and that their seeking refuge in the House of the Toad had been noted and now acted upon. Strangely, that thought did not make him in the least apprehensive. He was already aware that the drawing of the toad on his flesh conferred a great deal of power, and a power of quite a different order from that of mere functionaries of the Markgrave of Gleam.

Accordingly, he took his lead from Bufo. The intrusion of the crimson livery of Gleam had not discountenanced the old man a whit; nor even, it seemed, aroused any noticeable interest. Even so, Tobias withdrew to a shadowy corner, partly to observe more freely, and partly to allow the others to conduct their business unimpeded.

Martin Sculldung stepped into the room, pausing at the threshold. Bufo, still seated before his heavy refectory table, looked up without expression and then gestured with a finger for the man to approach. Years of service to the Markgrave had taught Sculldung well. Whatever feelings he felt in the presence of Manfred Bufo, he betrayed none by as much as a flicker. There could be read just a hint of curiosity in the glance he directed towards Tobias Swallow, but thereafter nothing.

'You will forgive this intrusion, good sir,' began Sculldung.

Bufo nodded.

'The Markgrave, my master, has a small matter he would like to discuss with you,' said Sculldung. 'I have been sent to arrange a time you could meet.'

It was difficult for Tobias to contain his astonishment. The Markgrave of Gleam had the power of life and death over all citizens of this benighted city. He could have had Bufo dragged before him. Such grace, such politeness, as this was not usually associated with the Citadel.

Bufo nodded again, but said nothing. Clearly he was waiting for the arrangements to be announced. Sculldung swallowed and added, 'At your mutual convenience.'

Bufo turned from the envoy and glanced towards the mullioned window, as if the small panels of glass were keeping an alien country at bay. 'I am an old man,' he murmured.

These had been Manfred Bufo's first words, but Sculldung understood their meaning. 'It may be possible,' he said.

Bufo allowed himself a faint smile. 'Good,' he said. 'Tell Master Twyll I will see him tomorrow evening.'

It was deftly done and Tobias was all the more astonished. Amazingly, the old man had, albeit with great subtlety, commanded the Markgrave of Gleam to appear before him.

The audience was obviously over. Martin Sculldung bowed slightly and announced his leave. Then, as if in the presence of the Markgrave himself, he backed with long-practised obeisance to the door before bowing once more, turning on his heel and leaving. Gull appeared briefly, to close the door, and Bufo and Tobias were left.

After a brief silence, Tobias dared to ask his new master a question. 'What do you think the Markgrave of Gleam would be wanting to see you about?'

Bufo looked at him thoughtfully before replying, 'What they always want.'

'What is that?' asked Tobias.

'Somebody's death,' said Manfred Bufo drily.

Martin Sculldung strode through the streets of Gleam angrily, his two attendant guards scurrying behind. People on the streets, seeing the scarlet livery of the Markgrave and sensing the furious determination of the Captain of the Watch, moved hastily, fearfully, to one side like water parting before the bows of a flying skiff.

From time to time Martin Sculldung would see the word MAIDEN daubed on a wall and he would point silently towards it as he hurried past. His men understood. The motto would have to be removed, and as quickly as possible. They would pause to add the reminder to their jumble of mental notes and then hasten again after the long striding steps of their Captain.

Sculldung could not quite understand why he was so angry. Most probably it had been his reception at the House of the Toad. He was used to being condescended to by the Markgrave, that was his role. But to all other people Sculldung was accustomed to being an object of fear. To his men scurrying behind he was superior in every way: he barked; they jumped. He pointed; they followed. He frowned; they trembled.

In the House of the Toad he had been ushered into the presence of a man, a man whose name he did not even know, a man who had treated him as a mere functionary, who had been uninterested in his rank and position or name, who had manipulated him as a child manipulates a cat's cradle. The Captain of the Markgrave of Gleam's Watch had been nothing more than a length of string. Worse, the man had been so supremely self-possessed and sure of his power that Sculldung was convinced the power actually existed; and Sculldung was uncomfortably aware, too, that the power was of a much higher order than the authority invested in the Markgrave.

This knowledge made him furious and he worried at it. What power could be greater than that of the Markgrave yet exist within the great walls of Gleam? Religious power? Sculldung almost snorted out loud. The Bishop of Gleam was the Markgrave's lapdog, a man whose interest in grace was rather less than his interest in favour, less than his interest in veal, ham and red wine, a man chosen to do the Markgrave's bidding and offer God's blessing to his most vicious projects. Somehow, Sculldung sensed that the old man whose presence he'd just backed obsequiously away from was not a man to do anybody's bidding, not the Markgrave's, not the Patriarch's, not the Emperor's himself. This sense troubled him, diminished him, and made him angry.

Now he was charged to go to the Citadel and report to Evan Twyll that he, the Markgrave, had been summoned to appear before one of his own citizens! The fact of this risk-ridden duty made him angrier still, and he paused and pointed to yet another MAIDEN and cursed his men as he did so, as if they had been personally responsible for its presence.

Then there had been that other figure, that slip of a youth sitting arrogantly in the room, witnessing his humiliation. Sculldung felt a surge of rage. Undoubtedly it had been the student, Swallow, who had some connection with the House, a connection that seemed to bestow protection.

All of these disconcerting events: the graffiti, the legend of the Maiden, the arrival and strange disappearance of the man Cassin, the disappearance of Dagonet the Fool, an event which had plunged the Markgrave into a sullen depression and made it even more perilous to be in his presence. Twyll had seen Dagonet's vanishing as a personal betrayal and his mood verged between something like the grief of loss and a lust for bitter vengeance. Altogether, there was more volatility in the throne room than Sculldung could ever remember.

All of this bile, all of this anger, of course, Sculldung had to swallow before he made his report. To his surprise, however, Twyll did not seem discountenanced by the intelligence that he would be received at the House of the Toad; the line of his scar did not gleam livid as it was wont to do in times of anger. Quite the contrary. The Markgrave seemed gratified. He nodded, gave a grim smile and then clapped his hands lightly as if a solution to a nagging problem was in the offing.

Before he dismissed his Captain, though, he made one further inquiry: 'That musician, the man the fool Mulbert attacked, was he…?'

Sculldung shook his head. 'I couldn't say, sir. I did not see him. Nor any sign of Dagonet. That's not to say, of course…'

The Markgrave nodded.

'I did see the student, Swallow, sir – the man you saw from the tower who had been with Cassin that night we pursued them as far as the House. At least, there was somebody who looked very much like him in attendance to the old man.'

The Markgrave of Gleam nodded again. 'I see. It is very likely those two are Brothers. We were wise to have nursed the musician's hurts and offered him no harm.'

Sculldung felt confident enough to raise a questioning eyebrow, but the Markgrave was not prepared to explain further. Instead he merely repeated, 'Very wise,' and raised a couple of fingers to signal that the Captain was dismissed.

Chapter Twelve
TO LAMARIA

Alissa Larch straightened her back and, shading her eyes against the light from the setting sun, peered into the distance. The dusty road wound down the valley and she could see two figures making their way towards her. They were black with the sun behind them, but all the same she could establish that one was tall and one was very short, a child perhaps.

Almost certainly the figures would be visitors, for the road led nowhere: theirs was the last settlement before the road petered out into a mountain trail used only by hunters or goatherds. Alissa waited patiently so that she could welcome the guests. She felt little fear that the strangers could be sinister, for Lamaria was a vale of tranquillity: its wealth was in things of the spirit, in music and craftsmanship, not in gold or in objects that could easily be plundered and seized by force. Visitors to Lamaria were invariably those who sought that peace of spirit, or who wished to hear or purchase the beautiful lutes for which the valley was famous.

Alissa squinted against the light. The taller figure was walking purposefully, but the smaller figure seemed to be less directed, to be dancing about, and again Alissa wondered whether or not it was a child.

Gradually, something in the manner of the first figure began to reassemble itself in her memory and she was able to guess who it must be. Her father, Abel, had spoken of a visit from Hugh Cassin of Blackfell, and whenever he'd mentioned the name he had given her a brief teasing glance and Alissa would drop her eyes from his smile. She did like Hugh Cassin, for he was a gentle man, kind and good; but he was old, closer to her father's generation than hers. She did not like it when, on his previous visit, her father had nudged Hugh and spoken of her in her presence so that Hugh had glanced at her with new interest. She feared that only Hugh's shyness had spared her the embarrassment of his closer attention, and she felt a twinge of alarm now, seeing his purposeful stride. Her father, she knew, felt the match would be a good one, despite the differences in their ages, and would continue to encourage the musician. Alissa dreaded the likelihood of having to deal a double hurt: first to her father, and second to the man he'd chosen for her.

Once she was certain that one of the figures was Hugh Cassin, Alissa turned on her heel and hurried up the steps of the rambling wooden house she shared with her father and brothers and their wives and families. It was not right that she should greet the musician alone. She would tell the others of his arrival and remove herself as discreetly as possible.

The night following their escape, Hugh found himself utterly lost in the maze of reeking back alleys in deep darkness on the far side of Gleam. To make matters worse, he was aware that he was out on the streets long after curfew: even if he had not been a fugitive already he would have been arrested by any passing patrol. Having escaped through the dungeons with Dagonet only made his position more dangerous.

He knew of no house of safety. He knew of no house at all except the House of the Toad and he had little confidence of being admitted there. From the glint of the stars above, the night looked to be long and dark and cold. Even when the grey light of dawn arrived there would still be the gatekeepers to consider, and Hugh realised there would be little chance of his passing through any of the gatehouses unnoticed; certainly not now that he had the company of Dagonet the Fool with his distinctive scarlet motley, strange dwarfish appearance, and his readiness to break into squawking riddles, half-songs and nonsense.

They sheltered in the doorway of what seemed to be a deserted hovel for some time to take stock.

'Why?' Hugh asked.

'*Why not?*' came the mocking reply.

Again Hugh felt a mistrust about the motives of his companion. 'Why did you come with me?' he asked.

Hugh Cassin was not a selfish man, but neither was he a particularly brave one. He was not angry with Dagonet for having forced himself upon him, but he was extremely troubled by the possible consequences. Dagonet had deserted his post. He was, presumably, a favourite of the Markgrave, and now he had betrayed him. Moreover, he had betrayed him with the help of Hugh Cassin. The Markgrave's reaction would be only too predictable: fury and a demand for vengeance. For this action, Dagonet had almost certainly put his life in forfeit – and also the life, Hugh had thought sourly, of anyone who had helped him escape.

'I am a bitter fool,' Dagonet said simply. 'And a better fool would not have been a bitter fool. Bitterness had bitten my wit: my doom was written in it.'

Hugh nodded. When the wit turned bitter, the foolishness became foolhardiness. Sooner or later Dagonet would have blurted one wrong thing too many, and provoked such a rage he would have been thrown to Garth the Simple like a fried chicken.

Suddenly, close by a dog started barking agitatedly, and almost immediately another joined in. 'We can't stay here,' Hugh whispered.

While they were huddled in the doorway, the only plan he could think of was to get to the harbour somehow, in the hope that the *Firefly* would still be in port. 'This way,' he whispered, taking charge, and they crept into the dark cobblestoned lane, making their way cautiously along the shadowy verges, negotiating potholes and door steps as silently as possible.

They had been proceeding thus for half an hour or so when, at a corner, Dagonet pointed. There was a balcony on a second storey. Silhouetted against the dark sky flapped the darker shapes of washing. 'Wait!' the jester whispered.

He hurried forward. The next thing Hugh could make out was the dark outline of the little jester shimmying up a balcony support as quickly and silently as a monkey. Then Hugh saw the shape clambering over the fretwork of railing, quickly grabbing at the washing and flinging selected items over the rail. Hugh darted forward to gather the falling clothes and by the time he had done so, Dagonet was standing beside him once more, puffing slightly from his exertion.

'The rug!' whispered Dagonet.

A coarsely woven rug in some dark material was passed over and Dagonet pulled it about his shoulders and over his head. He tied a pair of hose about his middle, and stuffed one or two other stolen items down his front. Now he looked exactly like a tiny monk. 'Let us continue our pilgrimage, Brother!' he hissed, and, deep within the hood formed by the rug, Hugh could just make out the gleam of his grinning teeth.

'*But a better brother, brother*!' the little man laughed wildly.

They continued, moving as quickly and quietly as the darkness would allow, working only to the plan of putting as much distance between themselves and the door out of the Citadel as possible and taking the right-hand turn at every opportunity so that they would be moving in a circle and, with luck, ultimately find their way to the harbour. It was a nervous time. Twice they had to slip into back alleys to avoid the flickering lanterns of the watch. At other times dogs woke and let loose a wild volley of barks, and on one of these occasions a window was noisily unshuttered and a drunken voice screamed a curse into the night. On two occasions, as well, they found themselves trapped in cul-de-sacs, and were forced to feel their way out, praying that they wouldn't be accosted by the officers of the watch before they found the relative safety of the street.

Eventually, the strategy worked. Perhaps an hour and a half after they'd burst through Garth the Simple's door, Hugh Cassin felt a movement of air, a breeze, and with it sensed a faint saltiness in the atmosphere. The sea was close by. The lanes that had been higgledy-piggledy up and down gave way to a broader thoroughfare which sloped downwards.

'That way,' Hugh whispered, glancing back over his shoulder. Rising behind him was the black bulk of the Citadel and on top of it the cross-hatching of the tower. This was the view he remembered from the night of their pursuit. 'The port must be down there,' he decided.

Now that they were clear of the warren of lanes and alleys, there was more danger from the watch, and they maintained a course through the darkest shadows. Then, suddenly, they were in a small square and Hugh recognised the Gut and Cuttle tavern, now shuttered, the brazier in the cresset long extinguished. On the brickwork and clearly visible in the moonlight were scrawled the words THE MAIDEN IS COMING. Up the adjacent street was the main gate to the Citadel itself with its forbidding portcullis. This street, Hugh knew, continued through the square to the harbour.

He seized his companion's arm. 'Come on,' he whispered. 'I know where we are now. There was a ship called the *Firefly* in the port some days ago. If it's still there we may yet find safe haven.'

The little figure in the monkish costume nodded. In the cloudless sky above, the two green moons hung in a cold sky. Dagonet looked about him and up at the iron portcullis at the entrance to the Citadel. 'Garth the Simple,' he muttered. 'His simplicity has served us well.'

'What do you mean?' Hugh asked.

Once again, Dagonet grinned from the recesses of his monk-like cowl. 'He will only do what he knows, and he only knows what he can do. He has been told never to leave his door unattended.'

Hugh nodded. 'So he will not have told anybody yet of our escape?'

Dagonet replied: 'He will not budge. He will be sitting there like a top stopped spinning. Nobody will discover we have gone until they take the food to the prisoners in the dungeon. Nobody will trouble Garth until then, and Garth will trouble nobody.'

'Not us, at any rate,' Hugh smiled.

'Not us,' Dagonet repeated.

This had been cheerful enough intelligence, and with more confidence in his heart, Hugh led the way down the shining street towards the harbour.

More cheerful still to Hugh was the sight of the *Firefly* still berthed beside the stone quay. Signalling to Dagonet to follow, he crept cautiously up the narrow gangplank towards the yellow light of two low-wicked oil lamps where he was challenged by the man on watch. He told him who he was and of the first mate's offer of some days before, and then the two of them were allowed on board. It disappointed but did not surprise Hugh to learn that Tobias Swallow, a student bound for Aser, had not yet come on board. They were led across a deck strewn with ropes and mysterious objects to the steerage compartment in the stern and there they were shown a couple of empty hammocks.

'Stow yourselves in there,' the seaman grumbled. 'Captain will see you in the morning.'

Gratefully, Hugh clambered into the hammock and swung there gently, waiting for sleep. His legs were weary, his head racing. The night had been an exhausting one for a man just out of his sick-bed and he was grateful to be wrapped about in the safety of the sweet-scented canvas. The wooden vessel, even at its mooring, creaked and groaned, and the suck and slap of the water was constant. From all about him came the heavy breathing and the occasional sleep-whimpers of other bodies. Thus sleep eluded him for a long stretch.

Whatever plans Hugh Cassin had made of finding Tobias and dissuading him from the madness of giving up his medical studies with Master Portcullis at the University of Aser were now in tatters. Hugh would certainly be a wanted man. Sooner or later Garth the Simple would explain his story and the hunt would be on. His only hope would be to get as far away from the city of Gleam as possible. Hugh's mind tumbled with fears and apprehensions. So far the little jester had clung to him and shown no sign of leaving off. Grateful as Hugh was for his help so far, he did not trust the jester. His oddness alarmed him and his motives were complex and suspicious.

Hugh worried also about his sister, Posy Beet, and his niece, Johanna. His connections with Flintside could well be discovered, and in the event of a manhunt these innocent people could find themselves in peril. Tobias, too, although Hugh's instinct told him that Tobias's position was more secure.

All in all, his best hope would be to secure a passage on the *Firefly* and be dropped off on the Lamarian coast. He would seek shelter in the valley with Abel Larch. Dagonet the Jester could carry on to Aser and lose himself in the towers of that university town. Thus it was that with the valley of Lamaria soothing his thoughts, Hugh Cassin fell asleep in the small hours of the morning.

Chapter Thirteen
CONSULTATIONS

When Evan Twyll did call upon the House of the Toad, attended by Martin Sculldung and a number of other officers, Master Gull ushered him with all due civility into the presence of Manfred Bufo. This time, however, Tobias had not been invited to be a party to the discussion. He remained below in one of the workrooms with the *Books of Leaves*, great leather-bound volumes with beautifully mounted botanical specimens. Here he spent a contented few hours patiently memorising the characteristics of various medicinal and poisonous herbs.

When Sculldung, in his turn, attempted to follow his master, Gull made it quite clear to him that this was to be a private audience by pointedly pulling the door shut behind the Markgrave. Sculldung shrugged, sensing not only the futility but also the risks of protesting too loudly, so he merely stationed his men at intervals along the hallway. He himself found a low stool near the library doorway, and he sat there arrogantly, his long legs stretched out before him.

Evan Twyll, too, was a tall man, and he knew how to use his height to intimidate underlings. He had never been a particularly good judge of character, and the judgement he did possess had long been blunted by absolute power. All the same, whatever faculty remained quickly told him that here was a man who could not easily be intimidated. Bufo was calm, almost serene in his presence, something the Markgrave had rarely experienced. His every movement was slow, considered. He looked up steadily as the Markgrave strode in and rose carefully, in a gesture of mild politeness.

'It was good of you to come,' he murmured, as if he himself had requested the meeting – as if the Markgrave were doing him a great favour.

Evan Twyll nodded, wiping the air with his hand, dismissing the implication.

'Will you take some wine?' Bufo offered.

The Markgrave shook his head. 'It is not my custom,' he said, meaning *it is not my custom to drink untasted wine*, and he might well have added *in such a house as this...* He glanced around him curiously. He had hardly ever been in a house beyond the Citadel. He saw the ceiling-high shelves of books, the gold lettering on their spines gleaming in the lamplight, the scatter of rugs of some oriental origin, and the deeply coloured tapestries with their strange themes: a pair of crouching toads with heavily embroidered toadstones fantastically patterned on the tops of their heads; a pair of love snakes bound in twisting symmetry and about to strike in opposite directions; a brilliantly stylised dagger with a double blade and a toad-headed handle shining in the green glow of the double moons. Turning back, Evan Twyll found the grave eyes of Manfred Bufo studying him with equal curiosity.

'How can this House be of service to you?' he asked.

It was an unusual way to put it. The words *this House* suggested not an individual, but a community, and the Markgrave wondered again momentarily at the nature and size of this community whose aid he had come to enlist. He knew of the House's reputation, of course, but he could not know how much was fact and how much was dark legend. Bufo gestured to an oaken carver chair on the other side of the table, and as soon as the Markgrave was seated, he sat down himself, clearly waiting for the Markgrave's response.

'The century,' began Evan Twyll, 'is, as you know, about to end.'

Bufo nodded. He knew of the touching faith that people put in arbitrary numbers. Label a year and call it a beginning. Or call it an ending. He could understand how knowing that his people were thinking about beginnings and endings could unsettle a ruler, especially a ruler such as Evan Twyll. However, he said nothing, merely waited patiently for the Markgrave to continue.

Evan Twyll glanced towards the window and the line of his scar was presented to Bufo. 'There is a story abroad,' he continued, 'a story of a so-called Maiden who will arrive with the new century and bring with her the destruction of my house, my dynasty.'

Bufo nodded again.

The Markgrave faced him once more, angered by what he felt compelled to report. 'It is arrant nonsense, of course. The splashings of the swill. Superstitious stupidity. But it is a story that seems to have taken hold. There has been much tavern talk, my spies tell me, gossip. The story is embroidered, developed, you know how it goes. And my men report that each night the walls of the city are disfigured by the word "Maiden".'

'I see,' said Bufo.

He could see the Markgrave's growing agitation, and he could understand it. The whispers, the tale passed from hand to hand, and with each passage growing from a tale to a myth, and from a myth to a certainty. He could see how belief in such a story could alter the hearts of men and women, make them dangerous with hope, wild with expectation.

'It is like a brush fire,' said Evan Twyll. 'It is growing beyond control. There is no way… I cannot see how to extinguish it.'

'If you ignore it?' asked Bufo. 'Let the century end willy-nilly?'

The Markgrave shook his head violently. 'It is the idea of the Maiden. It is the idea that gets stronger and stronger. Such an idea can move people to madness, to insurrection!'

Bufo nodded once more. So that was why the Markgrave of Gleam had sought the help of the House of the Toad. He did want a death, but not an ordinary death. He was more than capable of arranging an ordinary death himself.

'How do you kill an idea?' demanded the Markgrave.

There was another silence as Bufo considered this problem. He made his characteristic cathedral of his fingers, and looked for a time almost to be praying. Finally he looked up at the angry man before him. 'I think it can be arranged,' he said simply.

Evan Twyll leaned forward in his seat. There was a stillness in the room that he found calming. The pulse in his temple had stopped throbbing, as it was wont to do at times of angry frustration. 'How?' he asked.

'Oh, very simply,' said Manfred Bufo. 'If you want to kill an idea, first you must make it incarnate.'

The Markgrave frowned. 'What do you mean?'

'You must make it flesh.'

'I still don't understand.'

'Think about it,' said Bufo gently. 'The citizens of Gleam want a Maiden? Then we must give them a Maiden.'

'Give them a Maiden?'

'Yes,' said Bufo, as if explaining a very simple proposition. 'We give them a Maiden. A real live flesh-and-blood Maiden.' Even as he said this he thought of his new apprentice, and he remembered the evening the young man had knocked at his door. He remembered the older man with silver hair and a beard. And he remembered the young woman in a green cape. The sister of the young Swallow. Although the light had been dim he recalled that she had been fair and of surpassing beauty.

Evan Twyll stared at the old man, who had suddenly seemed quite abstracted.

Manfred Bufo was recalled by the Markgrave's stare. 'And then we kill her,' he added.

‘We expected you some days ago,’ said Abel Larch, shaking Hugh Cassin warmly by the hand then pulling the musician to him in an affectionate embrace. Releasing his friend, he nodded curiously but amiably at Dagonet the Fool.

They were standing in the porch of Abel Larch’s workshop. Sweet-scented shavings swept about their feet and from the doorway wafted the cloying smell of oils, hot glue and resins. Hugh Cassin breathed it all in gratefully, glancing about the Valley of Lamaria as the evening settled. The wooded hills, the craggy peaks, the tumbling stream: all these wrapped him about with a sense of safety, of fellowship. Dagonet had, on the night of their escape, used the word ‘pilgrimage’, but this was a genuine place of pilgrimage. Where Hugh was standing now had stood the most famous troubadours of the age, men more than willing to take the long journey to this secluded valley where they could obtain the legendary lutes of Lamaria. These hills would have echoed to their songs and stories.

‘I was held up in Gleam,’ explained Hugh. ‘My nephew, Tobias… I will tell you in good time. He is in trouble, and I fear that I too am in trouble and may have brought trouble to others.’

Abel raised his eyebrows. They were white and bushy and, like his hair, tufted alarmingly. He was a large man with walnut wrinkles, and he wore a long leather apron of great age. ‘In good time, then,’ he said. ‘And Master Dagobert, is it? Welcome, good sir, to the valley. Any friend of Mastersinger Cassin…’

‘Dagonet!’ said the jester. ‘Dagonet!’

Hugh glanced at the little man hopelessly. Was Dagonet a friend? It seemed he had become more of a burden, and a heavier burden than his bag and borrowed lute. He had hoped that the little jester would have carried on with the *Firefly* to Aser, but when the vessel anchored in the Gulf of Lamaria and the longboat lowered, Dagonet clambered on board as well, expressing his intention of staying with Hugh in terms almost hysterical. So upset was he that Hugh was forced to calm him down and promise he’d not be abandoned. And so he had followed Hugh. He followed him through the streets of the little town of Lamaria, stayed with him at the inn, then dogged his path along the roads crossing the lowland plains and then up the pathways of the valley.

Dagonet was neither servant nor friend. He was shadow. His personality seemed to shift with each mile. The further from Gleam the more taciturn and erratic he had become, and the more dependent on Hugh. His purpose it seemed, had disappeared along with his foolscap and scourge, and he appeared to lose both conversation and independence. From time to time, though, he would make brief barking comments as if he blamed Hugh entirely for his present predicament.

'You're welcome, anyway,' said Abel, grasping the jester's hand.

'I've told you already,' said Dagonet querulously, '*I'm Dagonet*!'

Abel Larch was examining, with a professional eye, the lute Hugh Cassin had brought with him. 'This is the work of Alessandro of Nieves,' he said. 'A beautiful piece of craftsmanship, though not in good repair.' He paused, expectantly.

'It came from the Citadel of Gleam,' explained Hugh. 'Dagonet found it for me. He wanted me to play for the dungeon master.'

Abel shook his head. 'And thereby hangs a tale,' he murmured. 'Did you play for this dungeon master, my friend?'

Hugh nodded. 'Oh, yes. A lovely lullaby your daughter once taught me.' Alissa looked up from her embroidery, and Hugh hummed a few bars, then smiled wryly. 'It worked, too.'

'The Citadel, you say?' said Abel. 'Then this could well have been Vendula's instrument. It was said he displeased the Markgrave of Gleam.'

There was a silence after that. There was no need for comment. All knew what the displeasure of the Markgrave of Gleam meant.

It was that period of quiet companionship before sleep. Earlier they had eaten well, and drunk well, then first the children, and then Abel's three sons and their wives had departed for bed. Now only the old man, Alissa, Dagonet and Hugh remained in the large gallery that served as a meeting place in the old rambling house of Larch. Alissa sat by the grate, nudging the flickering logs every now and again to nurse the last of the fire. After dinner both she and Hugh had sung, Hugh delighted at the beauty of the sound of the new lute Abel had created for him, and delighted, too, to be able to hear Alissa sing once more. He had forgotten how achingly sweet and pure her voice was, and how cleverly she could weave descant harmonies about his melodies. The others had listened in great contentment, Dagonet squatting cross-legged on top of a high cabinet, just as he had in the chamber in the Citadel, and Abel leaning against a bolster, fondly imagining again that Alissa and Hugh could one day marry.

After Alissa had finally risen to say her goodnights and departed, Abel poured a measure of rowanberry brandy into three wooden goblets and proposed their mutual good health. Later, as he sipped at the fiery liquid, Hugh was able to tell the lute maker of all that had happened in the city of Gleam, and of his worries about the safety of Posy Beet, Johanna and the baby Ellen; and of his fears for his nephew, Tobias Swallow.

As he described the House of the Toad and all that had happened there,

Abel's face grew grim and guarded. 'A toad, you say?' he asked.

'With a hexagon or a shape something like on its head.'

'The toadstone,' murmured Abel Larch.

'What's that?'

'I fear your nephew is in terrible danger,' said Abel Larch.

Hugh glanced up at the cross-legged figure of Dagonet the Fool. He remembered that he had said much the same thing as they had prepared to leave the Citadel.

'The Brotherhood,' murmured Abel Larch. 'He is no doubt in the process of becoming a brother. He will be lost.'

Again this talk of the brotherhood, of brothers. Hugh remembered the mad riddling of Dagonet: *Are you a brother, brother? Not my brother… Brother's brother? Hugh Cassin the Mastersinger, let them believe you're a brother.*

Hugh shook his head, glancing again at the squatting figure. 'What do you mean by this talk of brothers?'

Dagonet spoke for the first time since their supper. '*Brother saved your life, no brother*!'

Abel turned and gave him a bewildered look. He was unused to these wild and whirling words. 'Think of the toad,' he said, returning to Hugh. 'It is a creature no other creature will willingly harm because it is so poisonous. You eat it: you die. Or it spits at you, or you rub against it: you are poisoned. You suffer. They say there is a precious stone embedded in the head of certain toads which is the only safeguard against its venom: the toadstone. An antidote embedded in the poison, like a jewel set in a nest of vipers.'

'What has this to do with…?'

'Patience, patience,' said Abel. 'This Brotherhood we speak of is a dark and mysterious thing. From antiquity it has been well known in certain circles, and yet not well known. People know of it, but little about it. It has taken the toad as its emblem. Like the toad it is a creature of dark vapours and mystery. The Brothers dabble in the dark side. They are necromancers, experts in alchemy, in poisons, venom and death. Like the toad the Brotherhood enjoys a certain immunity. To harm them is to invite certain retribution… Even as grown men avoid scorpions, so men of great power avoid the Brothers.'

'But Tobias is not like that. He could never…'

Abel put out his arm and gripped Hugh's sleeve. 'Friend,' he said, 'I do not know your nephew, but he is young and easily impressed. The young are intrigued by mystery and fascinated by power. You said he seemed wild and madcap the day you left Gleam. I suspect he had been given a taste of the power, enough to get you out of the city, through the gates, and I suspect he was intoxicated by that.'

Hugh nodded. He remembered the feverish excitement that had seemed to have gripped Tobias. He remembered the sudden change in attitude of the Markgrave's men from grim-faced gatekeepers to almost fawning servants. 'You could be right,' he said slowly.

'I fear I am,' said Abel. 'And I fear more. I fear, as I said before, that he is lost.'

'Lost?'

'Once he has been with the Brothers, once he has learned their secrets he will never be free. Should he try to escape it would mean certain death.'

Hugh looked at the old lute-maker with horror. 'Then we must free him at once. We must free him before he becomes entangled in their web!' he exclaimed. 'He cannot become a brother!'

'*Brother saved your life*!' cried Dagonet once more.

Hugh stared into the flickering embers in the fireplace, thinking of toads, of Tobias, of this strange brotherhood.

'*Saved your life*!' Again Dagonet's parrot-like chorus. Again Abel looked at him in consternation.

Hugh, however, suddenly realised what the jester meant. 'Oh my goodness,' he whispered. 'So that's why I was treated with such civility. Why the man from the tavern was thrown into the dungeon. They feared I was a Brother.'

'*I told you! I told you*!' chanted Dagonet.

'But you didn't tell me why!' exclaimed Hugh. The enormity of it suddenly struck him. 'They were afraid of me!' he said, wondering at it. 'The Markgrave of Gleam himself, afraid of me. Oh, but if they had known.'

'They'd have chained you to the wall,' cried Dagonet. 'Like an apple tree for plucking!'

There was a long silence as the other two allowed Hugh to digest this strange news. In the grate of the huge stone fireplace a sudden draught caused a swirl of sparks to lift and shine like a brief sailing constellation against the sooty backdrop of the chimney.

At length he murmured, 'I wonder…'

'What do you wonder, my friend?' asked Abel, trickling another measure of rowanberry brandy into Hugh's goblet.

'Will they still be afraid of me?'

There was a flurry from the dresser and, with great agility, Dagonet the Fool launched himself cross-legged into the air to land safely crouched on his feet between the two men. All at once his parrot-language was forgotten as he turned to Hugh.

'You escaped from the Citadel,' he said, 'through the dungeons. You disappeared from Gleam, without passing through the gates. What else could that be but the darkest necromancy? Hugh Cassin, they will be more convinced than ever!'

There was another long silence as Hugh considered Dagonet's words. Finally, he murmured, 'Then, I can return to Gleam.'

Dagonet looked at him in alarm. 'No, Hugh Cassin! I am the fool. Don't play my part!'

Abel Larch looked troubled. 'Think on it, Hugh. It is not wise to tempt fate so.'

Chapter Fourteen
JOHANNA

As the Markgrave took his leave he turned and addressed one further question to Manfred Bufo. 'Tell me,' he said. 'There is a musician. A man named Hugh Cassin of Blackfell. He has silver hair and a silver beard and an unpleasing countenance. A sly shifting fellow.'

Bufo remained expressionless.

'Is he, how shall we say, of your company?'

The question was bluntly put and Bufo was in no doubt of Evan Twyll's meaning. However, it was not in his nature, nor in the code of the Brotherhood, to respond to such an inquiry. The old man gave a faint shrug and said drily, 'I believe I know the man.'

Evan Twyll gazed at him a moment trying to read his impassive face, and then he gave a fleeting smile. 'I thought as much,' he murmured. Then he turned on his heel and pushed through the door, nodding curtly to Martin Sculldung as the Captain leapt in a flurry to his feet. 'Come!' he ordered. The Markgrave wanted out of this House and the feeling it gave him, even as he was congratulating himself on his good fortune in not having harmed a hair of a Brother given to him for safekeeping.

Shortly after the departure of the Markgrave and his men, Bufo was sitting at his table thoughtfully. He looked up at a soft knock at the door.

Master Gull entered quietly, closing the door behind him. 'They have gone,' he said.

Bufo nodded. 'Where is the boy?' he asked.

'He is downstairs,' said Gull, 'with the *Books of Leaves*.'

Manfred signalled to the stooped figure to approach. 'Tell me,' he asked. 'Is he ready, do you think?'

Gull pursed his lips for a moment, then shook his head. 'He is still intrigued,' he said slowly, as if thinking aloud. 'Fascinated. He is certainly desirous of the power, but in my view he is nowhere near ready to pay the price of that power. It is a heavy price,' he added with a bleak smile. 'Who is ever ready to pay it?'

Bufo did not reply immediately. Instead he looked towards the oriel window, and his shadowy reflection stared back. Finally he murmured, 'No matter. The business is now pressing. The pot will have to be stirred.'

'It is often the best way,' said Gull.

'It is often the only way,' said Bufo.

'True. That's true enough,' whispered Master Gull, as he too turned towards the window and its dark reflections, but it was very clear he was thinking of events long past, but not forgotten.

The mood in the little cottage by the River Flint was of increasing gloom. There had been no news. Whenever they heard the sound of a traveller on the dusty road that led to Gleam, Posy Beet or Johanna would run with expectancy, but each time these small spiralling hopes were dashed. Mistress Beet was no longer prepared to ask her husband to seek news in Gleam, despite his oft-stated willingness to do so. She knew what she must do, and every time she looked at her niece's downcast head or lost faraway expression the certainty hardened.

After some days, she knew the time had come. She turned to the young woman. 'Johanna, would you know this house again? The place you sought shelter that night?'

Johanna looked up thoughtfully. 'I think so,' she nodded. 'It was on the waterfront. A very large house with a stone porch. I remember thinking it could have been a monastery.'

'We've heard nothing,' sighed Posy Beet. 'My brother may well have left for Lamaria, or something else.' She did not want to put those fears into words. 'But as for Tobias – we know that from what he said to Gabriel he was going back to that house.'

'Yes, the wooden toad.'

Mistress Beet nodded. 'My dear,' she said firmly, 'I think the time has come for us to pay that house a visit.'

Master Gull reached high up into the shelves of the dimly lit laboratory and with both hands brought down a large glass jar stoppered with a waxed cork. Carefully, he manoeuvred it on to a large work table and then he rested for a moment before dusting the jar clean with a soft cloth.

In the windowless room there were deep shadows all about, the only light coming from a small oil lantern. In its glow the liquid in the glass shone with a honey-gold colour, and as the dust was polished away Gull could see his distorted image, ancient and yellow, peering back at him with huge sturgeon's eyes.

Inside the bottle could now be seen a collection of wrinkled roots, like narrow parsnips, except that each root was forked, giving the appearance of spindly, disembodied legs. Dancing legs, you'd think, as if a kicking frenzy had been frozen. Master Gull nodded. It was good. He fingered at the grimy yellowed label and peered forward to read the legend. *Mandragora*, it read: *Mandrake*.

Leaving the jar, he then moved over to a bookshelf. Holding the lamp aloft he scanned the shelves, then finding what he was after, removed a heavy volume bound in dark vellum and returned to the table.

What was it Doctor Bufo had said? Stoke the fire? Stir the pot? Stir the pot! That was it. The young man, Swallow, had much potential. He could see that, and so could the Master. There was a recklessness in him. A swagger. An arrogance. There was also a keen intelligence and a will to power. A good combination. All important attributes.

There was certainly the possibility of a Brother there. Gull sighed, and pondered. The young man in his guilelessness, his foolishness, so much wanted the authority of a Brother. How he thought he would enjoy the flash of fear in the eyes of those who glimpsed his badge, his crouching toad. How he would secretly exult knowing how their mouths would dry, their pulses quicken. He did not yet know the terrible price he must pay for such power, nor that having paid that price he would never exult in anything again. For at some point, and now quite soon (the pot must be stirred; the point must be sharpened) Master Tobias Swallow must be brought to commit the unthinkable without thinking, perform the unspeakable without speaking; for the Brothers were those who lived with enormities so terrible their only human shelter, their only refuge in a world made mad, was the Brotherhood itself.

Opening the book, Master Gull turned the heavy pages carefully, looking for his reference. Then picking up the lantern he returned to the shelves where the flasks, jars and jeroboams were housed. Master Gull soon found what he was looking for: an equally dusty jar of serpent wine. He placed it on the table beside the jar of mandragora roots and dusted it clear to check the contents. It was also good. The head and neck of the albino-like snake rose from its coils as if locked in the act of striking, its bared fangs glinting icy in the lantern light like death frozen.

With a slight shudder, Master Gull turned away from the snake and back to the mandrake roots. Even more than in the glass jar of the mandragora had he seen his reflection in that jar of serpent wine. He preferred to study the forked roots. Preserved in their liquor they had never known daylight, had never been touched by human hand. Generations before, under the eerie light of the two green gibbous moons a doomed black dog had tugged their forked legs from the red earth. Used in the right measure they could drive men and women to wild excesses of passion, or drug them to insensibility. Used another way and with certain other substances, they could, say, render an ambitious young man as pliant as pastry-dough, to be shaped, pulled, rolled, and stretched, if need be, into an assassin.

It was good.

Sighing once more, Master Gull took a razor-sharp knife and began to scratch carefully at the brown wax sealing the cork.

'What is the Brotherhood?' asked Tobias.

The last time he had asked this question, Manfred Bufo had dismissed him. Tobias had bided his time, conquering his impatience. He had been given tasks and he had performed them. He had picked up the threads of his studies at Aser, for the House of the Toad was well endowed. He found the library excellent, the herbals and collections more than adequate, and Bufo as learned in the far reaches of medical knowledge as Doctor Portcullis himself. Still, at the heart of the House of the Toad was a mystery. There were silences there, and secrets. Anonymous visitors called at strange hours and the inhabitants of the house were shadowy and fleeting. The knowledge here was hermetic, sealed off. Truly, he himself had been given access to it, but he had stumbled into the house by accident; he was a windfall who had been picked up, perhaps, and polished a little, but he knew he was a lucky exception. Moreover, he realised he had only been given permission to sift at the surface of things: the deeper things, the darker places, the cabbala, had been denied him. There were doors with locks, cabinets with locks, locked drawers and secret compartments. There were Brothers here, but they were evanescent, unseen. He was only able to connect with the tall gaunt figure of Master Gull. The others drifted along different, more dimly lit corridors, worked in different places and, when they passed each other along the way, made Tobias feel like a child caught in a forbidden orchard.

Bufo considered his young acolyte carefully before replying. 'Would you be a Brother?' he asked.

Tobias said, 'I do not know. I would know more of the Brothers, and then I could decide.'

Bufo said cryptically, 'To know of the Brothers is to be a Brother.'

Tobias stared at him helplessly. 'This is a circle. You're arguing in a circle.'

'It *is* a circle.'

This was an impasse. Tobias remained silent.

'What would you have?' asked Bufo.

Tobias thought. What was it that had brought him here, back to this dark forbidding house? That had drawn him so urgently from Flintside, causing both hurt to his family and the scattering of his intentions to return to Aser? The answer, he realised, was drawn on his arm. Faded but still visible. The image of the toad, and the magic that image had wrought. Again he saw the face of the gatekeeper and how his sneering superiority had wilted before that little picture, how the toad had transformed the man into a frightened lapdog. And as he saw that transformation yet again, Tobias knew the answer to Bufo's question. 'Power,' he said.

Bufo gave a faint smile. 'And what is power?'

Again, Tobias considered. He remembered the freedom he had felt. The surge. The glint of triumph as he had unrolled his sleeve. He remembered the gatekeeper's slightly widened eyes, the barely audible catch in his breath. What was that freedom he'd felt? Freedom from…?

'Freedom from fear,' he said, and again Bufo smiled faintly, as if a catechism had been correctly learnt.

'There are two ways of obtaining that particular freedom,' he said. 'The ignorance that is innocence; or the knowledge that is certainty.'

Tobias nodded.

Manfred Bufo formed his fingers into a cathedral. 'The Brotherhood,' he said, 'deals in certainties. You would be a doctor, yes?'

Tobias nodded again.

'As a doctor, as a Master Portcullis, you will deal only in possibilities. You will deal with that most volatile of human commodities: hope. Hope which is, as often as not, doomed despite your best intentions. If you are an honest physician your life will be one of constant fear.'

'As a Brother?' asked Tobias.

'There will be no need for hope. Hope is irrelevant. There will only be certainty. Doubt is irrelevant, too. We represent that which is inevitable.'

Tobias's eyes widened. He began to realise.

'This century,' added Manfred Bufo, 'is almost at an end. Its end was inevitable, and what is to come is inevitable; and yet the foolish citizens of this benighted town insist on visiting the occasion with much significance – of investing the moment with hope. That is the way of superstition.'

'Death?' asked Tobias.

'That certainty,' said Bufo looking over his joined fingers at Tobias, 'is our comfort. It is our security, and that certainty and our, how shall I say, *knowledge* of the subject, makes all others quail before us.'

At that point there was a soft knock at the door. Both men looked up as

Master Gull entered bearing a tray with a glass decanter and two glass goblets. 'You called for wine, sir?' he murmured.

On the road to Gleam, Posy Beet wondered again at her niece's determination. It was difficult to identify: there had been no scenes, no nagging, no open manipulation, and yet there had been a growing inevitability about this journey, and somehow, quietly, surely, it had been Johanna who had determined it.

Over the last few days, Posy had grown to know Johanna as the woman she was becoming rather than the child she had been, and she had come to love her dearly, as a sister more than as an aunt.

Johanna, despite her physical resemblance to Tobias, was unlike her brother in almost every other way. She shared the height, the same shock of fair hair, the almond-shaped green eyes and high cheekbones of the Swallows – the Cassins were ever short and dark – but their personalities were quite at odds. Whereas Tobias was excitable and impulsive, Johanna was calm and collected; whereas Tobias was given to excess, Johanna was restrained; where he was a creature of appetites and selfishness, she was sober and selfless. Tobias was obvious, but Johanna, Mistress Beet was beginning to appreciate, was subtle.

It was typical, thought Posy, that on a mad whim, Tobias should have left his aunt, his Uncle Hugh, and his loving sister without so much as a goodbye or a passing thought; and typical that since that sudden departure, Johanna should have thought of little else but *his* welfare and the trouble he may have got himself into. For Tobias was in trouble, of that Posy Beet was sure. Of the House of the Toad she knew very little except vague murmurs and cloudy rumours. Although she knew full well that Dame Rumour was never to be trusted, there was usually some starting point of truth. Whatever she'd heard always pointed in the direction of evil, of darkness, of death. None of this she mentioned to Johanna, but somehow or other the younger woman had been sensitive enough to pick up a hint here and a suggestion there.

Posy had watched her determination grow as she had dandled baby Ellen with an instinctive love, as she had taken over household duties to give her aunt more time, anticipating and covering in a quietly responsible and intelligent way. She had even, by good humour and gentle charm, managed to get Gabriel to his feet and into the woods where from time to time Posy could hear the sound of his axe rather than the click of his whittling knife.

That morning, Posy knew the time had come. Carefully she packed some provisions for the journey, and then tied her swaddled baby into a harness which she tied to her front. 'Look after the house, husband,' she'd said. 'Johanna and I must to Gleam. It is time. We will be back before nightfall.'

Johanna gave her aunt a quick, grateful smile and rushed to fetch her long green cape, for the days were growing keener with the year's end and the wind would be cold off the sea.

On another road many miles to the west strode Hugh Cassin, his bag slung over his right shoulder, and his new lute slung over his left. Hurrying behind was the tiny figure of Dagonet the Fool, who seemed determined to dance attendance on the musician, even if this journey had seemed to fill him with fear.

'There is no need! There is no need!' he had cried, when Hugh had made his intentions of returning to Flintside clear.

'No need for you, it's true,' Hugh had replied, 'but I need to see my sister and my niece. They'll be worried I haven't returned from Gleam. They'll be wanting news of my nephew.'

Privately, Hugh hoped that his decision to return towards Gleam might rid him of the jester, who had steadfastly remained at his side like some querulous shadow. Alissa had taken the little man under her wing and had even fashioned ordinary clothes for him from his stolen rugs so that he could discard his jester's motley. Her meticulous needlework ensured that the jacket and jerkin fitted perfectly, but all the same there had been only a marginal improvement in Dagonet's eccentric appearance. Partly it was his size, but mostly it was his unpredictable way of moving and his oddly intense manner. It was not easy to discard the jester along with the foolscap and motley.

Dagonet had lived most of his life in the Citadel as a creature apart, one who spoke in riddles and double meanings, who tweaked authority and danced away. He had no recipe for dealing with such ordinary folk as Abel Larch and his household. He frightened the children and worried their mothers. He was sensible enough to avoid the menfolk but increasingly he irked Hugh. Only Alissa seemed not to mind him. She humoured him and listened to him and, to reward him when he was less wild, she occasionally sang to him.

Despite his terror of Gleam, though, he had rushed after Hugh Cassin when he had set off on the road down the valley, and remained with him after each crossroads. Hugh thought he may have been able to persuade him to stay in the small town of Lamaria or take another road towards the east, but Dagonet remained, albeit complaining all the while of the dangers they were unnecessarily exposing themselves to.

Hugh had been given courage by the knowledge that he had been mistaken for a Brother, and from time to time he had reminded Dagonet of this. 'You said they will be frightened of me?'

'You are not Brother, Mock Brother!'

'They will not know that.'

'The Brothers will know that, Not Brother!'

Hugh had not thought of that. Still, he'd reasoned, he had not really been impersonating a Brother. He had been mistaken for one. It was not a claim he'd made. It had been their error. Surely there would have been no blame in that? He still had only the vaguest notion of what a Brother was, anyway. And that thought reminded him of the plight of Tobias and of the need to make for Flintside as quickly as possible. He lengthened his stride yet again, prompting another squawking protest from Dagonet.

'There is a visitor, Master,' said Gull.

Manfred Bufo looked up.

'Or rather, three visitors – a young woman and an older woman with a baby. The young woman is very fair. She claims to be Master Swallow's sister.'

Bufo suddenly became more alert. 'His sister, you say? Astonishing! Incredible. The arrow quivering in the bull and I didn't even draw the bow,' he murmured. He raised a finger, gesturing Gull to wait, while he thought quickly. 'Where is the boy?'

'Down below. He is sorting through the specimen drawers of amanita.'

'Lock that door,' ordered Bufo, suddenly decisive. 'I do not want them to meet. Then bring the girl to me.'

Gull nodded, and was about to withdraw when Bufo said, 'Wait.'

'Doctor?'

'Almost certainly,' said Bufo, choosing his words carefully and giving a thin smile to the old man, 'I will need them to stay overnight. It would be very convenient if one of them could fall sufficiently ill.'

Master Gull nodded expressionlessly and departed. As he did so, Bufo reached for his blue skullcap and, with great satisfaction, pulled it over his straggly white hair. Such a visit was an unexpected boon. All the same, matters would have to be hurried along. There was much to think about. The outline of a beautifully elegant plan had been fashioning itself in his brain, a plan which would serve both the Markgrave of Gleam's need to eliminate the idea of the so-called Maiden, and his own desire to initiate Tobias Swallow into the dark night of the Brotherhood. The boy had all the promise but was still free. If things worked out well he would shortly be fixed in the dark amber of forever. And things were suddenly working out very well. All the elements in his plan were assembling themselves beneath this very roof of their own free will. It was astonishingly convenient, almost as if ordained.

Still, to take advantage of this luck, he would have to arrange things carefully. Brother and sister must not encounter each other. Master Gull would have to be given instructions: the women must stay here; Tobias

Swallow must be conditioned. Most important of all he himself must consult with Evan Twyll. This night.

Such rapid planning coupled with the wonderful pattern of the plan was almost enough to put Bufo in a mood approaching good humour as he rose to greet Johanna and Mistress Beet when, a little later, Gull ushered them in.

Chapter Fifteen
GATHERING

Hugh Cassin knocked at the door of the cottage at Flintside. He pulled his mantle over his shoulders and rubbed his hands. It was mid-morning but the watery sun had done little to warm the day. At length the door opened and Gabriel Beet peered blearily out. His hair was tousled and Hugh gained the distinct impression he had just woken up.

'Brother-in-law?'

Gabriel's eyes widened in recognition and he smiled in welcome. This was a good sight. Posy would be pleased, Johanna too. He knew how both had been worrying about not having heard from Hugh. Then he caught sight of a strange little creature clutching at the back of Hugh's cape and his smile faded. A boy? Too old for a boy, but too small for a man.

'This is Dagonet,' explained Hugh, seeing Gabriel's slightly alarmed look. Thinking better of saying 'The jester', he added, 'My travelling companion. How are you, Gabriel? Has there been any news? What of Tobias?'

'Come in! Come in!' said Gabriel, ushering them into the small parlour.

Hugh slung off his bag and lute and made himself comfortable while Gabriel busied himself preparing them some food, but Dagonet wandered around the room inspecting everything carefully.

'You have just missed Posy and Johanna,' said Gabriel some time later, handing his guests each a pannikin of gruel. 'They left for Gleam earlier this morning with baby Ellen. They will return this evening, though.'

Hugh looked up at. 'You have had some news?'

Gabriel shook his head. 'Nothing. That is why they went. I myself have been a number of times to no avail. This time they were going to go to that house.'

Hugh looked at him with alarm. 'They should not have gone there. It is a place of evil.'

Gabriel shrugged.

'The only hope,' said Hugh bitterly, 'is that they'll not get in there. The door was shut fast as a tomb against me.'

Dagonet, who had so far been more interested in the cottage and Gabriel's little wooden figures displayed in various corners, was alerted by Hugh's bitter tone. 'What door? What house?' he asked.

As if in reply Gabriel reached into a willow basket by his seat and took out a small wooden object. He held it out towards Dagonet. 'This house,' he said. Crouched in his palm was a beautifully chiselled wooden toad. Its mouth seemed fixed in a hideous grin and its globulous eyes stared sightlessly at the suddenly horrified jester. The light in the parlour was gloomy, but even in that gloom the wood shone like butter.

Dagonet leapt back as if stung. 'Hugh Cassin! Hugh Cassin!' he cried, jumping to his side and clinging at his arm. 'They should not go into that house!'

Shrugging off the clutching Dagonet, Hugh moved to the table and picked up the wooden toad. He studied it curiously, both repelled and attracted.

Seeing his interest, Gabriel said, 'It is the same as that drawn on Tobias's arm.'

Dagonet's gasp was audible.

Hugh cradled the toad in his hand. 'Would you sell it to me, Gabriel?' he asked. 'I would have this little monster…'

Dagonet whispered, 'No…'

It had been on the tip of Gabriel's tongue to say generously, 'You may have it, brother, as a gift. As a homecoming present.' But the idea of Hugh's pennies turning themselves into creaming ale overcame him. 'Of course,' he said.

Manfred Bufo stared intently at Johanna, a gaze the young woman found quite unnerving.

She was ideal, Bufo thought. Ideal. She possessed a perfection of form that not even the folds of her long green cape could conceal. Her hair was long and fair; her eyes wide, green and luminous. Above all, she radiated that innocence that was so often associated with saintliness. There could be no more striking contrast to the swarthy, scarred and bitter figure of Evan Twyll, Markgrave of Gleam. Johanna Swallow seemed everything he was not. She seemed perfect.

'Come in. Come in,' he said, as Johanna and Posy Beet stood at the doorway unsure of what to do, given the old man's intense scrutiny.

Ideal was the word, thought Bufo. For those deluded fools who demanded a Maiden this young girl provided a vision of maidenhood that could satisfy any prescription.

'Come in,' he repeated, and finally Johanna and Posy were persuaded to cross the threshold and enter the library of the House of the Toad.

Posy looked about her in wonder at the size of the room, the light from the oriel window, the books, the rugs and the tapestries. Then she glanced at the figure before her, his blue skullcap and his deep-blue clerical-looking gown. He had an ageless face: it did not seem lined or wrinkled as had that of the old shambling man who had shown them in, but there seemed an ancient knowledge there, especially in the sharp dark eyes which studied her niece in such a calculating way. Only the white hair, which he wore long so that it sprouted and tumbled beneath his cap, told you that this man was no longer young.

Posy was proud of her intuition, and she immediately recognised that something about this man made her feel very afraid, that it had been a terrible mistake to intrude into this forbidding domain. Instinctively she crossed her arms about her baby who was still sleeping on her chest, and then she hurried after Johanna who was making her way towards the large table where the man sat, a large volume open before him.

'I am sorry, sir, to trespass on your kindness once again,' said Johanna, her voice steady, maintaining a formality which seemed appropriate to the library.

Manfred Bufo nodded, but did not reply.

'You may remember offering us shelter one night not long ago. I was with my uncle, Hugh Cassin of Blackfell, and my brother, Tobias Swallow.'

'Yes, young lady,' said Bufo. 'Indeed I do remember, and I was happy to offer the assistance of this House to those in need.'

Posy wondered. The sentiments were warm, but the voice was dry and chill. She wondered also at the way the man had referred to the house. It was almost as though the house itself possessed a personality. Once again she glanced around at the library, this time imagining what sort of character the house had. Something quite unpleasant, she was sure. Oppressive. She could not understand why her nephew would have willingly returned to such a place.

For the first time Johanna's composure faltered. Why had the man not volunteered any information about Tobias being here? Why this cat and mouse game? 'We believe,' she said, then began again. 'We think that my brother may have returned to this house.'

Bufo looked at her expressionlessly.

Johanna faltered once more. 'He left us. The next morning. After we reached Flintside. His intention was to return here.'

Bufo raised his eyebrows as if surprised. 'Really, young lady? Why would he have wanted to do such a thing? Did he leave something here perhaps?'

Johanna gave Posy a quick disappointed look, then turned back to the old man. 'He is not here?' she asked directly.

However, Bufo did not immediately answer, because at that point Master Gull entered the room with a tray of sweetmeats and a decanter of wine.

'You will take some refreshments, surely,' murmured Bufo. 'I fear you have come a long way with high hopes.'

Johanna nodded, finding speech difficult.

'Your brother is not here,' said Bufo. 'It was my understanding from our conversation that he intended to return to Aser. In fact I remember giving him my best wishes to pass on to my old friend, Dr Portcullis.'

Posy glanced up at the tall figure of Master Gull and refused a goblet of wine, but she could not resist the softly coloured cubes of confection.

'You are certain?' insisted Johanna.

Bufo shook his head. 'I am sorry,' he said. 'Your brother did not return here.'

There was a short silence as Johanna sought to make sense of what she had been told.

'I wish I could be of some assistance,' said Bufo. This time his tone was almost gentle, and Posy wondered whether her earlier misgivings had been a moment of foolish panic. Perhaps his manner was simply overly severe, that of a scholar cut off from human contact. He could possibly be a kind, considerate man. 'But I am old,' added Bufo, 'and I rarely leave the House.'

Johanna nodded. 'I am sorry to have given you this trouble,' she said. 'It's just…' Suddenly she brightened. The man had said something about Aser, and Dr Portcullis. Of course. Tobias must have joined his ship. That made sense. The *Firefly*. He would have met Hugh then joined his ship and sailed on to Aser. Hugh must have gone on to the valley of Lamaria. They had been worrying for nought. Putting two and two together – Tobias's sudden disappearance, the whittled toad – and making five. Not hearing from Hugh had made them think the worst.

She rose, giving Bufo a warm smile.

She is ideal, he thought. Ideal.

'Come, aunt,' said Johanna. 'We must not impose ourselves any longer.'

'Wait,' insisted Gull. 'You have clearly come a long way and I know you must be tired. I do implore you to have something to drink and something to eat.'

Johanna glanced at Posy, and her aunt nodded. Baby Ellen was stirring in her harness, and would need to be nursed before long. This room provided some comfort and warmth for this.

'Thank you,' said Johanna, looking up at Gull with a small smile. He bowed his head slightly and passed her a small goblet of red wine, waited for her to take one of the coloured cubes, and then he passed a goblet to Bufo.

The little repast was awkward. Neither Gull nor Bufo made any attempt at conversation and Johanna could think of nothing to say that could possibly be of interest to the two old men. She sipped at the thick sweet wine in quick little bursts, eager to be finished and to be out of the room which she found increasingly oppressive. She was compelled to wait, though, as Posy had put her baby to her breast and was murmuring endearments of encouragement softly. Eventually, she was done and she bound baby Ellen back to her front and gave Johanna a small grateful smile.

Pleased to be able to leave at last, Johanna rose to her feet. As she did so, however, the room seemed to sway and she seemed to keep on rising, higher, higher. She stared at the oriel window. Its hexameters of glass were turning around in a clockwise direction, speeding, slowing, stopping, and then they began to spin in an anti-clockwise direction, splashing the room with gobbets of light. The light fractured into prisms and the library was suddenly full of rainbows. It was beautiful. She had stopped climbing and paused, reaching, with a cry of delight, towards the beauty of the rainbows, but they retreated before her fingers and she fell forward, slowly, slowly, and the rich red rug with its patterns of diamonds and triangles rose inexorably towards her.

Tobias had been absorbed in his study of the *amanita*, the evil toadstools of the dark places. He had studied both the actual specimens collected, mounted and neatly labelled in the wide flat drawers of a cabinet in the collection chamber, and the beautifully inked drawings of the death caps, death cups and destroying angels. So absorbed had he been he had not noticed the faint click of the key when Master Gull had locked him in the chamber.

He had been feeling oddly light-headed throughout the morning and wondered whether he was suffering a mild fever, for despite the cold which had prompted him to wear extra layers of clothing, he found at times he was perspiring slightly and at other times was possessed of a chill so penetrating it almost caused his teeth to chatter.

Just as he had not heard the earlier click, nor did he hear the second click when, an hour or so later, Gull unlocked the door once more. Tobias looked up with some surprise when Gull entered the collection chamber. He was carrying a tray with the same decanter of wine that had been served to him in the library. To his further surprise Master Gull gave him a faint smile as he placed the tray, decanter and goblet on the table.

'Doctor Bufo is concerned you may be feeling cold, Master Swallow,' he said, 'and would have me bring you a little something to warm the inner man.' He then deftly poured a generous measure of wine into the goblet.

Tobias, watching him, smiled. 'Tell him the inner man is grateful; and the outer man too.'

Gull bowed slightly as Tobias took from him the proffered goblet and lifted it to his lips.

Posy clambered to her knees beside the prostrate body of her niece. She looked up wildly at Manfred Bufo who had hurried to her side from behind his table. Master Gull stayed in attendance, but kept back in the shadows.

The old man knelt awkwardly beside Posy and took up one of her limp arms and felt for her pulse. 'She has fainted,' he said.

'Fainted?' cried Posy. 'Are you sure.'

'Dr Bufo has more knowledge of medical matters than all the leeches of Gleam put together,' observed Master Gull.

'Tell me,' asked Bufo, 'is she with child?'

Posy looked up at him angrily. 'She is not,' she declared. 'She is my niece and a maiden of great virtue. It is a vile suggestion!'

'That it may be,' said Bufo drily, 'but it may well be true nonetheless.' He looked again at the slumped body, considering it gravely. 'It is better she should rest. She will come to consciousness soon.' Indeed, Johanna was already making light whimpering sounds and was beginning to breathe noisily. 'All the same,' Bufo added, 'I feel she should not exert herself too soon. What were your plans, Mistress?'

Posy said stiffly, 'We planned to return to Flintside as soon as possible. The baby…'

Bufo nodded. 'Naturally. However I deem it most unwise she should attempt such a long walk this day. May I suggest that Master Gull here show you to a room where she could rest? Indeed, you must remain here this evening. If your niece is feeling stronger you could journey home in the morning. It may well be better for the little one, too.'

Posy nodded. She did not like to have to stay so long away from Flintside, but Gabriel was capable of looking after himself. It was far more important that Johanna recover her strength, and for them to make their way home after that. Bufo's reminder of baby Ellen mollified her somewhat, as well. Looking after Ellen was demanding and she couldn't do that job as well if she had to help Johanna. 'Thank you,' she said. 'It is a kind offer.'

'It is nothing, I assure you, Mistress,' replied Bufo with just the faintest hint of a gracious smile. Then he turned to the ancient figure of Master Gull. 'Fetch Mistress Quail,' he said. 'She will help the young lady to a room when she is well enough, and Mistress Beet and her little one too.'

Gull nodded politely and, stepping carefully around Johanna, left the library.

Bufo made himself comfortable in the wooden chair the Markgrave had provided for him, and drew the dark blue monkish hood off his head. Then he looked up. 'I believe I am now in a position to solve your little problem,' he said.

'Tell me more.'

'That is, to eliminate this so-called Maiden that seems to have blighted your life.'

'The devil!' exclaimed the Markgrave, staring at his mild-mannered visitor, admiring his sang-froid, and grinning with the surprise of it. 'The devil! This is all very sudden.'

The two men were in a private chamber in the Citadel. There were no servants in attendance. Few in the Citadel would have been aware of the visit of the old man in the long blue habit, as Martin Sculldung had brought him briskly to this place by rarely frequented passages.

It was already evening and bitterly cold outside, but the room had the chill taken off it by a log fire burning in an iron-basket grate and by rich red hangings covering the door and windows. Evan Twyll had drawn the chairs close to the fire and had called for a bottle of wine that now sat on a small table between them, its dark ruby red gleaming in the firelight.

'Events have fallen into place extremely fortuitously,' said Bufo. 'However,' he continued, 'there will be certain conditions I must insist on being fully observed.'

'Oh, yes?' said Evan Twyll. He was not used to people insisting on conditions. These were, though, unusual circumstances, and if this strange figure could deliver what he promised then he was more than prepared to listen.

'You see,' explained Bufo, 'your little problem also provides me with a small opportunity. If I solve your problem, I will be able to take advantage of this small boon I have been offered.'

The Markgrave nodded, although he did not follow. Instead he poured himself a glass of wine, and offered one to Bufo who declined with a small wave of his fingers.

'It gives me the chance of assaying a potential Brother,' explained Bufo, although this explanation still did little to allow the Markgrave to understand.

'What does this mean for me?'

'It means I will provide a Maiden. Ideal for the part, in fact. Ideal. I will also ensure that she is recognised as such by the citizens, after which you will arrange to have her arrested.'

'Where?'

'In the main market square of Gleam.'

'When?'

'Tomorrow.'

'So soon?'

'So soon. Station your men. There will be a signal. The time should be about noon. Bring her to the Citadel.'

'There will be a cause?'

'Clearly,' murmured Bufo, 'the woman will be a witch.'

Evan Twyll nodded. 'It is good. It is excellent good. As a witch we can put her to death in full view. The flames will show the people. The bishop…'

'No,' said Bufo urgently, 'you will not put her to death. This is one of my conditions. You must allow our Brotherhood to put her to death.'

Evan Twyll frowned. 'What would you have me do, then?'

'I would have you imprison the woman. Bind her, and bundle her well. Put her in a dark cell. Shortly, I will arrange a person who is to dispatch her. Allow him full access and freedom of movement. It is most important to my cause that this man be the one and no other.'

The Markgrave of Gleam shrugged. 'It is a small matter, I think. But how should I know the fellow?'

Bufo in reply pulled back his sleeve and the image of the toad squatted there, bulbous eyes glaring at the Markgrave. 'He will bear the sign of the toad,' he said simply. 'One more thing. I need a man you trust, one to whom I can give some special instructions.'

'Martin Sculldung. My Captain of Guards.'

Bufo nodded. 'Is that the man? When the maiden is well within your care, send him to me. I will give him further instructions. Do not fail me in this.'

Evan Twyll flushed a little at having yet again been given a direct instruction, but gave his assent.

'Good,' said Bufo. 'All is most satisfactory then, is it not? Once I have met with your Sculldung I will be in a position to send you our man.'

'There remains the problem of the people,' said the Markgrave. 'Her death will have to be shown to them. How will they know she is dead?'

It was Bufo's turn to shrug. 'You will decide. You will of course have the body. Display it any way you like. Hang it in the market. The head could be left on the traitors' spikes on the city wall. My only demand is that my man is, shall we say, the executioner.'

Evan Twyll nodded. 'Good. Good. It is a small thing. And if it means an end to this nonsense…'

Bufo said, 'It could hardly be otherwise. Is it agreed? You agree to these conditions?'

'I do,' said Evan Twyll. 'Clearly they serve our mutual interests. Mine. Yours.'

'Then,' said Bufo, 'all are satisfied. There is a pleasing symmetry in these arrangements. A satisfactory design. But it would not do,' he added warningly, 'for there to be any rearrangement, any dislocation.'

'Oh no,' said Evan Twyll looking directly at the old man, raising his glass in a pledge and letting the ruby liquid trickle into his mouth. He swallowed, then said, 'I agree. Two birds then, with one stone.'

'Exactly,' said Bufo. 'Exactly. Two birds. One stone.' And for the first time he allowed himself a faint smile.

It was, as he had said, a beautifully symmetrical design. The Markgrave would be provided with his Maiden. She would be revealed, made flesh momentarily, and then plucked away to be revealed once more, dead. As cold and dead as the hopes she once represented. And the assassin, the destroyer of those hopes, would be her own brother, by which act he would be bound inextricably to the Brotherhood he so foolishly craved. Such an act, so unnatural, so barbarous, was an ideal initiation. It would cut him off from all he knew, from all claims and kinship, and he would be confronted with the choice every member of the order had had to face: death, or the Brotherhood.

Each Brother was bound to the brotherhood by an act of such enormity. Each Brother had to bear a real toad of horror forever. Even after so many years, Bufo could scarcely bear to think about his own toad without a shudder of despair. He stood up. There was no ceremony in it.

The Markgrave of Gleam stood as well. All protocols had been ignored. This man seemed somehow beyond them, and strangely the Markgrave did not feel offence. None had been intended, he knew. The man seemed beyond human fear. Beyond, if it came to that, humanity itself.

'I will have my captain show you out,' he said.

It was not until very early the next morning that Johanna returned to full consciousness, although she had wandered in and out of coherence at various times. She was, however, still very weak and disoriented. Posy had sat with her all night in the little chamber Master Gull had provided, mopping her when she was feverish, calming her when she was given to wild ramblings. Posy had been very grateful to the strange old man, Gull, for despite his somewhat forbidding and rather remote manner he had visited the room regularly to inquire after Johanna and to offer any other assistance. He had brought rugs to help stave off the chill of the small hours, a ewer of water and a cloth to help cool Johanna's brow when she was burning, and he had regularly checked her pulse and murmured encouraging words. Clearly he had not been to his bed at all that night. On a couple of occasions Posy had been visited by Mistress Quail who had brought a steaming bowl of chicken broth and insisted that as a nursing mother she should drink. Posy was sure, too, that this act of kindness had been at the instigation of the old man, Gull.

Later when Johanna was helped to her feet and took her first few unsteady steps, another bowl of broth was delivered and Master Gull returned and encouraged Johanna to take a few drops. He persuaded her to stand once more and inspected her tongue carefully, made her roll her eyes, and then once more took her pulse. Then he looked at the two women.

'I am pleased to say,' he said gravely, not looking at all pleased, 'that Miss Johanna is well recovered and should be able to make her return journey after another three or four hours. At midday, perhaps?'

Posy nodded, and gave him a quick grateful smile.

'Make sure she takes as much broth as possible, then,' said Master Gull. 'It will build her strength.' Then, with a formal bow of his head, he left the two women, closing the door carefully behind him.

Chapter Sixteen
AT THE MARKET

True to Master Gull's prediction, Posy Beet, baby Ellen and Johanna left the House of the Toad half an hour or so before noon. Johanna was feeling almost returned to her usual strength but even so, Manfred Bufo had insisted on both Gull and Mistress Quail accompanying the two women to the East Gate.

When they had visited him just before leaving, Bufo had been courteous and concerned. As she had sipped at the small glass of sweet liquor he had offered them as a 'tonic for their journey', Posy Beet had considered how she had misjudged the man. It was shocking to suggest that Johanna might have been pregnant, but, she conceded, if he were a medical man then it must have appeared a possibility. First appearances had been deceiving: he had been gentility and kindness itself. Finally he had ushered them out, wishing them good luck in their efforts to make contact with Tobias.

Now, as they approached the East Gate and came upon the small market, Posy glanced at her niece and felt more confident. Johanna was looking better all the time: her colour had returned and there was much more purpose in her step. She looked, in fact, far fitter and better equipped for walking than her two escorts. The old man, Gull, moved slowly aided by a gnarled stick and the Mistress Quail waddled awkwardly. Posy could see from her distorted boots that she had bunions like knotted lumps that must have been very painful.

The market was noisy and crowded. Shouting vendors stood behind benches or tables piled with coarse sacks of grain and root vegetables. Eventually they reached that section of the market where the butchers were selling their joints of pig and beef and where the cobbles were littered and greasy with bits and pieces of animal, bits and pieces not even the wildest entreaties of the vendors could persuade people to buy: split hooves, fragments of bone, tattered snatches of hide, globs of fat and gobbets of blood. The smell was horrendous; a reeking sweet scent of death, and the air was filled with the whine of flies and the hoarse cries of the butchers.

Posy glanced anxiously at Mistress Quail. She was looking quite unwell, and she wondered at the folly of these two ancient retainers escorting such young and relatively fit women, for Johanna continued to improve and was pressing ahead of the party, relishing in her return to good health.

Worried at the old lady's appearance, Posy pushed her way through the throng, trying to establish a path so that Mistress Quail would not suffer too much jostling, and she slowed so that the old lady would not be compelled to move so fast. By this time Mistress Quail had taken Master Gull's arm and the two made their way like an ancient and grotesque bride and groom. And then Johanna, from her three or four yards ahead, heard a curious double cry: a pained whimper from Mistress Quail and a cry of alarm from Master Gull. She turned hurriedly to find Mistress Quail lying sprawled on the dreadful cobblestones, and the old man clambering to his knees beside her.

'Posy!' called Johanna in alarm. Posy, clutching at baby Ellen, was staring, frightened, at the body of the old lady. Then to Master Gull, Johanna cried, 'What ails her?'

Master Gull looked up at Johanna, his rheumy eyes filled with fear. 'I think she's dead!' he whispered.

'Oh no!' gasped Johanna, death being strange and mysterious to her. 'She cannot be.' It was something she could not make sense of. How could this old lady, tottery as she was, be alive one moment, and suddenly dead the next? How could she, who had been walking seconds before, now be so still, so completely motionless? Johanna instinctively dropped to her knees beside the old lady whose eyes were closed, whose mouth hung slackly open, with her skirts fanning out over the stones.

Master Gull, who had been holding Mistress Quail's wrist, let it drop like an unwanted fish. 'No pulse,' he whispered ominously as he made room for Johanna.

Johanna, white-faced, glanced up at Posy who was standing at the front of the gathering excited crowd.

'Is she…?' whispered Posy.

Master Gull nodded

Already the gawping onlookers had begun to multiply and press around the prone figure, gazing at it with that horrified fascination which the living reserve for the dead. Master Gull climbed awkwardly to his feet and swayed against them. A buzz, not of flies, but of human excitement spread through the crowded market and the butchers faltered in their shouting, sensing that somewhere there was meat more attractive and that they had lost their audience.

Johanna reached for the limp, discarded wrist and picked it up gently, seeking with two fingers for the telltale throb. She was unused to this, but remembered how her brother had looked for the tiny heart beat in her own arm.

Posy looked at the scene with a mixture of feelings. She was a good-hearted woman, and distressed for the old lady, but she sensed how this tragedy was causing the crowd to push and shove in its curiosity and she felt increasingly concerned for baby Ellen's safety, strapped to her front. She pushed them away but ever closer the people pressed, poking, pointing, and murmuring. Master Gull, too, blindly shook his hands at them, croaking ineffectually, 'Back! Back!'

From somewhere, then, came the cry of 'Fetch the watch! Fetch the watch!' and the call was taken up. Meanwhile, Johanna's fingers gently tried to read the withered, wrinkled wrist, but there seemed no more life in it than in one of Gabriel Beet's dried sticks. She looked up helplessly at her companions. The old man, Gull, now appeared to be in a complete daze, and Posy was looking about her with alarm. It was a very awkward situation. The old lady was clearly beyond help, but they could hardly leave the old man.

It did not seem long before the authoritative footsteps of the watch arrived, and the crowd fell away before five figures cloaked in scarlet. Beside the kneeling Johanna lay the body of Mistress Quail. Her grey-white shawl spread over the cobbles like an open cowl, and from her long skirt of rough-spun blue serge, her bunion-filled boots stuck up like turnips.

'What's happened here?' demanded a tall figure, the leader of the watch.

Johanna stared up at a brown-bearded man who towered over her. 'I think she's dead,' she said, wonderingly.

The word sounded heavy and strange in her mouth. Death was something Johanna had been largely sheltered from. Since her father's death, when she was but a child, there had been deaths of course: of animals, of neighbour's children, of elderly villagers; but Johanna had always stood at their outskirts. The awful reality of kneeling beside one who, now pitched into death, had been lurching along before her minutes before, was something quite disturbingly new.

The man waited.

'She just fell,' said Johanna, holding out her hands as if to demonstrate that the old lady indeed had just fallen, never to rise again.

The man nodded, and glanced around him. 'Get back!' he barked at the crowd.

It was almost too late for such an order. Those pressing at the front were inclined to obey, but were prevented from doing so by the press from those behind. However, the venom in the man's voice and the scarlet cape of the

Markgrave's Watch were sufficient to effect a shuffling movement backwards. And thus for a prolonged moment there was something of a tableau in the market square. The stretched still body of the old lady, the kneeling Johanna looking up at the tall officer with her arms raised in supplication, and crouched behind her the crow-like figure of Master Gull. These four were circled by the growing crowd craning across an invisible line established by the authority of the Markgrave of Gleam.

At that moment of stillness, however, completely unexpectedly, the stretched body of the old lady gave a spasm, a shudder, and then, as those in the crowd who were closest gasped and pulled back in fear, her elbows drew back and she half-rose to a sitting position. She gave a low moan, opened her eyes and looked about with wide, wild eyes.

Johanna closed her eyes briefly in gratitude. 'She lives! She's alive!' she whispered, opening her eyes and lifting her head. The cry was taken up by all about her, but by none more so than old Master Gull who clapped his hands in ecstatic joy and leapt about with a clamouring enthusiasm that belied his arthritic awkwardness of before.

'She lives!' he cried in a quavering voice. 'It's a miracle! She has come back from the dead! The Maiden has saved her! She lives!'

He danced about the reclining figure grabbing the outstretched hands of the now buzzing crowd. The word *maiden* seemed to have a galvanising effect. Like a kind of talisman the word was passed backwards through the crowd until it overwhelmed all others, so that when Johanna eventually rose, helping the miraculously recovered Mistress Quail to her own feet, she found herself the object of a reverential gawping from a crowd now strangely stilled and whispering. No longer was Mistress Quail the object of attention, now it was Johanna whom the onlookers craned to see, and, as the whispering grew, to reach for, and touch.

'Maiden! Maiden!'

The word was taken up and passed from one to another like some strange polished object, as if it were something mysterious and powerful. Gathering courage from the power of the word people on the outer fringes pushed further towards the front.

'Back!' cried the Captain of the Watch furiously.

The crowd swayed, indecisive, as the word danced and tumbled amongst it.

'Maiden! Maiden!'

To all of this, Johanna seemed perfectly oblivious. Her attention was still with the old lady whose unsteady figure she was helping to her feet. Mistress Quail rewarded her with a ghastly smile and a gaze of adoration, then made a grotesque curtsey and reached to touch Johanna's cheek in part homage, part blessing. 'Thank you, Maiden,' she whispered hoarsely. Loud enough for those in the immediate vicinity to hear the word, seize it, and pass it quickly form one to another.

The word spread throughout the crowd, and again and again the Captain of the Watch was forced to roar to quell the mounting excitement.

Posy Beet, meanwhile, had found herself manoeuvred away from Johanna by the surge of the crowd and although she attempted to get back to her niece her efforts were blocked by a wall of legs and backs, a wall that swayed back and forth as its courage and curiosity, its desperation to get close to the Maiden grew before quailing once again before the ferocity of the watch.

Suddenly Posy, trapped as she was, heard another set of urgent sounds. Shouts, and running footsteps. Somewhere she could here a bell ringing with desperation. A tocsin. The galloping footsteps grew louder and Posy realised the watch was being reinforced. There were shouts and more fearful cries and Posy fell to the ground as those about her tried blindly to escape the wrath of the Markgrave's guards. She instinctively curled into a protective ball wrapped about baby Ellen, who had jerked into wakefulness and was squalling angrily. Posy finally felt more space about her then opened her eyes, struggled onto her knees, then clambered to her feet, whispering to her crying baby, stroking her little head. Already the crowd was dispersing as people scattered pell-mell to avoid the heavy boots and flying clubs of the guards.

As she stood and stared about her in a thinning crowd Posy saw with horror a contingent of guards with drawn swords make straight for Johanna, who stood in confused isolation. She saw her seized brutally and dragged crying across the cobbles. She could hear her cries of fear and outrage. Posy screamed and stumbled towards her niece, but found her way barred by a grim-faced figure who swung a cudgel at her.

'Back woman, if you value your life!' he snarled. 'Get away home. Can't you see the Maiden has been taken, you fool!'

The blow would have struck Ellen but instead struck Posy against her upraised forearms and she fell once more to the cobbles, gasping with the pain of it. When she raised her eyes again she could see the market square clearly. The spectators had scattered, stallholders had returned to their booths, and members of the watch and other guardsmen, there were so many now, were driving the last of the stragglers away. A knot of guards in the distance was pushing a stumbling figure before them. Johanna. Arms bound. Driven towards the citadel by taunting guards.

In her shock, Posy saw, standing to one side, the tall hollow-looking figure of Master Gull, no longer prancing with excitement. He was standing not far away from the old lady, Mistress Quail, none the worse for her apparent death and resurrection. Clutching her throbbing arms across her chest, Posy stumbled towards them. 'What has happened?' she cried. 'Why have they taken Johanna?'

The old man turned towards her, as if surprised she should still remain. Suddenly, to Posy, he seemed taller, straighter, less shambling and fragile. 'Get home with your child, woman, while you can,' he said in a voice of steel. 'The other young woman is quite lost to you now!'

'What do you mean?' cried Posy, chilled by the old man's tone and manner.

'I mean she is dead,' said Gull, and his words were all the more terrifying for his calm matter-of-fact manner of saying them. Then he turned abruptly, dismissing Posy Beet with a flick of his hand as if she were a troublesome insect.

Chapter Seventeen
THE WOODEN TOAD

Almost blind with grief and trouble, Posy stumbled down the narrow road that led to Flintside. Baby Ellen hadn't stopped her angry agitated crying since the violence in the market. So beset was Posy that she almost collided with her brother, Hugh Cassin, before she looked up to realise who it was.

'Oh, Hugh,' she cried. 'Something dreadful…'

'What is it, sister?' cried Hugh, catching her in his arms.

'Johanna… Johanna… She has been taken!'

'Taken? How do you mean, taken?'

'By soldiers of the Citadel. By the guard. They dragged her away from the marketplace, and Master Gull, he said…'

'Master Gull?'

'Master Gull from the House.'

None of this was making any sense to Hugh, so he stepped back from his sister but still held her firmly at arms length. 'Quiet, Posy,' he said gently. 'All these wild whirling words. I can't begin to understand what you're trying to tell me right now. You must calm yourself and start right at the beginning.'

Thus saying, he led her gently to the side of the road where there was a low bank overhung with wild bracken, and he sat her down, taking a seat beside her, but he kept his hand in hers. Dagonet, strangely subdued in the face of Posy's and her baby's distress, climbed up beside Hugh and swung his little legs from side to side. As he did so, Posy was finally able to calm Ellen by putting her to her breast, and Ellen's suckling in turn calmed Posy. After some time she was able to recount the whole story of how she and Johanna had gained admittance to the House of the Toad. She told Hugh how the strange old man said he knew nothing of the whereabouts of Tobias, but had assumed he'd gone on to Aser as he had planned, and how this had relieved Johanna.

At this, Hugh shook his head. 'No, sister, it is too soon for relief. Tobias did not join the *Firefly*. This little man and I found safe haven on the vessel. Indeed, we left Gleam on it. Tobias certainly was not on board.'

Posy Beet's distress increased visibly.

'But go on,' insisted Hugh. 'What of Johanna?'

Posy continued her tale: how Johanna had fallen strangely ill and had to be nursed through the night, and how kind and considerate the people in the house had been. Then how the old man Gull and the old woman Mistress Quail had accompanied them through the market on their way to the gatehouse, but how in the market Mistress Quail had collapsed. How she had been pronounced dead; and how somehow, even as Johanna was holding her, she had been returned to life.

'Astonishing,' murmured Hugh.

'Yes, but what followed was terrible,' cried Posy, her voice quivering with the horror of the memory. 'The old man Gull shouted about it being a miracle and how the Maiden had performed it. There was a crowd. They all began shouting and crowding and all I could hear was 'Maiden' and 'miracle' and somehow in all of the buffeting and in the press of the crowd I lost Johanna. I think they would have swept her away, they seemed so filled with joy. But then the watch moved in, and then more soldiers arrived. There was shouting and there were pikes and cudgels. I was feared to my heart for Ellen. They clubbed the crowd aside, seized Johanna and dragged her away as if she were a common felon, not a sweet young thing who had simply been trying to help a poor old woman who had collapsed in the street.'

'I don't understand this,' whispered Hugh. He turned to Dagonet, but the little man shook his head in equal bewilderment.

'What can we do?' cried Posy. 'She will be killed. Johanna will be killed.' Her eyes filled with tears once more, and she wiped at her face with her sleeve.

'Oh nonsense,' said Hugh gently, 'you surely can't believe that.' Once again he turned to Dagonet for reassurance, but the jester stared at him wide-eyed and would not give him reassurance. Hugh felt a surge of fear. 'Why do you say that?' he demanded.

Posy, red-rimmed, stared at her brother. 'It was the old man,' she whispered. 'The old man, Gull. He said Johanna was lost to us. That she was dead.'

Hugh sank his head into his hands. He did not understand. Abel Larch had told him he feared Tobias was lost to the world and now Posy was telling him that Johanna had been taken by the guard and would be put to death. How could he ever return to Blackfell and bring such news to his sister, Joan? The sister who had farewelled her son and daughter with such high hopes for Tobias at Aser and for Johanna at Flint. The sister who had entrusted her children to him, knowing the high-spiritedness of the one and the gentleness of the other.

Posy stood up. 'I must to Flintside,' she said. 'Gabriel will be…'

Hugh stood up as well. 'Of course,' he said. 'Of course you must and we…' He did not know what he and Dagonet would do. The world suddenly seemed darker and less able to be shaped. His hand brushed his pocket and felt a shape there. A weight. Idly, he put his hand into the hole and felt again the wooden object he had paid Gabriel for.

He drew the toad out and studied it. Gabriel had cleverly whittled it from willow and oiled it into a yellow smoothness. The grain flowed around its squatness widening around the knobby eyes as if the wood once had knuckles there. It sat in his hand complacent and perfect and Hugh recalled why he had purchased it in the first place.

Dagonet saw Hugh studying the toad in his hand and his eyes widened with anxiety. He jumped from the bank crying, 'No! No! It is a foolishness in your mind. You must not!'

Hugh looked at the little figure, shaking his head at the man's terror. There was a grim determination in his voice though when he said, 'But I am the fool now, remember?'

'You mustn't!'

'I have no choice. This little bauble may be our only chance.'

'Our?'

'Suit yourself,' said Hugh coldly. '*My* only chance.'

Posy did not understand what the men were speaking of, but she could feel the fear emanating from Dagonet and it alarmed her. 'What would you do, brother?' she asked.

'I will to Gleam,' said Hugh. 'I was going there at any rate to find Tobias, but it seems there is work of even greater urgency I must do.'

'No!' cried Dagonet.

Hugh ignored the jester and seized Posy by the hands. 'Goodbye sister, goodbye little Ellen,' he said. 'Give my regards to Gabriel.' Then turning on his back he set off grimly down the road towards Gleam. Posy sighed heavily, and turned the other way and began her journey once more to Flintside. Dagonet stayed where he was in an agony of indecision. First he made as if to follow Posy, then stopped and took a hesitant step or two after Hugh. Then he stopped, turned and ran after Posy once more. His steps faltered, though, and once again he stopped, looked anxiously over his shoulder at Hugh's retreating figure, then with a wail of despair he began to scamper after him.

'You will die, Hugh Cassin!' he gasped as, puffing with the effort, he fell in a two-to-one skipping run alongside Hugh's long strides.

'We will all die,' said Hugh Cassin shortly.

'That's what I fear most,' cried Dagonet, but this time he was not driven to stop again. His mind, it seemed, was now made up.

The odd pair negotiated the gate with some nervousness, but although Dagonet did attract a curious glance or two from the guards whom Hugh did not recognise, they were not otherwise challenged. It was early afternoon, and most of the market stallholders were already packing away their tired goods and wilted produce for another day.

'What will you do, Hugh Cassin?' whispered Dagonet, who seemed in a state of permanent apprehension and was staying as close to Hugh as was physically possible.

Hugh shook his head helplessly. His own courage was fragile enough, he knew that. Frankly, he did not know what to do. Now that he was actually inside the city walls his mind was jumbled. Nothing suggested itself except the fact that in the bright daylight they were undoubtedly in danger of being recognised. 'We should get off the streets, I suppose,' Hugh said. 'It is foolishness to be so conspicuous.'

'Yes! Yes!' cried Dagonet.

Just how they should get off the streets, though, remained a problem for some time, until Hugh, looking down a narrow lane off the main thoroughfare they were on, spied the peeling paint of a hanging board. 'The Sign of the Two Fishes' was clumsily lettered above an equally clumsy painting of a pair of alecost leaves. 'That tavern,' he whispered. 'We could wait there until dusk.'

Dagonet leapt excitedly. 'Yes, Master Cassin! Yes!' he cried with relief.

Even in the shadows of the lane Hugh felt slightly safer. He glanced absently at the word MAIDEN painted crudely with whitewash along the stones of the building and then pushed into the gloomy interior of the Two Fishes tavern. Apart from a pair of grizzled men playing dominoes at a table near the door and an old woman standing guard behind the counter, the tavern was empty.

The woman smiled at him with a ghastly toothless smile. Its mocking black emptiness so frightened Dagonet that he ducked behind Hugh to escape it. The old crone chuckled at the strange little man and raised an eyebrow at Hugh. There was a small tapped cask before her on the counter and Hugh nodded at it. 'Would you draw us two tankards of your good ale, mother,' he said, 'for we've walked a good distance and we have a great thirst between us.'

'Sit yourselves down, good sirs,' the woman lisped. 'I'll bring it you bye and bye.'

Hugh saluted the woman and followed Dagonet into the darkest corner of the room, ducking his way between the low heavy beams of the ceiling. Shortly afterwards the old woman brought them their ale, and still later the watery stew they had asked for to assuage their hunger.

'You are travellers then?' she asked.

Hugh nodded.

'What brings you to Gleam, travellers?' the woman enquired in her harsh lisping voice. Dagonet had given a quick warning glance at Hugh, but Hugh was already suspicious of the woman's interest.

'Nothing brings us to Gleam, mother,' he replied carefully. 'We are just passing through.' He did not elaborate.

'Ah,' the woman sighed. 'It is a sad day for Gleam. A very sad day for Gleam, master traveller. They have taken her.'

'Taken her?'

'The Maiden. Poor thing. She'll…' Suddenly the woman, as if realising she'd spoken too much, grew suspicious in her turn. 'Travellers,' she said. 'Where is your luggage? Your bundle?'

Hugh lifted a hand. 'Do not fear us, mother. Our luggage is safely stowed with my sister near the River Flint.' He did not elaborate.

The woman then looked at him briefly and gathered the empty tankards. Something had been established, however. The existence of safety, perhaps. But neither she nor Hugh made any further attempt at small talk. This Gleam, thought Hugh, is a scurvy graceless place where people chase shadows for comfort and silence for safety and would sell their beldames and grandfathers if they dared.

The long afternoon passed slowly. At times the two men muttered together about their best course of action, at other times they slumped back against the wall or leaned forwards on their arms in an uneasy slumber. Customers came and went, but there were few of them and little notice was taken of Dagonet and Hugh in their dark corner. When the shadows had grown so long that the hostess thought of lighting a couple of smoky oil lamps, Hugh rose heavily. 'It is time,' he whispered.

The old lady, noticing their movements, asked, 'Will ye not be needing a bed then, sirs?'

Hugh thought quickly. It would not do to leave an oddness in the woman's memory. Travellers should not be setting out at darkness. Quite the reverse. He made a quick decision. 'Yes, good mother. But we will return later. There's an old friend we will try to find betimes.'

His explanation seemed to satisfy the old woman, and she nodded, treating them both to yet another ghastly grin. Hugh made as if to leave her then, but as he did so, surprisingly she reached with an ancient hand and seized his sleeve and he was jerked back to find his face locked hard against her walnut wrinkles. 'Ye may be needing help, mightn't ye, master traveller?' she whispered.

Hugh could not help himself. Unnerved by the crone's closeness, he nodded, swallowing.

'Ye'll find it at the Two Fishes then,' the woman whispered, and then she released him. Hugh gave her a small frightened grin, then with Dagonet scurrying behind him, he pushed through the door and into the shadowy twilight of the lane.

Their course of action, insofar as they had been able to decide upon one in their long hours within the Two Fishes, was to try to locate that rear wall of the Citadel and the dungeon door from which they'd escaped some days before. This would mean bearding Garth the Simple, but that seemed easier somehow than attempting to bluff their way through the main entrance and down through the bowels of the Citadel from the inside. If Johanna were still alive, almost certainly she would be imprisoned in one of the dreadful cells on the other side of that door.

It was a plan fraught with danger even so, and one with only a remote chance of success. For all that, it was the only chance they had.

They would have been just a little cheered to learn that on each of their premises they were correct. Johanna was still alive. She was lying in fear on the floor of one of the dank little rooms that made up the domain of Garth the Simple.

Earlier that day there had been a clatter of steps and one of the Markgrave's men dragged the terrified figure of Johanna, whose hands had been roped in front of her, into the passage of the lower dungeon. Martin Sculldung himself followed.

At this sudden intrusion Garth the Simple lifted his great bulk from his stool and as the visitors arrived one after the other he stood there mutely, his small eyes shifting from the soldier to Johanna to Sculldung. The dungeon master had been living in a state of guilty bewilderment since that moment some days previously when for the first time in living memory he'd allowed the door behind him to open and for living bodies to pass through. Bewilderment, because his entire existence was governed by very simple rules and the most elemental of these had always been *do not permit passage past the door.* And yet, despite his allowing the jester Dagonet and the lute-player with the lilting voice and the silver hair to trick him into sleep, itself a terrible failure of duty; and despite this failure in turn leading to the far more awful fact that these two had then stolen his key, slipped past his defences and through the door itself; despite this succession of broken rules, there had been no fearful consequences. Garth had always understood that such failure in the line of duty would result in his being thrown into his own dungeon, in his being manacled to a dank wall and denied food and drink, possibly until he died a slow and painful death.

There had been no punishment at all. Quite the reverse. Garth knew of the Markgrave's fury, and for letting the door open he should by all that was right and proper have suffered the very worst blast of that fury. And yet the Markgrave had not flown into a rage. Instead it was as though he had been grateful that Garth had allowed the two men to slip through his clutches, rather than breaking their bones to splinters in his terrible grip. It was all very confusing and quite beyond Garth's limited powers of understanding. For many days now the world had not seemed as easy and as uncomplicated as of yore.

'I want,' ordered Sculldung, 'this maiden to be secured in a cell.'

Garth nodded dumbly. Then he stepped forward and lifted Johanna's cape to look at her. To Johanna, her eyes still unused to the gloom, Garth would have appeared nothing more than a threatening blob, but all the same she recoiled instinctively from the acrid living stench of him as it gusted towards her.

'Pretty,' said Garth happily.

'You will not touch her,' said Sculldung sharply, and Garth stepped back, feeling the rebuke. Then, taking a ring of heavy keys, he moved past his visitors and found a small empty cell, which he unlocked. The soldier following pushed Johanna roughly through the doorway. He did not bother to untie the rope binding her wrists. Johanna gave a short sharp cry, tripped and fell to the floor. Immediately, Garth pulled the door shut and locked it.

'A word,' said Sculldung, following the shambling figure back to his stool. Garth, who'd already settled into his usual position before the door, looked up smiling.

'The maiden,' said Sculldung simply, 'is to be put to death.' At this satisfying news, Garth smiled even more broadly and pulled at the fingers of his left hand until they clicked ominously. 'But not,' continued Sculldung, 'by you.'

The smile faltered.

'The executioner will be a stranger to you. He will be allowed access to the maiden. He will be a Brother.'

Garth nodded, but his face betrayed complete incomprehension. He was still climbing out of the disappointment that he would not have the pleasure of killing the maiden and all of Sculldung's information was coming rather too quickly for him to keep up with.

'You know of the Brotherhood?'

Garth shook his head. He did know 'brother'. There was once a time, he vaguely remembered, when he'd had a brother. But he did not know 'brotherhood'.

Sculldung sighed. 'The executioner will be a stranger,' he repeated. 'You will know him because he will show you a sign of a toad.'

Garth nodded.

'You know 'toad'?'

'Toad,' repeated Garth, nodding again. He knew toads. Small squatting creatures with hanging bellies and big pimply eyes and great wide mouths. They crouched in dark corners and croaked. To show Sculldung he understood, he squatted and made happy croaking sounds. The sight was grotesque and Sculldung looked quickly away.

'Yes, yes,' he said impatiently. 'That's a toad. Now stand up for God's sake!'

Garth stood up beaming at his own cleverness.

'But I repeat,' Sculldung added wearily, 'do not touch her yourself. Only the man with the toad.'

Garth nodded. Not to touch. Man with toad. He understood.

Night had not long fallen when Hugh and Dagonet once again found themselves in the cobbled street at the rear of the Citadel. Its black basalt stones reared above them, reaching it seemed right to the rags of dark cloud that almost but not quite hid a thin sliver of pale green moon. It was fiendishly cold.

Now that they were so near the Citadel, Dagonet, frightened as he was, had somehow been returned to the jester who had lived within its walls for so many years. His voice took on that prancy dancy quality of before and he once more was given to wild riddling utterance.

'*Hard hearted*
Garth hearted.
Hey ho and he'll break our bones!'

'Be quiet,' hissed Hugh.

'*Pardon us, your fastness, your hardness, your lardness.*'

They inched along the black wall until they located a darker recess. 'I think this is it,' whispered Hugh. Within the recess he could feel the broad oaken planks of a door. At least he presumed it was a door. There was no handle that he could discover. As his hands traversed it, however, he felt a square aperture at eye-level and remembered the peephole. If this were the door, then even now, the terrible figure of Garth the Simple was only a matter of inches away on the other side of the wood. The thought was enough to hush Dagonet completely.

'What do we do?' whispered Hugh.

'*Birds and insects*!' whispered Dagonet.

'What?'

'*Fly! Flee! Fly flee flo flum. Any second Garth will come! He'll play snap with us!*'

'Oh God,' groaned Hugh, then summoning up his last resources he banged heavily at the door.

Garth's great chins were sagging down on to his chest when a peculiar sound seeped through his consciousness. It sounded like a banging at his shoulder. It couldn't be. There was only the door behind him, and nobody as long as he could remember had ever attempted to gain access through that door. It was used only for departures and, except for that one recent bewildering occasion, those who departed through that door were beyond knowledge of its dimensions, were beyond anything of this world as a rule.

He opened his eyes, and listened.

The noise came once more. It *was* a banging. It was a knocking on the door. Garth shook his head in puzzlement and his jowls quivered. He stood up, and his stool clattered to one side. 'Yes?' he asked, confused. Then realising that his voice would not be heard he turned to the door. He kicked at it. It knocked back at him. Garth scratched at his head, and then he saw the peephole and remembered. It was not something he'd often had reason to use before. He reached for it tentatively and felt for the iron slide. It was difficult to move so he banged at it with his fist and tried again. This time it slid across easily.

He peered out into the darkness. 'Yes?' he said again.

A voice replied. 'Garth?'

Garth smiled. Somebody knew him. 'Yes?'

'We are looking for Johanna.'

'Johanna?' Garth was confused.

'A maiden.'

'Ah.' Garth was no longer confused. A stranger would come. A toad. A Brother. Carefully, he found the words to ask: 'You are a Brother?'

On the other side of the door, Hugh paused. The voice of Garth the Simple, even so close, seemed somehow divorced from his fearsome bulk. The voice, nevertheless, was not hostile. 'You are a Brother?' the voice had asked. Hugh had thought immediately that he had meant brother as in relation, as in Tobias, but then he recalled the darker resonance of 'Brother'. The power invested in the word. A little unsteadily, Hugh replied, 'Yes, I am a Brother.'

'You have come to kill the maiden?' Garth asked. It was more a statement than a question.

Even distorted as they were through the peephole, the words were chilling. Dagonet grabbed fearfully at Hugh's sleeve. Hugh swallowed. He must go through with this hideous charade. Somehow he forced himself to utter the dreadful words. 'Yes,' he said. 'I have come to kill her.'

'Toad,' said Garth, remembering his catechism. 'You have the toad?'

Hugh felt in his pocket. The wooden shape nestled in his hand. He withdrew it and held it to the peephole. Garth's great powerful fingers pale in the darkness pushed through and wriggled there like crab's legs. Hugh pushed the wooden toad towards the fingers and allowed them to feel the shape of the head and the bulbous eyes. Apparently satisfied, the fingers withdrew and Hugh could hear a key being inserted into the door. There was a click and a creak and suddenly the door was being pushed open. Dagonet, who had been clinging ever more tightly to Hugh's coat, suddenly broke away and fled for the shadows.

The cell into which Johanna had been flung was not far from Garth the Simple's station. All the same it was very dark, for little if any of the greasy light from Garth's lantern penetrated into it. There was no stool or bench, merely the damp flagstones of the floor, and it was on these that Johanna lay, wrapping her green cloak about her in a futile effort to stem the cold and moisture that seeped from them. Despite being numb with exhaustion, she could not sleep. Over and over she revisited the confusing events of the morning, but nothing made sense. It was clear only that some appalling mistake had been made, that she had been mistaken for some criminal. How suddenly the wonder of the woman Quail's recovery had turned into the horror of her seizure. It must have been a monstrous mistake. Yet all of her efforts to point this out had been in vain. Her captors had seemed grimly deaf. She understood nothing of the *why*, but all too dreadfully she had come to understand the *what*.

There was no doubt about this at all. There was a determination in the air. She was to be killed. She was to die, probably in this hellish place of darkness, of dripping walls and seeping floors with the smell of excrement and terror all about. Escape was beyond her dreams. The grotesque giant into whose hands she had been given would protect her from all hope, except the hope that when death came it would be swift and complete.

The interminable hours passed. Johanna lay there, bundled in her cloak and shivering, all nerves and senses alert to any noise. The scrabble of some small creature. A long low moan from some anonymous fellow prisoner. Then after what seemed an aeon, she heard with a start a sudden muffled knocking, then the clatter of Garth's stool falling across the floor, then his voice in conversation. It was a weirdness. She had been expecting the ringing of boots coming down the stone steps and corridors, but there had been nothing like that. Straining still further she was sure she could hear the creak of a door.

There were more muffled voices, too murky to make any sense of, and what seemed to be a chortle that could only have come from the giant dungeon master. Then, unmistakably, Johanna heard footsteps coming towards her cell. The footsteps were of more than one person.

Finally, through her bars there came the erratic illumination of a swaying lantern, its yellow light chasing shadows across the floor and up and down walls. Johanna stared fearfully from her huddle. She was now very frightened, but some deep reserves of courage forced her not to betray the fear she felt by screaming or sobbing. Somehow she did not want indignity to be a measure of her death.

All at once the lantern itself swung towards her, held in front of the huge shambling figure of the jailer. There was a smaller shape behind him. She heard a jangle of keys, then one key twisted in the lock and the door swung open.

'Here she is,' said Garth the Simple happily. 'You can kill her.'

Johanna felt faint, but gripped her fingers tightly against the swoozy feeling. She stared up at the light as a figure, her assassin, stepped around the jailer's bulk and reached for her.

'All in good time,' the voice muttered. 'Stand up, Johanna,' the voice whispered.

She was dreaming. The sound of the voice did not make sense. In the echoing dripping darkness it had sounded not unlike the voice of her uncle. Her uncle's voice, but strained and tight with apprehension. Then she was sure of it. Hugh Cassin. How could he be here in this place of lost souls, of those whom the tyrant of Gleam had damned? He too must have been captured and brought here to wait for the release of death.

'Uncle?' she asked.

Garth's gurgling laughter. 'Not uncle!' he cried. 'Not uncle. Brother!'

She must have been dreaming. She could see him now. It was a wild careering nightmare. She suffered Hugh to draw her to her feet. Her side was stiff and her legs felt unsteady. Garth was still chuckling to himself. He recognised the figure of the Mastersinger once he'd lifted the lantern to inspect the wooden toad more thoroughly. There was no forgetting that silver hair. He understood then. This Brother had the protection of the Markgrave himself. This Brother could come and go as his own will demanded.

'You tricked Garth,' he grinned. 'But you've come back. You have a chicken?' Hugh shook his head, confused by Garth's amiability. 'The fool Dagonet?' Garth asked. 'You bring the fool Dagonet?'

Hugh shook his head. 'Where is the maiden?' he had asked. These pleasantries were unnerving him. He attempted to speak with as much authority as his own fear could muster, but his voice was so dry he could barely articulate. However, Garth the Simple had been strangely compliant and welcoming.

It was almost as though he had been expected. Shrugging at these strange events, Hugh followed Garth.

It was then, as he was standing beside his trembling niece, still thankfully alive, in the horror of her cell, that one major problem presented itself. Garth the Simple, vast, grinning and ghastly behind his lantern, stood blocking the only way out.

'Kill her,' he said.

Hugh turned to him appalled. Garth stood there like a man licking his lips before a banquet. Clearly, he expected Hugh to despatch Johanna then and there and right before him. He waited there grinning like a child. Hugh felt despair. To have come this far.

'I do intend to kill her,' he said. 'I do.' He faltered then, his mind racing desperately. As he did so he remembered that other desperate plight. The foolishness that had first brought this smothering darkness into their lives. He remembered running from the watch. The drumming of their footsteps and the wild sweep of torches. Then again he saw the dark portal. The heavy door. The stone toad above the lintel; and then Hugh remembered the wooden toad in his pocket. It was his only chance. He said. 'But she must be put to death in the House of the Toad. She is, after all, our guest.'

Garth's smile faded. He lowered the lantern in disappointment. He nodded in disappointment and turned. Hugh found Johanna's hand and took it and she gave him a quick little smile in the darkness. He could feel at her wrist her racing heartbeat and he began to think for the first time that escape might just be possible.

Together they followed Garth's great slumped shoulders back towards the heavy studded door. Hugh remembered the chicken Dagonet had given Garth to tear apart. That unpredictable ferocity. The decision not to put Johanna to her death there and then must have been as if Hugh had plucked that chicken away from him. Hugh stiffened. They were still not through the door.

Hugh was not to know that, for all that, Garth was not prepared to risk the wrath of the Markgrave. Sculldung had been quite clear. *Garth not to touch. Brother to kill. Toad.* Garth the Simple sighed. What must be done, must be done. He unlocked the door and pushed it open. 'Take her,' he said.

Trying not to move too quickly, Hugh assisted Johanna towards the opening. Suddenly, Garth seemed to change his mind. 'Wait!' he demanded.

Hugh's heart filled with dread. Things had gone so miraculously well. Too well. He steeled himself for whatever was to come.

Garth the Simple was pointing at Johanna. He patted his own foetid fat-stained jerkin. 'Maiden not need her cloak,' he grinned. 'Not where she's going. Garth have her cloak?'

Such a little thing. Such a small price. Threads for a life. Despite the chill,

Johanna glanced quickly at Hugh then pulled frantically out of her long green mantle. She stepped back from the giant and thrust it at him. Garth grabbed it, chortling and tried to pull it around his vastness, and as he was doing so, Hugh and Johanna slipped swiftly out of the door and on to the cobblestones of the street. Johanna gasped in the cold clear night, suddenly aware, as Hugh had been before her, that stars, constellations shone beyond the fastness of the studded door to the dungeons.

'Hurry!' cried Hugh, taking her arm. 'Hurry! We must fly!'

In their haste, Johanna seemed hardly aware that they had been joined by another small prancing figure who chased after them muttering to himself. 'Nowhere to go. Nowhere to go. Must get to Nowhere as fast as we can. Twill be hard. Twill be hard. Twyll will be angry. Twyll will be angry. Angry. Angry…'

Chapter Eighteen
MANDRAGORA AND THRALL

The library of the House of the Toad was dimly lit. Heavy blue curtains had been drawn across the windows, and candles rather than lamps illuminated the room. They flickered here and there, one on a table, others on shelves, another on a sideboard – all like tiny lighthouses on some dark ocean, and they gave the room an air of even greater mystery, of ceremony.

An hour or so before, Master Gull and Mistress Quail had returned to the House of the Toad and reported the morning's events to Manfred Bufo.

Gull had rubbed his hands together with the satisfaction of a job well done. 'Mistress Quail made a remarkably convincing corpse,' he had said, nodding happily. 'And her resurrection was quite, quite miraculous. It set the market abuzzing and squawking and our little maiden was lauded and applauded to the skies. Such a pity the guard arrived in such numbers to drag her away in such a very public fashion.'

'You have done well,' Bufo had replied. 'We have fulfilled our side of this bargain to perfection. It only remains for Twyll to fulfil his.'

Now, Bufo sat behind a long refectory table, his back to a wall of ancient volumes. A candle underlit his face, carving it into slabs of light and shadow so that he seemed sculpted from some grim dark marble. He played idly with a gold chain. The heavy weight at one end of the chain swung back and forth across the light of the candle. It was a golden toad, squat and beautifully crafted, no bigger than a child's fist. Shining in its head there was embedded a deep red ruby.

Bufo glanced up as the door opened. In the darker shadows just beyond stood Master Gull. He paused, not yet entering.

'Is the boy ready?' Bufo asked.

Gull nodded.

'Then show him in,' said Bufo, taking the weight of the toad into his hand and allowing the chain to fall into his fingers like a trickle of gold.

Silently, Gull stood to one side and gestured to a figure behind him. Tobias Swallow entered the room.

'Approach the Master,' whispered Gull, adjusting Tobias's direction with a hand at his shoulder. 'Sit before him.'

In front of the table, directly before Bufo, was a high-backed chair. At Master Gull's nudge, Tobias started walking in an oddly stilted way. He approached the chair and, without even giving it a glance, took his seat and then stared across at Bufo, waiting for him to speak. Gull followed him, but sat down in a chair almost lost in the shadows, some distance from the table.

Bufo did not say anything for some time. He sat there contemplating Tobias, lifting the chain every so often before letting it fall into his fingers once more. He was satisfied with the appearance of the boy. It looked as though Gull had performed his preliminary tasks well. Tobias's face was expressionless and his eyes wide. In the dimness of the library, his pupils were huge and dark, but without life. Bufo's continued silence seemed not to discountenance him at all. He merely sat there waiting with the patience of the hopeless or the very old.

'Well, Master Swallow,' Bufo said at last, 'it is good to see you once more. Your studies? They are proceeding well?'

Tobias nodded, his eyes never leaving Bufo.

'Good. Good. And you would still be a Brother?'

Tobias stared at Bufo.

'Master Swallow?'

Tobias nodded again. 'I would be a Brother.' His voice was thin and the words came slowly as if individually sought for and found.

'Good,' said Bufo, lifting the chain, and letting it drop. The boy was in a state of thrall. Gull's judicious application of mandragora and other secret herbs had gradually drained him of many human emotions. However, that emptiness would not motivate him to the task that lay before him. More was needed. Much more. The emptiness would have to be filled with a very active brew: a brew made up of disgust, ambition, the will to power, steel of purpose, and a sense of invulnerability.

'Good,' said Bufo. 'If you would really be a Brother, Master Swallow, we must prepare you for the first test.'

'I am ready,' said Tobias.

'Oh, no you're not,' murmured Bufo. 'But you will be. You will be.'

Gull stood silently and moved about the room. He stood before each candle, then slowly and deliberately licked a forefinger and thumb after which he squeezed at each flickering flame in turn. One by one the candles were extinguished. As each one died a deeper darkness settled on the room until only one candle remained: the low candle that stood on the table between Bufo and Tobias.

'What would you kill, Master Swallow, in order to become a Brother?' Bufo asked, one hand held in the air as if in benediction. From the hand the glittering chain hung. Tobias did not reply. Imperceptibly at first, then more clearly, as if it were a pendulum, the chain and toad began to move from side to side. With each arc the golden toad passed over the candle's flame. Out of darkness, into the flickering light, then into the darkness, back into the flickering light, and back into the darkness. Automatically, Tobias's eyes followed its sway and shine. Back and forth. Dark. Gold. Dark.

'Would you kill a mosquito?'

The toad turned black and tiny. It grew long inky legs like slender threads and it fashioned pinpoint eyes for itself. It whined with a narrow insolence and landed on Tobias's wrist. Momentarily its wings stilled as it leaned and then sank its mouthpart deep into the forested landscape of Tobias's flesh. Instinctively, he slapped at his wrist and then what had once been mosquito was suddenly a simple smudge of crimson and black. Mosquito flesh. Mosquito blood. Tobias's blood.

Tobias looked up at Bufo. Their eyes locked. Once more the golden toad was swinging back and forth, the toadstone shining red each time the candlelight caught it.

'Would you kill a fly?'

Tobias followed the toad as it moved. For a time it swung from the light to the darkness and then back again from the darkness. As he watched, though, the direction seemed to change. Now it was moving back and forth, front and back not left to right and it was all at once black and gleaming blue with great compound eyes, a thorax and tail. The room became loud with its noise. Then all movement stopped and it hovered, buzzing. Treading the air momentarily. A second or so later it dropped out of the air and alighted on the table before Tobias. He watched curiously as the fly crouched before him. Somehow magnified, the fly's head moved from side to side and then it vomited a tiny dollop of yellow that glistened moistly on the polished wood of the table. To Tobias's surging disgust the fly immediately began re-ingesting this vomit through a feeding tube like a thin black straw. Tobias could not help himself. He raised his right hand in horror and brought it crashing down upon the filth of the fly and its filthy meal. There was some satisfaction in having the creature crinkle and splatter beneath his palm, but he could not feel completely uncontaminated until he had rubbed and rubbed away every vestige of its damp remains against the front of his gown.

He was still shuddering and rubbing up and down at his gown when he heard Bufo's dry voice asking yet another question.

'Would you kill a rat?'

As the long, dark minutes passed, Tobias was asked to consider an ever-growing number of loathsome creatures. The golden toad swung back and forth, and the strange catechism continued. It was a ladder, and rung by rung, Tobias climbed. Higher and higher.

An hour or so later, Manfred Bufo caught the swaying frog in his left hand and allowed the chain to fall upon it once more. He nodded at Master Gull who rose and left the room.

'We have done enough for now,' said Bufo. 'Your answers have been more than satisfactory. Gull will bring us something to drink and then we shall rest for a while, for there is still much to do.'

Sure enough, within a few minutes Gull returned with a tray bearing a bottle and three goblets. He busied himself at a sideboard and then brought the tray and its contents over to the table, handing one goblet to Bufo and another to Tobias. Bufo and Gull lifted their glasses slightly and, with their eyes only, silently acknowledged each other. Tobias was clearly excluded from this tacit toast, and in any event was quite unaware of it. He had raised his own goblet to let the fiery bitter liquid trickle down his throat. This was some kind of wine flavoured with wormwood along with certain other acrid herbs he could not yet identify. A strange complex brew which enabled him to see again with startling clarity the succession of hateful creatures he had been more than happy to put to death: the mosquito, the fly, the rat, the weasel, the rabid dog, the ringworm-infested cat. Then the human filth he'd been pleased to deal with: the murderers, the degenerates, the wretched and the dying. As he'd expunged each piece of leprous, scabrous refuse, the world had seemed a safer, cleaner place. The toad had glowed with a richer gold and the ruby had shone like a beacon of redemption.

Tobias drained his goblet to the dregs, and felt suddenly very, very tired.

'The boy needs to rest,' murmured Bufo. 'Gull, take him away and let him sleep.'

Even as he uttered the words there was a far-off knocking. 'Attend to the boy first, Gull, and then attend to the door. I will make ready for our guest.'

Gull left the room then, one arm supporting a limp and exhausted Tobias, while Bufo rose from the table and drew the heavy blue drapes aside. Light seeped into the room from the late afternoon sun. Bufo sighed, satisfied, then retrieved a small package from a cabinet and returned to his seat to wait for his visitor.

'Your visit no doubt means you have the Maiden quite secure?' Manfred Bufo murmured, staring across the refectory table at the Markgrave of Gleam's Captain of the Watch. A towel of white linen was bundled on the table beside a small vial of deep blue glass standing on its reflection.

Martin Sculldung misheard him. 'Skewered? Not as yet… sir.' Sculldung was uncomfortable. He did not know how to address this man who seemed somehow to possess an authority even the Markgrave was prepared to bow to. 'I thought you'd reserved that task for yourself.'

'I have had reports that she has been taken,' said Bufo easily, ignoring Sculldung's discomfiture.

Sculldung nodded. 'She is at present housed in a cell at the Citadel. I escorted her there myself and gave her into the charge of the jailer.'

'Good,' said Bufo. 'It has been well done.'

Sculldung nodded, fighting back his curiosity. It was beyond his imagination why this man and this House should have become so involved in the matter. He understood that somehow this remote, scholarly looking man had given assistance to the Markgrave, so much so that Evan Twyll had for a day or so been almost cheerful. The problem of the Maiden, which had plagued and tormented him, had apparently been solved. And the solution had come from this House. Well and good. But that should have been all. Why should this man, who seemed so particular, so fastidious, wish to drench his hands in the Maiden's blood?

He understood why Evan Twyll needed her death. The century could then turn on its spiked wheel. There would be no other change. Sculldung thought of the frightened figure he had bundled down the narrow steps of the Citadel. All the while she had protested her innocence. The foolish girl. How could she have known that it was this very innocence that demanded her extinction? Her voice had been sweet with reason and did have a certain heart-stopping quality. But it was pure reason in its coldness that had betrayed her. He could not tell her this. It had been better not to respond lest her loveliness move him. For she was a beautiful creature. In another world… He sighed. She'd kept insisting that there had been a dreadful mistake, had even cried for an audience with the Markgrave. But there had been no mistake, and the Markgrave… It would have been better to have struck her down in the marketplace where all could have seen her death.

'This,' said Bufo, 'is the way her death will be arranged. It must proceed this way. Afterwards, her body will be Twyll's to do as he pleases with. This we have agreed.'

Sculldung stared at the man. Astonishing. Never had he heard the Markgrave's name pronounced with such disdain. Sculldung had gained his present rank cutting down those who had failed to tremble sufficiently at the name of Twyll.

'When you return to the Citadel,' continued Bufo, oblivious, 'you will go to the Maiden's cell.' He reached across the towel and picked up the blue vial, exhibiting it for Sculldung to see. 'This is what you must do. This little bottle contains a very powerful sleeping draught.' Bufo up-ended the vial, which was stoppered with a waxed cork, and mimicked pouring its contents over the towel. Sculldung nodded. 'Smother the girl's face with the towel,' said Bufo. 'She will fall into a state of unconsciousness for many hours.'

Sculldung looked at Bufo, a question in his eyes.

'The Maiden is beautiful,' Bufo said. 'Her beauty could move a man to pity. Her voice could shake a man's resolve. Even one of our own. I would have her drugged and lifeless. Put her to sleep. Shroud her. Swaddle her. In the darkness she will be a mere shape. Mute. No eloquence.'

'I understand,' said Sculldung, reaching for the towel and bottle. 'When would I do this?'

'Before I send our man. He is almost prepared. But some hours yet. Expect him at the darkest hour, so do your work before then.'

Sculldung did not understand all of these odd words: *prepared*? Still, he wrapped the vial in the towel and bundled it beneath his jerkin. 'It will be done as you say,' he said. Bufo looked up, beyond Sculldung towards the door. It was as though the Markgrave of Gleam's emissary had been forgotten already.

'I will take my leave then,' Sculldung said, rising and backing towards the door. Bufo nodded at his voice but no further eye contact was made, and when Sculldung turned it was to find Master Gull already standing before him, ready to escort him from the premises.

'Would you kill a felon?'

It was late evening. The drapes had been drawn once more and the single candle lit. The golden frog swung slowly from side to side. Manfred Bufo watched carefully as the blank-eyed figure opposite him appeared to consider the proposition carefully. Then the blank eyes widened and glittered with determination; his mouth drew into a grimace of intense purpose. His right hand lifted, fist clenched as if gripping the handle of a dagger, and then the imaginary dagger swung down and quivered through the sinews of the real table.

Bufo glanced across the room to where Master Gull was sitting patiently. The old man had done a good job with his drugs and tinctures. Tobias had been very well prepared. When Bufo bowed his head slightly, Gull quietly rose and slipped out of the room. Some minutes later he returned bearing a dull leather scabbard in both hands, holding it before him like an offering. He approached the table and moved to Bufo's side. Bufo took the proffered scabbard and lay it on the table. A knob on the handle gleamed gold in the candle light and as Bufo drew the dagger from the scabbard and lay it before him Tobias saw that this knob was in fact a crouching toad, not unlike the toad that had swayed like a pendulum over the candle.

'It is beautiful?' Bufo murmured.

Tobias nodded. The dagger was beautiful. The shaft beneath the toad-knob was tightly bound in a golden thread, and the shining silver blade wriggled on the dark wood like the ripple of a snake through water. It must have been a dagger of Darkland's origin. The scabbard suggested a straight edge so the wavy blade was a surprise. So much more sinister somehow, and twisting to a merciless point.

'Would you use it to kill a felon?' Bufo whispered, and Tobias nodded soberly, although he did want to tell the Master that no felon was worth the deadly beauty of this blade. It was magnificent. Then he did not want to tell the Master anything; he wanted only to take the blade, to test it against his finger. To feel the point of it. To blood it. Any felon would do.

All of this Bufo observed. 'You will get your chance very soon,' he said. 'A felon waits for you, already prepared for death. Master Gull will escort you to the Citadel. There the toad will give you entrance and you will be taken to where you may use this blade for its ordained purpose. Listen to Master Gull carefully, for he will show you how and where to drive the blade. This is a ceremony, Master Swallow; a ceremony of great moment for it may well admit you into the Brotherhood. It must be conducted with all due reverence and respect.'

Tobias nodded. 'I hear your words,' he said. 'Reverence and respect.'

Bufo looked at him for a moment, then closed his eyes briefly. Opening his eyes once more, he carefully twisted the blade back into the scabbard, and pushed it across the table to Tobias. 'Take it,' he said. 'It is of the Brotherhood. Return it to me when you have done what must be done.'

Chapter Nineteen
THE TWO FISHES

The three figures fled from the Citadel through the narrow streets and winding lanes of Gleam. The night was dry, but a bitter cold prevailed. Hugh led the way, dragging the stumbling figure of Johanna along behind him. She found it difficult to move quickly. Her body was exhausted, stiff and cramped, and without her long cloak of green, the cold lay its icy hands upon her. Hugh was unrelenting, however. He knew that their safety, their survival, depended on flying as far from the dungeons of the Citadel as they could manage.

Bringing up the rear in a jinking, jumping prance was Dagonet the Fool who still, to Hugh's dismay, kept up his mad riddling in a piping voice. Hugh was fearful enough of the clatter of their footsteps and the gasping of their breath – it was folly in the extreme for Dagonet to add to their peril with his mad commentary.

'*Danger! Danger! Dagonet must fly!*
Cold! So cold! Dagonet needs fire!
Must fly! Needs fire! Fly! Fire! Fly! Fire!'

'Quiet! You fool, Dagonet!' hissed Hugh, over his shoulder.

'*Fire! Fly! Fire! Fly!*
Firefly! Firefly!
No Firefly for us tonight!'

Suddenly Hugh realised what the little man was telling him. He pulled up, puffing heavily, leaned his back against the brick wall of a building and sucked in great draughts of air.

The *Firefly*. That other time when on the run in Gleam, there had been the sanctuary of the *Firefly*. They had sought and obtained safety there, below its decks. There would be no safe haven in the *Firefly* tonight. No doubt it was navigating far-off seas, oceans away from the dangers of Gleam. And where else could they hide? There would be no getting through the gatehouses, certainly not tonight now that curfew was in place, and not tomorrow either. Sooner or later the fact that Johanna had been spirited away by mock assassins would be revealed.

The fat simpleton Garth had expected to witness Johanna's death. It was clear to Hugh now. He understood why he had been admitted: Garth the Simple had been expecting somebody. A Brother. Somebody from the House of the Toad. And that person, Garth seemed to expect, would put Johanna to death. Hugh trembled. How lucky it had been that he'd had Gabriel Beet's whittled toad in his pocket; how lucky it had been that Garth was a credulous fool; and how lucky they had been to arrive when they did. For there was going to be another visitor. That was clear. This very night. Another visitor from the House of the Toad. A visitor who might arrive at any time and who would be expecting to find Johanna ready for slaughter.

The House of the Toad. That evil place. Hugh smiled grimly at the horrible thought that in all of Gleam it was the only house he knew. That just a short time ago he had sought shelter there. Well, he would not be seeking refuge there this night. He would not be delivering Johanna into the hands of her executioners.

But where? Where could they find shelter?

He felt Johanna shivering against him. Now that they were not moving the cold was even more penetrating. And then Hugh heard Johanna whisper into the darkness. 'Who are you?'

Dagonet's small shadowy figure stopped moving. His head cocked. '*Who is truth! Who in truth? In truth in deed? Who indeed? Truth indeed is Dagonet no longer knows who he is*!' Dagonet's voice trailed away from his high piping foolishness to a sad cadence.

Johanna whispered, 'Dagonet?'

'A bitter frightened fool,' murmured Hugh, 'who escaped from the Citadel. He haunts me like a shadow.'

'Poor fool,' whispered Johanna, and Dagonet, hearing her sweet pity, ran up to her and swept his arms about her knees.

'See,' muttered Hugh. 'He is a leech!'

'Cold! Cold!' cried Dagonet. 'Maiden's cold!'

The little man was right. Johanna was cold. Hugh was cold enough himself. They would have to keep moving. But where in this grim and grimy city could they find the shelter, the safety, and the warmth they so desperately needed?

Johanna's gentle grip on his arm then reminded Hugh of another grip, a harsher more clutching grip and he remembered how his face had been dragged against the wrinkled flesh of the old hostess at the tavern where they had spent the late afternoon. What was it? The Two Fishes.

'Ye may be needing help.' Had the old woman really whispered that? Had those words really come out of her ghastly mouth?

He shook his head. It was, however, their only hope. Could he find it again? He reached down to Dagonet, still clutched about Johanna's knees as if trying to warm her with the power of his squeeze. 'Dagonet,' whispered Hugh 'the place today. The Sign of the Two Fishes. Could we find it?'

Dagonet released Johanna and darted into the middle of the lane. He jumped to the left, then he jumped to the right looking down the direction from which they'd come, then back to the left again. Then he pointed. 'That way!' he whispered.

Hugh had no way of knowing whether to believe him or not. Still, he was leading them away from the Citadel so that at least was sensible. 'Come along,' he whispered to Johanna. 'There may be a place…'

There may be a place. Just as Hugh had no way of knowing whether to believe Dagonet, he had no way of knowing or not whether the old crone's offer of help was a trap. His experience of Gleam tavern-keepers had not been very encouraging, he thought ruefully, remembering the crashing blow to the head he'd received from the knave at the Gut and Cuttle. He shuddered again with the cold. Nothing could be helped. Even a warm betrayal would be better than a frozen death on the streets of Gleam, he decided, and he quickened his step to catch up with Dagonet, who had already scurried on ahead,

Even as these three fled through the back streets of Gleam, another figure accompanied by two pike-wielding guards was striding along the waterfront from the House of Toad towards the Citadel. Martin Sculldung was not concerned about hiding his presence on the streets. On the contrary, he kept a professional eye open for any lurking curfew-breakers, who if they saw the Captain of the Watch first would shrink into their very souls with fear and trembling.

Beneath his jerkin he could feel the bulk of the towel the old man had given him, and inside the towel he knew lurked the little blue bottle. An odd business, he thought. Sculldung did not much like the idea of poisons and potions. It seemed unnecessarily delicate, effete somehow. He wondered idly why the old man in the House of the Toad should be so particular about the sensitivities of one of the Brothers.

He shook his head. It did not make sense. The whole point of taking the Maiden was to end her, and thus to end the stories and the hopes pinned on her. Surely the best way of doing this would have been to have hung her kicking and screaming from the tower of Gleam until she screamed and kicked no more.

This clandestine business in the depths of the dungeons was folly. But not, of course, his decision, Sculldung thought. His function was to carry out orders. His orders were to drug the Maiden and truss her up like a corpse before her time. And this he would do and do as efficiently as was his wont.

Then he turned a corner and he could see the huge darkness of the Citadel ahead. 'It will be done soon enough anyway,' he thought grimly. 'However it is done.'

'There,' hissed Dagonet.

Hugh peered into the darkness of the steep little lane. There was an icy glitter of moonlight on the damp cobbles for a deep frost was already falling. At first he could see nothing but then he felt he could just locate a darker, jutting shadow, which he guessed must be the dangling sign of the Two Fishes.

'Well done!' he whispered to Dagonet. 'You'll make a fine navigator yet!'

Dagonet reached through the darkness and timidly touched Hugh's sleeve. With a pang of guilt Hugh understood what the gesture meant. *Thank you*. Over the last few days, he realised, he had been sparing of kind words for the little man. He had in fact come to resent his clinging presence and had more usually been cruel and dismissive. Now, he remembered that despite his deep fear Dagonet had accompanied him into the dangers of Gleam, had returned to within inches of Garth the Simple, and now had led him all the way back to the possible haven of the Two Fishes.

Was the dingy tavern to be a haven, though? It was their only possibility. As Hugh stood outside the door through which no chink of light could be seen, he swallowed. It was all or nothing, but still he hesitated. Then a sudden noise from the street beyond the steep little lane decided him. It was probably the noise of a stray dog running for a cat, but there would no doubt be far more savage dogs, dogs of the two-legged type, hunting for the fugitives within hours or even minutes. There was no choice and no waiting possible. He lifted his fist and banged on the door.

It seemed to take a shivery forever for the door to open, but eventually he could hear footsteps, and some moments later the sound of bolts being withdrawn. Then the door slowly opened a fraction and a dim yellow light shone forth. The old crone held up a lantern and peered out. She did not seem surprised to see Hugh and Dagonet, or even Johanna for that matter.

'As I thought,' she muttered. 'Come on in. Come on in. You'll catch your death out there.' She hurried them in and quickly locked the door behind them. When she saw that Johanna had been out in the cold night without a coat or warm mantle she said with what appeared to be genuine concern, 'Oh, my dear, you're perished. You're perished. Come quick, over to the ingle.' She led the shivering girl to a large fireplace where a meagre fire still burnt. There was a stone nook around the fire and the old lady made Johanna sit there while she made off to find something warm for her.

Hugh and Dagonet, too, huddled near the fire and gradually its flickering flames drew the worst of the cold from their bones. They had glanced at each other in some surprise at the matter-of-fact warmth of their welcome, and the even more surprising feeling that they had somehow been expected. But all this was too difficult to work out and, anyway, getting warm again was their first priority.

Johanna looked up at Hugh, tears shining in her eyes. 'Oh, Uncle,' she whispered. 'I would have died. They would have had me dead.'

Hugh nodded sombrely. 'I fear so, Johanna,' he said wearily.

'But why?' whispered Johanna.

The old crone, returning with a heavy patchwork quilt evidently had sharp hearing. 'They would have had you dead all right, my girl. And wonderful it is that ye live. Right wonderful.'

Johanna stared at the old woman, but she didn't elaborate, merely muttering, 'Lean forward now.' As Johanna obediently did so, the old lady draped the quilt about her shoulders. 'Pull it tight, now,' she said. 'Have to get the warmth back into ye.'

'Why would they have had me dead?' repeated Johanna, but this time addressing the old lady.

'To kill ye, naturally,' she replied.

'This is a Dagonet riddling reply,' complained Hugh. 'What do you mean, mother?'

'There's been wild rumours for months, traveller,' said the old lady, 'of a maiden coming with the century's end, a maiden who will bring about the end of the Twylls.'

Hugh nodded, remembering all the wild talk in the Gut and Cuttle and his fears when Tobias began opening his mouth wider than was wise.

'Well,' said the old lady. 'Ask yourself! Suddenly in the market place, from what I've heard, and the whole of Gleam knows by now, a maiden arrives and first thing she does is bring back a poor lost soul from death itself. Is it *a* maiden? Or *the* maiden? Well, ask yourself, would the Markgrave of Gleam take any chances? Would he?'

Hugh began to understand. 'So Johanna was taken because she was thought to be this maiden creature?'

'Best way to end all the talk,' said the old crone grimly. 'Catch her and kill her. Kill her and kill all talk, all hope, all dreams.'

Hugh nodded. 'Oh my goodness,' he whispered. 'And we managed to get her away.'

Johanna reached for his hand and clutched it. 'But, Uncle, that means…'

Hugh looked at her gently. 'That means what, Johanna?'

Johanna was remembering the sequence of events that had led to her arrest: their reception at the House of Toad; her being taken ill and fainting after drinking the wine and drinking the sweetmeats old Gull had offered her; the tender ministrations of the old woman, Quail, and Master Gull; the walk next morning and the old lady's collapse in the market. Suddenly there were too many coincidences. She stared at her uncle. 'That means it was all planned,' she said carefully. 'That old man at the House of Toad. He told me Tobias was not there, but he lied, I'm sure he lied now. The old lady pretended to die. It was all planned so that it would seem as if I had saved her. The soldiers. They were there too quickly. It must have been planned. The man Gull – he was shouting "Miracle!" and "Maiden!" His shouting made the crowd so excited…' Johanna's voice, at the thought of it, had risen with indignation.

'Slow down, Johanna,' said Hugh. 'These are wild words. I don't understand what you're saying.'

'I do,' said the old woman grimly. 'And the girl is right to be angry. It is an evil House and if there was mischief afoot I don't doubt it was involved. But I cannot understand why the Brothers would want to help the tyrant Twyll. They would not usually lower themselves so basely.'

'*Lower ladder*
Twyll is bad as
bad as Twyll is
Brothers badder,' muttered Dagonet, half to himself.

The old crone nodded as she passed the little man on her way to the grate. 'I fear you're right, little man. I fear you're right.' She hefted a small cauldron on to a circular gridiron, lifted its lid and began stirring.

Johanna, too, had heard Dagonet's doggerel, and started a little at the last line. 'Why would the old man lie about Tobias?' she demanded. 'Does that mean he is still in that house?'

Hugh Cassin, recalling Abel Larch's sombre warning that Tobias was lost to them, nodded gravely. 'I fear he is,' he whispered. Then seeing the pain on Johanna's face, he gripped her hand more tightly and smiled. 'But we don't really know that and, anyway, we managed to get you away from that foul hole before God knows what might have befallen.'

The old crone cackled with delight. 'Oh, ye did all right, good master. Ye managed to get her away! By all that's wonderful.'

Despite himself, Hugh smiled at the old lady's pleasure.

'And Evan Twyll,' continued the old lady, cackling even more. 'When he finds out the Maiden has slipped through his fingers he'll be lost in such a howling rage we'll hear it from here!' She wiped her eyes at the thought of it.

But at the thought of the Markgrave's rage, Hugh's grin faded, and he felt Dagonet the Fool tremble and clutch at his knees once more.

'But why, mother, are you helping us?' asked Hugh.

They had eaten a supper of stew from the cauldron and now all four were sitting around a crude table drawn near the fire. There were tankards of ale before them, which the old lady had heated by plunging a hot poker into each in turn. Each time the poker had hissed like an angry cat and the room had filled with an aromatic steam of beer, yeast and a pungent hint of alecost.

The old lady had untied her shawl so that it hung loosely about her shoulders and wisps of greasy grey hair slipped free. She looked at Hugh for some time as if considering what she should say. 'It may be hard for you to understand, seeing me now, but I too was once a maiden like this one here,' she began, nodding at Johanna. Johanna glanced across at the old lady and could not help but flinch slightly, a movement the crone's sharp eyes quickly noted. 'Yes, and should you live this long you'll be glad to look as I do,' she said, 'for the dead look worse. Far, far worse, not that they care how they look.' Johanna dropped her eyes, feeling at once rebuked and at the same time reminded of how close her own death had been, and could still be.

'No matter,' continued the old lady. 'But I was a maiden a long, long time ago. So long ago that this vicious Twyll had not been born and his grandfather was still just a slippery-talking rogue of an officer in the Citadel. The empire held sway and Gleam was a happy bustling sort of a place where you'd hear laughter in the market and whistling in the street. The way things are today aren't the way things have once been, but I'm one of the few who remembers the old, old days. Most folk in Gleam can't even imagine things other than the way they are. My ancient memories might just as well be fairy stories. That is, fairy stories until this other fairy story of the Maiden came along and seemed to waken up folks' imaginations once again.'

Hugh stared at the old lady. She lifted her head and even though her faint smile was a sunken parody, her eyes shone in the flickering light and Hugh saw her for the first time as no longer ugly, but somehow resilient, like the old gnarled tree in an orchard that still produces the sweetest fruit.

'Thank you, mother,' he murmured. 'But what is your name? We owe so many thanks to your good name.'

The old lady glanced his way. 'You should call me Mother Grayling,' she said. 'That's what most folks do. And while this maiden lives, Master Cassin, so will people's imaginations.'

Hugh started. 'You know my name!'

'I know many things,' said Mother Grayling. 'And I also know one other thing: as I told ye before, as long as this maiden lives so the Markgrave's rage will grow.'

They sat soberly for some time digesting this, all knowing its truth.

Suddenly, there was a loud knocking at the door and Dagonet gave a little yelp of fear.

'This way,' said the old lady swiftly, and ushered them out of the room and into a small adjoining taproom. She pulled the door behind them and they heard her shambling footsteps cross the room to the outside door. Then there was a muffled conversation, none of which they could make out. It seemed to end with the old lady's voice raised sharply and then they heard the door slam and the bolt slammed home. They huddled in the darkness, scarcely daring to breathe until the door opened once more and the old lady beckoned them out.

'Was it…' whispered Hugh.

'No, no,' said Mother Grayling, grinning her fiendish grin. 'Just the local tosspots and topers. They can't understand why the Two Fishes is shut up and barred. They've been banging at the door all evening.'

'And why is the Two Fishes shut up and barred, mother?' asked Johanna.

'Because,' said the old lady, grinning once again, more to herself than to the company, 'I was half-expecting guests.'

The news seemed to have spread abroad that there'd be no hospitality at the Two Fishes that night, for they were not disturbed again and as the old lady and her visitors sipped slowly at their mulled ale Johanna told her story in greater detail. When she'd mentioned the House of the Toad their hostess shuddered a little, nodded and muttered to herself. Again, Johanna talked of how they'd been treated courteously and how considerate the old man was when she'd fallen so suddenly ill and how kind it was of him to arrange for the two retainers to walk them to the gatehouse. Her story added considerably to the version Hugh and Dagonet had heard from Posy Beet on the road to Flintside.

'It was all a sham,' Johanna said. 'I can see that now. Somehow they had arranged the whole thing.'

When she'd been dragged off by the guards, there'd been no explanation and no ceremony. No sooner had the Citadel door slammed behind her, than she had been dragged down the steps, down, down in an endless circle of stairs it seemed until she reached the bottom and the giant jailer had taken her into his honeycomb of cells.

'I can't believe Tobias could be a part of such evil,' said Johanna. 'If he were there he'd probably have been hidden away. He couldn't have known Aunt Posy and I were there. Or perhaps the old man was right. Perhaps he has gone on to Aser after all.'

Hugh shook his head. 'No, Johanna, as I said to Posy, he did not go on to Aser. He was not on the *Firefly*.'

Hugh then told Johanna of his search for Tobias and of the strange adventures he'd had, including his escape from Gleam with Dagonet. He did not tell her all of what he'd learnt from Dagonet and Abel of the House of the Toad, nor did he tell her how Gull had treated Posy after Johanna had been taken. Something dark and terrible was pushing at his mind, too insistent to be shut out.

'Then what do you think has happened to Tobias, Uncle?' asked Johanna.

Hugh glanced at Dagonet. He shook his head. 'I don't know,' he said, 'but I fear…'

'Fear?'

'I fear he did go straight back to the House of the Toad. I am sure he was there all the time while you and Posy were there, and I fear he is there now.'

'But why,' persisted Johanna, 'would the old man have told us such a lie? Why would he have done that?'

Hugh shook his head. Again the dark thought came crowding at him, and again by an effort of will he turned it way. 'I don't know,' he said helplessly.

'Ah, 'tis an evil place,' murmured the old lady. 'A place of evil repute. You were not wise to go there. Not wise at all.'

'He was so courteous, so plausible,' mused Johanna. 'He would have convinced a judge.'

'The wolf can be courteous to the lamb, given a reason,' said Mother Grayling drily. Then she nodded. 'And you just happened to fall ill in a house of necromancers and alchemists? Just like that?'

'I know,' said Johanna. 'And now I know why.' She shuddered. 'Even then they were plotting to kill me.'

Hugh said, 'I think so too. Everything that happened. The miracle. The soldiers. All too neat.'

'And you do believe Tobias may still be there?' asked Johanna.

Hugh nodded. 'Yes. We have no reason to believe anything the old man said, do we?'

Johanna looked at him slowly and shook her head.

Later the old lady showed Hugh and Dagonet into a small room with an ancient bed they would share. She would share her own bed with Johanna.

Once the taper was blown out, Dagonet, curled to one side and fell almost immediately into a restless sleep; but sleep would not come to Hugh. Instead, the dark thought that had been demanding admission finally shouldered through his defences and he submitted to its horror. He saw again and again Dagonet perched on the dresser in the Citadel. He saw the fool's finger draw across his neck and his bizarre warning: *let them think you're a Brother, brother.*

He heard Abel Larch's worried voice. *I fear he is lost…* And he heard Posy's distressed account of the old man Gull: *She is quite lost… She is dead.*

Hugh shook his head wildly and stared up at the dark shapes of the heavy beams pressing down from the low ceiling. Then came the worst voice of all, the slow silly voice of Garth the Simple: *Are you a Brother? You have come to kill her?*

Johanna. Tobias. Sister and brother. The thought would not leave him. Tobias. Johanna. Maiden and Brother. Tobias a brother. Tobias a Brother. *Are you a Brother? You have come to kill her?*

'No!' groaned Hugh Cassin, twisting back and forth trying to escape from the hideous thought. 'No, dear God. Not that.'

Chapter Twenty
CHOLER

Evan Twyll looked up as Martin Sculldung entered the room.

'Well,' he asked. 'What did the man Bufo want with you?'

Sculldung inclined his head then drew the bundled towel out from beneath his jerkin. 'This, sire,' he said. And reaching into the folds of the towel Sculldung retrieved the tiny blue bottle and held it up.

The Markgrave turned his head, the better to focus his good eye. 'What is that?'

Sculldung shrugged. 'He didn't say exactly. But something to drug the girl with, I understand. He wants her unconscious for the assassin, apparently. Doesn't want her beauty or her cries to put the executioner off.'

'The devil he doesn't,' exclaimed the Markgrave. 'I didn't think such people would be swayed by things of the flesh.'

Again Sculldung inclined his head. It wouldn't do for the Markgrave to learn that his thought wasn't original.

'Must be an uncommonly fetching piece of flesh then,' said the Markgrave, 'if she could move one of those cold reptiles.'

'She is certainly not unattractive,' murmured Sculldung.

'You say so?'

Again Sculldung nodded.

'Might be worth a look then with my riding boots on,' said the Markgrave. He added brutally, 'Won't be much chance tomorrow.'

'The assassin will arrive after midnight,' said Sculldung. 'The old man was most particular. I am to make sure the Maiden has been well drugged before then. She is to be wrapped up so that her beauty can not be seen.'

The Markgrave smiled wolfishly. 'Well, there's plenty of time. Let us go and see this Maiden then. See what all the fuss has been about.'

With Sculldung leading the way down the narrow halls and stairways, the two men descended into the bowels of the Citadel until at last they reached the dank domain of Garth the Simple. In the gloomy light of a single flickering lamp they eventually reached the huge figure himself, apparently asleep on his stool. But Garth the Simple was not asleep. Long years of his crepuscular existence had given him the nocturnal vision of a cat and such a finely tuned sense of hearing he was immediately alert to any sound alien to the warren of cells and corridors he ruled.

Long before the Markgrave and Sculldung reached him he had been aware that visitors were calling. All the same he made no move, no gesture. As was his habit he would do no more than open one inquiring eye should they require attention.

'Pshaw!' gasped Evan Twyll, lifting a great red kerchief to his nose to smother the rank stench of the place. In the darkness he could make out very little except shadows on shadows and the waxen figure of Garth wrapped about in a swathe of rags.

'We would like,' announced Sculldung, 'to see the Maiden. The Markgrave would inspect her, and I have something for her.' He gripped the small blue bottle.

Garth opened his eye. Widely. Something suggested to him that there was a difficulty ahead. A problem. But it was little more than a cloudy, troubling feeling, and he brushed it aside as he would a blowfly on his ear. 'Cannot,' he said, smiling.

The Markgrave started and stared. He was completely unused to underlings, and this underling was as low as any in his household, denying him anything, and actually smiling as they denied. 'What?' he said.

'Cannot!' repeated Garth, and again he smiled his idiot smile.

Sculldung felt a slight tremor of anxiety, an anxiety made sharper as his eyes became more accustomed to the gloom and he saw that the top layer of the rags swaddled about the giant looked familiar. A green cape stretched and twisted about Garth's huge body. He remembered how a green cape had been wrapped about the slender body of the fair woman they had dragged down the stairs. He looked sideways, briefly, listening, as if his ears could verify the presence of the Maiden, and then he turned back to Garth. 'Where did you get that cape?' he demanded.

Garth giggled slowly. 'From her. She be not needing it.'

Sculldung felt the gaze of the Markgrave on him, and he sensed Twyll's growing anger. He tried to concentrate on simple Garth and the problem. Then, as he beheld the great self-satisfied bulk of the jailer, an explanation suddenly occurred to him. Either deliberately or accidentally, Garth himself must have put the girl to death.

'What have you done to her?' he demanded, enunciating his words carefully, so that Garth could understand completely and give some sort of an answer that made sense.

'Nothing,' said Garth. 'Nothing to her.'

There was no mistake now. The Markgrave was definitely angry. Luckily, thought Sculldung, his wrath for the moment was directed towards Garth the Simple.

'Listen, you great dolt!' Evan Twyll hissed. 'I want to see this girl. I want to see her now. Take me to her cell immediately!'

Garth stared at him, his smile fading. Something told him this man with the Captain of the Watch was not to be trifled with. He did not understand why the man was angry. He had, after all, obeyed every order he had been given. He struggled to find a way to meet the expressed desires of this man with the strange dead eye. He realised slowly that the only order that he could possibly obey was the last. He could, at least, take the angry man and Sculldung to the Maiden's cell. Accordingly he climbed to his feet and swayed there before them.

'This way,' he said. 'Her cell is this way.'

Glancing at each other, the captain and the Markgrave followed the jailer's clomping footsteps out of the gloomy gallery and into another smaller gallery lined with oaken-doored cells. Each door had a barred window and Garth stopped before one not very far from the entrance. 'Her cell,' he announced.

Immediately the Markgrave peered through the bars into the dark interior. Try as he might he could make out nothing in the room, nor could he hear anything. 'Light!' he ordered.

Hastily, Sculldung passed the Markgrave his lamp and the Markgrave held it above his head as close to the bars as possible. Still he could see nothing. 'Unlock the door!' he ordered.

Obediently, Garth felt through his keys and then inserted a huge key into the lock, twisted it then pulled the door open. Evan Twyll stepped in, lamp held aloft, and stared about him, kicking at the scattered straw in one corner of the room. It was immediately clear to all that there was no Maiden in the cell.

Twyll turned with fury to the jailer. 'Where is she?' he shouted. 'What have you done with her. You said you would bring us to her cell!'

Sculldung instinctively stepped back. The Markgrave's fury had the makings of a tidal rage that could sweep all before it. A part of him felt sorry for Garth the Simple as the immediate victim, but a greater part of him felt apprehensive as he knew that he could be the next to suffer.

Garth the Simple could not understand. 'This is her cell,' he said.

A pulse began beating in the Markgrave's temple. 'Where is *she*?'

'I don't know.' Before the Markgrave could give full vent to his rage, Garth found sufficient inspiration to add, 'Perhaps with the Brothers?'

There was a silence. 'The Brothers?' asked Evan Twyll in a somewhat calmer voice. 'What on earth do you mean?'

'Brother came,' said Garth, sensing the worst was over. 'Brother came to kill her.'

The Markgrave shook his head. He turned to Sculldung. 'Does this make any sense to you?'

'No,' said Sculldung. 'It doesn't. My arrangement with the House was exactly as I explained. I was to drug the Maiden and swathe her. At some time after midnight the assassin would arrive and I would escort him to the cell. It is not yet near the time. Had any Brother arrived, I certainly would have been aware of it.'

'What Brother?' demanded Evan Twyll of Garth. 'When did this Brother come?'

'How did this Brother come?' added Sculldung. 'How could he gain access to the dungeons?'

These were too many questions for Garth all at once. He stepped back as if they were pepper thrown. 'Brother came!' he repeated obstinately. 'To kill her.'

'*How* did he come?' insisted Sculldung.

This at least Garth could answer. 'Through door,' he said.

'What door?' demanded Sculldung, his own anger rising.

'Door by stool,' said Garth unhappily. Clearly something was amiss. He could sense that neither the captain nor the one-eyed man was pleased with him. He did not understand why.

'The door by the stool?' whispered the Markgrave. 'What does he mean?'

Sculldung knew all too well. Garth meant the door to the street. The one escape door that his gigantic presence was supposed to render impassable. Yet already the door had been recently breached when the musician Cassin, who may have been a Brother himself, had taken his mysterious leave of the castle. Sculldung whispered, scarcely daring to announce it, 'The door behind him, sire. The door to the lane outside. Used to remove bodies.'

He sensed the Markgrave's sharp intake of breath. 'How do you know this was a Brother?' Sculldung demanded.

'Came to kill her,' said Garth, as if repeating a simple litany. 'Had toad.'

'A toad?'

'Wooden toad.'

'You doltish idiot!' the Markgrave shouted. 'You let her out of that door!'

'Came to kill her,' repeated Garth.

The full enormity of the Maiden's possible escape began to swell and pulse in Evan Twyll's consciousness. She had been arrested in as public a way as possible so that her death could be equally public. If she had escaped, the reverse effect would occur. She would be seen by all of Gleam to have powers greater than the iron bars and stone walls of the Markgrave's citadel. Her capture and escape would simply fan those flames her capture and death were supposed to extinguish. It would be seen as magic. A miracle. He stared furiously at the imbecilic giant whose incompetence had allowed this hideous reversal to take place.

A towering apoplexy overtook him. 'Fool!' he screamed. He reached into his jerkin and pulled out a stiletto, which he lifted so that its steel flashed in the lamplight. Then, stiletto raised, he rushed at Garth the Simple determined to cut him to pieces.

Nothing like this had ever happened to Garth before. He backed away from the advancing Twyll, his eyes widening with alarm. Almost immediately, though, his back met the solid resistance of the stone wall of the gallery. He raised his arms with a frightened wail as the furious Markgrave slashed at him with his knife. Seeing that his victim had nowhere to go, Twyll drew the knife back behind his shoulder ready to drive it into the chest of the cowering giant; but as he did so, Garth reached forward in a defensive reflex and seized the Markgrave's wrist. He gripped and then tightened the grip into a bone-crunching squeeze. And the squeeze in turn opened Twyll's fingers, and as he gave a yelp of agony the stiletto fell from his hand and fell to the stone floor with a clatter.

'Let go! Let go!' screamed the Markgrave, livid with pain and anger. 'You idiot tub of lard! You're breaking my hand. Let go!'

The fury and the shouting only frightened and confused Garth the Simple to a much greater degree. He did not like the angry noises the one-eyed man was making. He released his wrist and seized him by the neck instead. All screaming stopped. Then Sculldung heard the Markgrave's gurgling protest as Garth began to raise him bodily off the ground as if he were a chicken whose neck he was about to break.

'Garth!' Sculldung screamed.

Garth ignored him completely, and as the Markgrave's feet were lifted into the air the Captain of the Watch automatically drew his rapier, levelled it, then plunged it between the dangling kicking body of the Markgrave and Garth's left elbow. The sword drove deep into Garth's body and a jet of blood spurted forth. With an agonised squeal Garth dropped the body of the Markgrave and slumped down the wall, sat for a moment and then fell to one side, eyes frozen in startled surprise. He was quite dead.

Breathing heavily, Sculldung pulled his rapier from Garth's chest, and knelt by the body of Evan Twyll. It was difficult to believe that Garth's powerful grip and heave had not broken the Markgrave's neck, but by some miracle it hadn't. Nor had the life been completely squeezed from Twyll's body for, although he lay there unconscious, there was a faint pulse at his wrist and Sculldung could just detect a soft gargling breathing.

As he knelt by Twyll's barely alive form, Sculldung thought quickly over the events of the last few minutes. He had saved Twyll's life, but what of that? Gratitude was a feeling quite alien to the Markgrave. When he recovered consciousness all he would remember was the fact that Sculldung had witnessed his humiliation. This would add to his fury that the Maiden had escaped, a fury that he could no longer direct at Garth and would almost certainly direct at Sculldung.

The Markgrave lay there before him helpless and vulnerable. How easy it would be to despatch him then and there. How unfortunate that Garth hadn't tightened his death grip just a fraction or so more. The Markgrave's rage could have been silenced forever.

Almost absently, Sculldung noticed the towel on the floor that he'd dropped in his haste to pull his sword. He reached for it in order to wipe Garth's blood from his blade. However, as he drew the towel towards him, the little blue bottle fell on to the flagstones with a faint clink. Sculldung glanced from the bottle and back to the outstretched figure of the Markgrave. At that point, and with a grim smile at the poetry of the situation, he realised what chance had provided for him.

The Maiden had vanished. She who was to bring about the end of Twyll had been and gone. How appropriate that she could take Twyll with her. That the prophecy could be fulfilled.

He unstoppered the bottle and, holding it at arm's length, poured the contents onto the towel. A sickly smell of almonds was added to the presiding stench of human waste. Then, holding the towel before him, Martin Sculldung leaned towards the prone body of the Markgrave of Gleam.

Chapter Twenty-One
THE ASSASSIN OF GLEAM

Gull knocked softly at Tobias's door. 'Master Swallow,' he called. 'It is time.'

Tobias Swallow opened the door. He was wrapped about already in a long deep blue cape with a hood. If you were to pull back the sleeve of his left arm you would have found the sign of the crouching toad, a sign that Manfred Bufo earlier that night had fastidiously re-inked, and if you reached around his side you would have found hanging from his belt the beautifully tooled scabbard containing that twisting blade whose passage through human flesh would admit Tobias into the Brotherhood.

He was ready. Master Gull and Bufo between them had seen to that. Between Gull's tinctures and Bufo's suggestion, Tobias had been thoroughly prepared to carry out the task demanded of him. He understood that waiting for him somewhere in the Citadel lay the body of one who had forfeited all right to existence and that he, Tobias Swallow, had been charged with the simple task of putting all misery to an end.

Some hours before, Bufo had made a cathedral of his fingers and looked carefully over them at Tobias. 'When the deed is done there is one further thing…'

Tobias stared at him.

'You must draw the cape from the head and view your victim. It is a tradition of the Brothers. And you must bring me a description of what you find.'

Tobias understood. 'All will be done as you say,' he said.

The night outside the House of the Toad was chill, and the wind off the sea was filled with the sharpness of kelp and salt. It stirred Tobias to memories of that rush through the night with the watch in pursuit, and for a brief second a far-off image of Johanna came into his mind, an image he quickly brushed to one side as a distraction from his mission. All the same he was aware that this was the first time he'd been outside the walls of the House of the Toad for a long time and the night felt huge about him. There was a great bowl of glinting stars above and floating among them the twin green blades of the sickle moons.

'Come along, Master Swallow!'

Tobias started at the voice of old man Gull, and turned to follow him down the dark street. There were further memories stirred by the square and the abandoned Gut and Cuttle tavern, and then they were striding up the steep steps towards the very gates of the Citadel where two leather-coated watchmen stood leaning on their pikestaffs.

The first of these stepped forward, lowering his pike and barring their way. 'What would you, stragglers? 'Tis long past curfew!'

'I would have you tell Captain Sculldung that the visitor is come. He will know what you mean,' said Master Gull easily, not at all perturbed by the guard's brutal voice, nor the vicious-looking point of the pike.

The guard nodded. He seemed aware that a visitor was expected. He turned and opened a small door within the great door and disappeared. The other guard glanced curiously their way, and then resumed his position. At length there came the sound of footsteps and the guard re-emerged. 'Follow me, sirs,' he said in a much less belligerent manner.

Just before he stepped through the narrow door into the confines of the Citadel, Tobias turned his head for a last look at Gleam. At the end of the street was the square, and beyond the square the harbour where he could make out the black poles and spars of a number of ships at anchor. And beyond the harbour lay an immense heaving blackness he knew to be the sea. Beyond the sea lay Aser and what might have been his future. And what would there have been after Aser? He would have been a minor leech in a minor town, if he was lucky. This night would see him rise far above that, rise far above the petty low-life and flotsam of Gleam and Aser. Once he had performed this simple task he would be embraced by the Brotherhood and initiated into its mysteries.

Buoyed by the thought, he felt for the toad on the dagger handle beneath the leather of the scabbard and felt the power it conferred. This was good. Tobias then stepped through the door to find the guard waiting for him. In the dim light he saw the apprehension and respect in the man's face as he glanced at Tobias's shrouded figure and Tobias, although he stared at him coldly, felt a small glint of satisfaction.

'You have come, then,' said Sculldung, somewhat unnecessarily.

Master Gull inclined his head. There was no need to answer. Tobias stared ahead without acknowledgement. He had not removed his hood, and looked as anonymous as a monk.

'Well, shall we go?'

'I prefer not to, if you don't mind,' said Master Gull drily, 'I shall remain here. Bring the Brother back to me after.'

Sculldung nodded. 'Of course,' he said. 'Come along.'

He left the room and Tobias followed him mechanically. There was much of interest within the Citadel. The various chambers were lined with tapestries and prizes and spoil: stuffed animals, heads and skins, weapons from exotic places, and paintings. Tobias, however, glanced neither to the right nor to the left: he simply followed Sculldung's back like a shadow. Nor did he say anything at all. Sculldung was nervously excited and tried to disguise it, but after one or two abortive attempts at conversation, quickly realised that there was nothing to be gained from trying to parlay with his grim companion and thereafter stayed silent himself.

At the entrance to the nether regions of the Citadel, there was a guard and Sculldung demanded a lantern of him. Then with lantern raised before him, and Tobias shadowing, he made his way once more down into the noisome depths of the building.

Eventually, they reached the dungeon galleries. Some hours earlier, it had taken Sculldung all of his strength to roll the inert weight of Garth the Simple's corpse into a dark corner, where he had covered its staring face and much of the body with straw so that it appeared a mere hump of waste. Johanna's cape he had pulled off the body and this he had carefully wrapped about the unconscious Markgrave, whom he had in turn dragged into the cell the Maiden had escaped from. Sculldung had pushed the Markgrave against the far wall and wrapped the towel tightly about his face, then pulled the hood of Johanna's cape over the towel. The Markgrave was now disposed exactly as Bufo had instructed: swaddled and lying on his right so that the left side was exposed for the assassin's blade.

'Not far now,' muttered Sculldung, flinching against the oppressive atmosphere of the darkest depths.

And then they were there. Sculldung paused and put his arm out to bar Tobias. 'Wait here,' he whispered. 'I'll make sure everything is in order.'

Leaving Tobias standing silent in the foetid darkness, he turned into the gallery of cells where he had left the unconscious figure of Evan Twyll. Holding his lamp aloft, and listening closely, he crept forward. It would not do to find the Markgrave of Gleam stirring, or worse, already awake. If he were to be found conscious, Sculldung was already dangerously compromised. For him, the die had been cast as soon as he had poured the vial of sleeping mixture on to the towel and plunged it against the nostrils of Evan Twyll. There would only be one thing to do in such an eventuality, and to be prepared for it, Sculldung drew his rapier and held it before him.

He reached the door of the cell and listened. Hard. He could hear nothing. Cautiously, he held the lamp to the bars then peered into the room. It seemed that the Markgrave had not moved. Against the wall the swaddled shape still lay, he was sure, in the same position he had left it.

However, Sculldung was too cautious a man to take any chances. He felt through the keys he'd cut from Garth's belt and inserted them one by one until he heard a faint click and the mechanism turned. He quietly opened the door, then stood for several seconds to see whether the sound and movement had roused Evan Twyll in any way. Satisfied, at length, that there was no stirring, Sculldung stepped silently into the room and carefully made his way across to the body. Again he paused. Then he dropped to his knees and, laying his sword down gently, brought his head close to the shrouded face. There was absolutely no sound of breath and nor was there the slightest tremor of movement.

The Markgrave was deeply unconscious. So unconscious he might already have been dead. Which in a sense, thought Sculldung in a grimly satisfied way, he was. Picking up his sword once more, he rose to his feet and backed quietly out of the cell.

Sculldung rejoined the silent figure of Tobias, who seemed not to have moved an inch from where they had stopped.

'All is ready,' muttered Sculldung, lifting his lamp. Even so he could make out little of the features of the Brother who stood before him like a wraith: dark, silent, still and completely without human feeling. It's as if he were not real, thought Sculldung, scarcely suppressing a shiver. He had known brutality and cruelty all of his life, had been brutal and cruel himself, but he had never known the genuinely cruel or the merely brutal to act with such inhuman numbness before. Always, there would be pleasure in cruelty, or relish, or fastidiousness or even nervousness. There would be *something*. A host of feelings could come into play. But there would be at least some human feeling, even if perverted.

'Show me,' said the voice, without expression.

Sculldung nodded. 'Follow me,' he whispered.

The two men approached the cell where the body of Evan Twyll lay unconscious. Sculldung paused and whispered. 'I've left the door unlocked. No step. You know what to do. In there, lying against the far wall.' And saying this, he handed Tobias the lamp.

Tobias seemed unmoved by Sculldung's muttering. He took the lamp, inclined his head imperceptibly and pushed at the door, which fell open before him.

'Do you want me to…' whispered Sculldung. But he was ignored completely and he realised at once that the assassin did not care a jot what he did. That he was a complete irrelevancy. Some squeamishness took possession of him, all the same, and he backed well away from the door so that the deed might be done in private.

Tobias held the lamp before him and advanced on the swaddled form. In the darkness Johanna's cloak was not recognisably green, not recognisably anything. Tobias stood gravely for some moments, and then put his right hand to his side and drew the dagger from its scabbard.

Would you kill a rat?

The toad crouched on the pommel and the wired hilt felt cold in his grip. In the light of the lamp the wavy blade rippled to its deadly point.

Would you kill a rabid dog?

Then, swiftly steeling himself Tobias crouched beside the body.

Would you kill a felon?

He knelt there momentarily, like a surgeon beside a patient, then raising the dagger above the point Gull had described to him, he paused, then brought it down swiftly with all his strength, grunting lightly as he did so.

He may as well have been stabbing a sack of wheat. No golden grain, however, rippled from the body. Instead, a darker stain spread out like some living thing about the shaft of the blade where it had sliced through the material. With a twisting motion, Tobias wrenched the blade from the body and wiped it on the swaddling cloak. Then he stood up into an even deeper emptiness.

Behind him he heard a small cough, and he turned. The silhouetted figure of the Captain of the Watch had come to the door. 'Is it done?'

'It is done.'

Sculldung entered the cell and moved to the body. He dropped to his knees and examined it with a certain professional precision, noting the position of the wound. He felt for an arm and found a wrist. All was still. There was no pulse. 'It is done,' he echoed softly.

Tobias did not reply. He returned the dagger to its scabbard.

Sculldung stood up once more and turned his back on the body. 'Let us go,' he said. 'This is not a place to linger.'

'Wait,' whispered Tobias. He had remembered his final task. He knelt once more and pulled the hood from the head and shoulders of the body.

'Don't!' cried Sculldung, suddenly aware of what Tobias was doing.

Tobias ignored him. To his surprise there was yet another layer to remove: what should have been a face was still swathed in a white towel. Carefully,

Tobias drew the towel away and handed it to Sculldung.

'There's no need! There's no need!' protested Sculldung. 'I've felt for the pulse. There is none.'

Tobias glanced up at the blathering man. What was the matter with him? Tobias had his instructions and was determined to follow them. 'The lamp!' he ordered.

There was such icy determination in the voice that Sculldung gave up his protest and brought the lamp close. He had no idea what would happen when the assassin discovered there was no Maiden lying there, but he suspected it would not be pleasant. Instinctively he gripped his rapier and readied himself to swing the lamp into the Brother's face should that be necessary.

Unaware of any of this, Tobias pulled the body towards him. The face of Evan Twyll, the Markgrave of Gleam, flopped back and stared up. The clenched socket now looked less horrible than the unseeing single eye, which glared into the lamplight. In life, grown men had quaked to see it. In death it was still a fearsome thing. Tobias, hardened as he had been by the mandragora, still shuddered slightly at the ghastly stare.

'You know him?' Tobias asked Sculldung.

The Captain of the Watch stared in some surprise at the assassin kneeling beside him. He understood that the brother had come to kill a young woman, yet he seemed quite unperturbed that his victim was a man. He was surprised, too, that the unmistakable face of the Markgrave seemed not to register at all. Silently, and with great relief, Sculldung shook his head, and Tobias pulled the cloth over the face once more. 'He has the face of an evil man,' he murmured.

As he adjusted the cape, Sculldung's lamp caused the bronze medallion of the Markgrave's badge of office to shine. 'This will help us identify our man,' he whispered, and once again he revealed the hideous face as he drew the heavy chain over the head and dangled the badge from his fingers. Then he gave a short laugh, and dropped the chain over his own head.

Master Gull lifted his head impassively as the two men entered the chamber. 'Well?' he asked.

'The deed is done,' said Sculldung shortly. Already there was a new imperative in his tone as he fingered the medallion he had taken from the Markgrave's body.

Master Gull appeared to notice neither the medallion nor Sculldung's tone. 'Good,' he murmured. Then, somewhat surprisingly, he approached the silent figure of Tobias and placed a sad hand on his shoulder. 'It seems you have paid the price, my boy,' he said. 'The brotherhood awaits you.'

Tobias glanced at the old man, and nodded. He felt very tired, and wished to be away, out into the cold and glinting night where the air was not heavy with excrement and death.

Sensing his mood, Gull nodded. He turned to Sculldung. 'We shall go now,' he said, 'if you would be so kind as to escort us out. Please convey our regards to your master.'

'Of course,' said Sculldung, with a faint smile. 'Follow me, gentlemen.'

Chapter Twenty-two
THE MARKGRAVE OF GLEAM

The next morning Tobias was awakened by a soft tap at the door. It was quite late, as a watery light was already leaking through the small window of his room, but it was very chill. As he became aware of the faint knocking, Tobias also became aware of the piercing cold and gathered his blankets about him tightly. He had not undressed the night before and he huddled there for some moments wrapped in a confusion of clothes, bedclothes, dreams and strange memories.

He could remember the sharp ringing of boots on cobblestones, pikestaffs and chain-mail, armorial hangings and tapestries, and stone stairs going round and round and round, oily light and the stench of waste and suffering. And then a darker memory made up of huddled shapes, whispering, a raised arm, and an upturned face swathed in a white towel. Finally he recalled the face itself, gripped in death. A straggle of beard. An eyeless socket. A sightless eye hideously staring, and a ghastly grimace.

Tobias started at the memory, and at the same time the knocking became more urgent.

Some distance away Johanna woke alone in a narrow bed in a tiny room in the Sign of the Two Fishes. She glanced around in the gloom, noting the heavy furniture, the low beams, remembering the terrifying events of the night before.

It was cold. Johanna struggled deeper into the rugs and remembered sacrificing her long green cloak in the interest of escape. She wiped the wet tip of her nose, and felt a sneeze erupting. As she gave vent to it she could hear the clomp of footsteps on the wooden stairs, then the door creaked open and the old lady, Mother Grayling, fully dressed and with a grey shawl wrapped about her, stood there holding a wooden tray bearing in turn a steaming earthenware bowl. 'I have some broth, lady,' she announced. 'It is a cold morning and you must be famished.'

Johanna smiled at her. 'Thank you, mother,' she said. 'You are kind.'

'And you are still in danger,' said the old lady wryly. 'It is best you remain out of sight for some time.'

Johanna nodded, and made way for the tray. 'Then you must be putting yourself in danger too,' she said, 'to shelter me like this.'

'I don't feel danger,' said the old lady.

'What do you feel, then?' asked Johanna.

'Satisfaction,' said the old lady. She stood up and went to the small pebbled-glass window, which overlooked the lane. For some time she stood there silently, intent, as Johanna supped at the hot lentil broth. 'Something has happened,' Mother Grayling murmured.

'What is that?' asked Johanna, looking across to her.

'There are people running about like chickens from a fox,' said the old lady. 'I can see their frightened shapes. But there is no fox.'

'Perhaps,' Johanna faltered, 'they are looking for me, and my uncle.'

Mother Grayling shook her head. 'I don't think so. It could be that the news of your delivery has got out. But there is… I don't know,' she shrugged. 'Later, I will go to the market.'

'Where are the men?' asked Johanna.

'Warming themselves by the fire,' said the old lady. 'With my good broth. They will stay out of sight as well. Something has happened,' she added. 'I just know it.'

'Well, Master Swallow,' smiled Manfred Bufo, after Gull had ushered the young man into the library. 'Did you sleep well?'

'I don't know,' replied Tobias. 'I cannot remember sleeping and I cannot remember being awake, so I imagine I did sleep well.'

'Master Gull said you were hard to wake,' murmured Bufo, 'so I expect you slept the sleep of the dead.'

Tobias did not reply. He knew enough of the doctor already to know he rarely said anything without calculation and that the use of the word 'dead' would have been perfectly deliberate. Instead he nodded in tacit agreement. He did not feel well. His waking visions continued to visit him in short snatches, visions in which he seemed to be able to see himself as if he were a stranger. A dark stranger. As if somehow last night he had exchanged places with his own shadow, attached to what had once been his body but unable to control it, or even know it.

'Well,' said Bufo, 'if you can neither remember sleeping nor being awake what can you remember?'

'Of?'

'Of your task, my boy,' said Bufo. 'Of your task.'

'I carried out my task,' said Tobias. 'It was executed as arranged.'

'Good. "Executed", a well-chosen word. Good,' said Bufo. 'And Master Gull confirms it as well.'

Again Tobias nodded.

'But what do you remember?' insisted Bufo. 'This is most important.'

It seemed to Tobias that here was some kind of test, or perhaps some game he must play. Accordingly, to accommodate the Master, he frowned slightly and tried hard to remember the sequence of events from the night before. He began with the walk, the encounter with the guards at the entrance to the Citadel, the meeting with Sculldung and then the descent with him to the dungeon. Again he had the weird sensation that he was his own shadow stalking his other stranger self.

He became aware that Bufo was watching him very carefully.

'Then what?' Bufo sighed.

Tobias sensed that the sigh was feigned, merely a ploy to disguise a growing excitement, a tension. He had never known the usually impassive Bufo to be this way. He was like a child being told a familiar bedtime story, not being able to wait for the exciting part, and yet not quite wanting it to arrive.

Something of the horror he should have felt the previous night but had not experienced then came to Tobias now as he recollected the next sequence of events. He told how Sculldung had led him to a cell, how he had waited as Sculldung checked his victim, and then how Sculldung had let him into the cell.

The drugs Master Gull had administered were wearing off. Tobias saw the huddled bundle of flesh again, but as flesh this time, smelt the rank and rotting atmosphere, experienced again the swinging light of the lamp in the eerie darkness. Then he told how he had knelt beside the still form and taken out the twisted dagger. How he had located the spot as Gull had instructed him, but now, as he remembered raising the dagger, something of the enormity of what he had done came to him for the first time. The shadow was reabsorbed into his flesh. He had become the stranger he had been stalking.

'I killed him,' he whispered. 'I killed him. The blood...'

Once more he saw how the blood had puddled black in the half-light about the blade of the knife and how it had spread and seeped after he had withdrawn the blade. Tobias gasped at the horror of it. What had he done? Then it had seemed so matter-of-fact, so clinical, almost clean. Now the deed had gathered about itself all of the primal darkness of murder. The greatest prohibition had been broken. He had broken it. He looked about him, knowing that the world must see him differently now. He bore the curse of a murderer. A killer of men. There was blood on his hands. It would be clear to all. Tobias lifted his hands and stared at them.

Manfred Bufo was looking at him curiously. Without either sympathy or judgement. 'Carry on,' he instructed.

'I killed him,' repeated Tobias.

Manfred Bufo frowned at the word 'him'. 'You say you killed *him*,' he murmured. 'But there was more, wasn't there? Your task did not end there.'

Tobias stared at him. By now he was trembling.

'You uncovered the face, didn't you?' prompted Bufo. 'What did you see?'

To Tobias, as he uncovered the face for Bufo – cape pulled aside, towel withdrawn – the hideous visage was no longer the mask of a felon, but something human, ghastly but unquestionably human. He described the craggy lines, the hawked nose, the straggly beard, the grimace, but most of all he recalled the eyeless socket and the single sightless eye staring up at him.

Bufo listened to this with increasing astonishment. 'The devil!' he gasped. Tobias stared across the table. He had never known him so agitated. The old man stood up abruptly and swept around the table, and moved quickly across the room to the door. He pulled violently at the silk rope, ringing the bell which would summon Master Gull.

'He's dead!' cried Mother Grayling.

She had flung open the door of the Two Fishes tavern and morning light flooded in, so much light that Hugh squinted against it as he stared up at the silhouetted figure of his hostess. Before he had time to ask, the old lady continued triumphantly, 'Twyll is dead. The Markgrave is dead. The whole market is buzzing with it!'

Dagonet gave a cry of joy, and Hugh rose to his feet. 'Is this true?'

'No doubt about it,' cried the old lady. 'If it were not true nobody would dare open their mouths.'

'Astonishing,' murmured Hugh. 'And last night he would have had Johanna put to death!'

The old lady quickly closed the door behind her and leaned against it as if shutting the world out. 'Even the guards are talking about it,' she said. 'There is such a flurry out there, it's as if a new world has begun.'

Hugh stared at her, and it felt to him as if a great weight had fallen off his shoulders. He remembered his one audience with the Markgrave as brief and terrifying, and turned to Dagonet without whose help he would never have escaped Twyll's ghastly clutches. Dagonet was grinning and in his joy was jumping from one foot to the other.

'But how?' he asked. 'How could this thing be?'

The old lady shrugged. 'Who knows? Foul play most like. There's been no suggestion that Evan Twyll has been ailing.'

'I must tell Johanna,' said Hugh, and made as if to leave the room. It had been agreed that Johanna should remain in Mother Grayling's bedchamber until they could work out how best to escape from Gleam. This news clearly altered everything. At the door Hugh stopped and turned, a thought having occurred to him. 'But who will rule Gleam, now?' he asked. 'What of the Markgrave's sons?'

The old lady's face clouded somewhat. 'He had sons certainly. Two little boys. But they'll not see the succession, poor bairns.'

'Why not?' asked Hugh.

'They say Martin Sculldung is now wearing the Markgrave's chain,' said the old lady drily.

That name meant little to Hugh, but he saw Dagonet's excited dancing stop on the instant and the little man slump slowly onto a stool. 'Say it isn't true,' he cried, utterly woebegone.

'I could say it isn't true if you like,' said Mother Grayling. 'But who knows whether anything's truly true or not in Gleam?'

'I'll tell Johanna,' said Hugh, but his steps were not as excited as he trod up the narrow stairs.

By the time Master Gull had answered the summons, been engaged by Bufo in an urgently whispered conversation and then been despatched once more to the pharmacopoeia, Tobias had collapsed into a chair, his hands covering his eyes. It was no use. He could not blot out the upturned face of the man he realised he had now murdered in cold blood. As Gull's drugs faded, the distance he had felt from the world had shrunk and it and all its accusations had come tumbling back again. He could not bear it.

Bufo, meanwhile, was pacing up and down in agitation, impatient for Gull's return. When the door finally opened, he demanded of the old man, 'Do you have it?'

Gull nodded and handed his master a small bottle and a tiny goblet. Bufo turned to the young man huddled in the chair. 'Stand up,' he ordered sharply.

Tobias opened his eyes as Bufo approached. When he saw the doctor pouring some drops from the bottle into a goblet he instinctively shrank back. 'No,' he whispered. 'No.'

'Don't be foolish,' snapped Bufo. 'Nothing will harm you. What you told me just before does not make sense. Master Gull cannot understand it either. This is merely an aid to memory – a simple tincture from the Witch of Aboraxus and it will make everything that happened last night much clearer.'

Tobias did not want everything that had happened the previous night made clearer. It was, if anything, far too clear as it was. However, he sensed the dangerous determination in Bufo's voice and wordlessly took the goblet and threw the acrid liquid back. His mouth immediately filled with saliva and he swallowed repeatedly, trying to get rid of the bitterness.

'Sit down!' ordered Bufo. 'The effect will take some minutes.' Then he turned to Gull, who was looking confused at the turn of the events. 'Tell me,' Bufo said, 'exactly what happened after you entered the Citadel.'

'Certainly.' Master Gull inclined his head. 'We were shown into a room where we met the captain, Sculldung, as arranged. I remained there while the captain personally escorted Master Swallow to the dungeons. They were gone perhaps one half of an hour, perhaps a little longer. When they returned I asked whether the deed had been done and Sculldung confirmed that it had. He seemed satisfied.'

'How did Master Swallow seem?'

'As you would expect, sir. Calm, but tired.'

'Then?'

'Then I said we should leave, and the captain escorted us to the main gate and we returned to the House of the Toad.'

Bufo nodded thoughtfully, then moved to his usual position behind the long refectory table. 'Well, Master Swallow. Shall we go through the events again? Would you take us from the time you and the captain Sculldung left Master Gull?'

Tobias nodded. This time as he retraced his steps, the memory was sharper, clearer; he felt as if he were reliving every moment. He found he could repeat every one of Sculldung's scattered comments, recapture every footfall, every drip, every groan and creak. The overlay of horror was still there, however, and Tobias found himself gripping the arms of his chair as he re-entered the dungeon cell and yet again took out the knife. He described the murder, graphically, and how he had talked with Sculldung. Then he once more described his final task: raising the lantern above the uncovered face of his victim.

As he did so he noticed Bufo and Gull exchanging glances. Master Gull looked surprised, and then as Tobias described the one-eyed man with the hawked nose and straggling beard, Gull could not disguise his astonishment. 'But that's…' he gasped.

Bufo nodded. 'Tell me Master Swallow, for this is very important, did Captain Sculldung see this face?'

Tobias nodded. 'Certainly. He was with me. Indeed, I asked whether he knew the man.'

'And?'

'He indicated he did not,' said Tobias.

Again Bufo and Gull exchanged glances.

'There was one other thing,' said Tobias.

'Tell us,' said Bufo.

'The man was wearing a chain with a large bronze medal. Master Sculldung took it from his body and suggested it would be a help in identifying him.'

'Oh yes?' prompted Bufo.

'Then he placed the chain over his own neck.'

'The devil he did,' murmured Bufo. 'Did he say anything else?'

'He laughed,' said Tobias. 'That was all.'

'What is wrong?' asked Tobias.

Following the information that Martin Sculldung had laughed after putting the chain and medallion over his neck, there had been an awkward silence. Then Bufo had leaned across and conducted a whispered conversation with Master Gull. Clearly Tobias, although only a few feet away, was excluded from this consultation, and the longer he was excluded the more uncomfortable he became. It was in the silence that followed the conversation that he felt moved to ask his question. Ordinarily, such a question would have been considered a lack of courtesy, but this was not an ordinary situation.

Whether Bufo would have answered him Tobias was not to know, for at that moment there was an urgent knock at the door. This was another unusual event. Door-knocking within the House of the Toad was ever discreet.

'Come in!' Bufo called sharply.

The door opened and Mistress Quail stood there, her hollow cheeks sucked in with excitement. 'Doctor, masters,' she cried. 'Such excitement.'

'What is it?' demanded Bufo.

'The Markgrave, masters, is dead!'

If Mistress Quail had been expecting her news to be received with astonishment, she was immediately disappointed. 'Yes, Mistress Quail, we know,' said Bufo, with just a hint of impatience. 'And Master Sculldung has installed himself in the Markgrave's place, I believe.'

Mistress Quail stared stupefied for a moment, then nodded vigorously. 'Yes, Doctor. Yes he has. And they say the maiden… But how did you…'

'Leave us now, mistress,' said Bufo. 'It was good of you to bring us your news, but we are at this moment discussing far graver matters.'

Mistress Quail made an awkward and grotesque curtsey, and mumbling 'Thank you, Doctor,' backed hurriedly out of the door, closing it behind her.

Tobias had listened to this exchange with growing disquiet. Mistress Gull's announcement seemed too much of a coincidence. The Markgrave dead. The

Captain of the Watch installed in the Markgrave's place. 'Tell me,' he said. 'This felon I slew, was it…'

Bufo turned to him and nodded. 'It appears so,' he said. 'The face you described could only have been that of the Markgrave. The action of Sculldung with the medallion seems simply to confirm it. The man has behaved treacherously but with more guile than I would have given him credit for. How he managed to substitute Evan Twyll I cannot imagine.'

'Substitute?'

'Oh, yes,' said Bufo. 'It had not been arranged that your test would be killing the Markgrave.'

'Then who?'

Master Gull reached across to lay a hand on Bufo's sleeve, but the old doctor was relentless. 'No, it had been arranged, by the Markgrave himself, that you should kill the Maiden.'

'The Maiden? But the Maiden doesn't exist. She is just a fairy story, a myth.'

'Let us say she had been made flesh,' said Bufo drily. Almost as an afterthought he added, 'Into the flesh of a person I believe you are not unfamiliar with. Your own sister, Johanna, in fact.' The old man paused, staring expressionlessly at the young man sitting opposite him.

For a long moment Tobias Swallow seemed to hear a wild ringing in his ears and the room appeared to shake around him, so much so that he had to steady himself by gripping the arm rests on his chair. The previous night's events once more played before him with a sickening inevitability. He felt again that sense of calm deliberation, that sense of purpose, and he saw the shape of the body, trussed and wrapped around on the floor of the cell. It had all seemed so clear in the darkness: a matter of finding the spot, raising his arm, and bringing down the instrument of death. He squeezed his eyes shut.

'It would have been Johanna?' he whispered.

'It *should* have been,' said Bufo. 'And would have been but for the intervention of Sculldung's ambition. If she lives, your sister owes her life to the Captain of the Watch.'

'If she lives?'

Manfred Bufo raised his eyebrows. 'Who knows what has happened to her? She was supposed to have been in the cell. Instead Evan Twyll was there. Sculldung may have saved her from your knife, but Sculldung is not an especially humane person.'

'I would have killed my sister! You would have had me kill Johanna!' The awful enormity of what might have been crowded in on Tobias's racing brain. He rose to his feet, feeling a surge of bitter anger. The weight of the Moorish dagger at his side drew his fingers instinctively to it and he thrust his hand into his blue gown, drew it out and raised the serpent-like blade threateningly.

Bufo seemed not in the slightest way alarmed by Tobias's flourish of rage. He sat quietly, looking up at the raised dagger and Tobias's angry face. He murmured. 'So, Master Swallow, you have developed a taste for death? You would kill again so soon?'

Tobias stood for some moments, then realising that nothing could faze the two Brothers, implacable in their calmness, he felt himself sag. Feeling a little ridiculous, childlike with his melodramatic gesture, let the knife fall from his hands to the rug below.

'Have you no feeling?' he whispered.

'Feeling? You would have been a Brother. Feeling is a luxury. And a Brother is ever dispassionate. It is the source of our power, the power you would have had.'

'But…'

'We each carry a terrible burden. We each have been taken out of the world,' said Bufo.

Tobias stared at him.

'You were to be given your burden last night. Your sister's death would have been your weight. Being a Brother is a very heavy thing.'

'But I couldn't have killed her,' whispered Tobias in an agony.

Bufo simply stared at him gravely. He did not have to say, 'But you would have killed her last night.' That knowledge, those unspoken words, lay heavily in Tobias's heart, and he covered his face with his hands.

Chapter Twenty-three
THE LEPERS

The crowds in the market place shifted like water, leaving an island of space in the middle of which three strange figures made their halting way. Two tall figures wearing black face-masks with crude eyeholes were preceded by a smaller figure similarly masked, who moved from side to side in strange loping steps as if clearing a way for them. This figure flourished a gnarly stick and waved a wooden clacker which made a sharp warning sound. Passage was readily conceded by the crowd, who otherwise seemed to be enjoying a carnival atmosphere.

Until the arrival of this strange procession there had been merry laughter and excited talk. Much chatter had there been of the strange events of the day before. How a young maiden clad in a long green cloak had somehow brought an old lady back from the dead right here in the market square, and how she had almost immediately been seized by the guard from the Citadel and dragged away. Few doubted that she must have been the very Maiden there had been talk of for months, the Maiden who would deliver the benighted city of Gleam from the clutches of the Markgrave and his cruelty.

Now this. Twyll himself was dead, Twyll who had clearly plucked the Maiden from the market in order to destroy her and all she represented. Now strangely, miraculously, it was Twyll who had been translated into dust and the Maiden back into air. It was a wonder and it was wonderful.

The sharp clatter of the wooden clacker momentarily silenced the market-goers, but the passage of the small party of lepers took only a few sombre moments before the crowd quickly filled the space once more and the gaiety returned.

Thus it was, as a small dark cloud in an otherwise brilliant sky, that the trio made their way to the gatehouse and to the narrow road which led north to the River Flint and the countryside beyond.

Manfred Bufo stared thoughtfully at the young man. 'Your moment of anger seemed to pass quickly,' he said. There was almost a hint of curiosity in his voice.

It was now late afternoon. Shafts of mote-filled light angled into the library from the mullioned windows, and here and there on the floor were small prismatic patterns like tiny quivering rainbows where the sunlight had refracted through bevelled edges. The dancing colour was beautiful; as he looked at it absently, it occurred to Tobias that he might never know beauty again.

The two old men and the young man had sat quietly for over an hour. Bufo and Gull behind the refectory table, Tobias slumped in a chair to one side. There had been no conversation until this point, yet there had been a charge in the room, an edge: it was as if each of the three was waiting for something.

Tobias looked up at Bufo, thinking about his anger. Bufo was right. His rage had suddenly surged and then died almost on the instant. Many things had died with his anger. Since that moment, Tobias had known only a welling emptiness. A darkness as large and deep as night itself had overwhelmed him. Was this what Bufo meant by being taken out of the world? Was this absence, this darkness, his burden, and would he have to bear its black weight from now on?

'I did kill my sister,' he said.

Bufo nodded.

'I did kill her,' repeated Tobias quietly. 'She would have been there. It would have been her body and I would have lifted the knife above it and plunged it into her.'

He stared about him, without looking at anything in particular. 'She is no more,' he said.

'What would you do?' asked Bufo.

'Do?'

'Would you still join the Brotherhood?'

Tobias gave a short bitter laugh. 'Of course. Have I not joined it already?'

Bufo nodded slowly. 'You have begun to join it,' he said. 'It is a long journey. A difficult path.'

'What choice do I have?' asked Tobias. 'There is no other path.'

'No,' murmured Bufo. 'There is no other path really, except death itself.'

He looked around to Master Gull. 'Go,' he said. 'Fetch the needles.'

It had been Mother Grayling who had thought of the idea. 'The city is in a buzz of excitement,' she said. 'Everywhere there is talk of the Maiden and talk of the end of Twyll. Such a coming and a going. Even the guards seem in a state of confusion – it is as if a hand of iron has been lifted.'

'Then we might well walk from the city?' Hugh asked. 'We could walk and smile and bow to passers by?'

Mother Grayling shook her head. 'No, no, no,' she said. 'You could not do that. Johanna could be recognised. Would be recognised. And mobbed. The crowd's love would cause a commotion and the watch would come. We have no way of knowing what Sculldung would do.'

'If Sculldung had a heart it would be a heart of stone, but Sculldung has no heart,' Dagonet added. 'Sculldung has none.'

Hugh looked at the little man appreciatively. 'I don't know whether that's altogether good to know, but we need to know it,' he said. 'So what do we do? Wait until nightfall?'

'No,' Mother Grayling said in her raspy voice. 'With all the turmoil, there's sure to be a curfew. Extra guards on the watch.'

'Sculldung will bind the city tight,' Dagonet said. 'He will test his new grip.'

'Then what can we do?' Johanna asked. 'We cannot stay here. Good Mother Grayling has put herself in more than enough danger for us already.'

It seemed a conundrum, until the old lady's face brightened. 'There is a way,' she whispered. 'If you dare…'

'Dare what?' Johanna asked.

'There is a way you could drive people from you, rather than draw them to you,' Mother Grayling said. 'I think I have it.'

She opened the door of the small anteroom where the three fugitives had hidden the night before. Hugh followed her to the doorway, watching as she raised the lid of an old chest. She lifted out armloads of black garments and returned with them to the room.

'You think we could disguise ourselves as priests?' Hugh asked.

The old lady shook her head. 'My late husband, Grayling, was a tailor,' she explained, 'and he clothed priests fat and thin, but priests won't repel folks. Not all folks, anyway. Come here, my dear,' she instructed Johanna. 'I'll show you something that will.'

While Johanna stood before her, the old lady took a length of the black cloth and arranged it as a long shawl over Johanna's shoulders, then with a smaller piece of cloth she made Johanna a headscarf which at first hid her long fair hair and then, with a twist, was pulled around to hide her nose and mouth. Johanna turned and gazed at the men with only her eyes showing.

'Bend your shoulders,' Mother Grayling ordered.

'I see,' Hugh whispered. And even though he knew full well it was really Johanna, his niece, he was unable to repress a slight nervousness at the leprous figure who seemed to bend before him.

'I'll make headscarves for you as well, and we'll cut eyeholes in them. Then I'll find you some staves for walking sticks,' the old lady whispered. 'And I even have a rattle and a begging bowl some fool of a friar once exchanged for a pot of ale.'

In this fearsome disguise, Johanna, Hugh and Dagonet made their trouble-free way through the lanes and streets of Gleam and across the market square towards the gatehouse. Individuals gave them a wide passage, and even when they came across excited crowds, suddenly those crowds dispersed and parted leaving a clear pathway. Dagonet rattled his clacker with a wild enthusiasm, and his natural prancing gait seemed ideal. The little hunched figure seemed to unnerve people particularly. In his wake Hugh and Johanna slouched in a less fantastical manner. Nobody dared come within twenty feet of them.

In a perverse way, Hugh almost enjoyed this negative authority of the leper. He knew that lepers were dead to the living world. Alive, they were given funeral rites after which they were denied the sacraments of the living. Even the doors of the churches were closed to them. For the brief minutes of their procession through the streets of Gleam Hugh enjoyed the power of driving people from him as a shepherd drives sheep, and even though he kept his eyes fixed on the ground not too far in front of him, he knew that not even the most powerful dared stand in his way. Johanna held the begging bowl before her, but nobody came within the distance of a penny.

Thus they reached the gate in the wall of Gleam, but here there was no ceremony for them. The guard lowered his pike and brusquely signalled for them to hurry through and out of the city. Then he stepped well aside, fearful of contamination.

Apart from snarling, 'You should not be inside the city walls. You people know the law!' as they hurried through, he did not dare say another word. In no time at all, the three found themselves beyond Gleam and its dangers, and on the winding road to Flintside.

Master Gull carefully wiped Tobias's arm with a soft cloth. Already it was drenched with blood. He laid the cloth down on the bench beside the small wooden box which contained a bristling collection of needles and a pair of small hammers. Adjacent lay a small pottle of black ink and another of scarlet.

As the blood was wiped from Tobias's arm the black outline of a toad emerged, crouching indelibly there. Once, Tobias had exulted in the coloured toad Bufo had inked onto his arm. Now he gazed at this monochrome version with a slight feeling of revulsion. It seemed like a crouching curse.

'The only colour permitted yet,' murmured Bufo, who had been watching the operation from behind the shoulder of the old man Gull, 'is the scarlet of the toadstone.'

Tobias nodded, scarcely daring to utter a sound. The tattooing had been long and painful and he was pleased the final minutes had arrived. The toadstone was duly hammered home and Gull applied the brilliant scarlet to the small spot at the centre of the image's head. Tobias winced and wiped at his brow as once again Gull padded his arm with the bloody cloth. He then bandaged the arm loosely and said, 'There will be discomfort and scabbing for some days. Don't play with the wound. Time will both heal and reveal.'

Tobias understood, and he nodded again. Time might well reveal, he thought bitterly, but time would not heal. Eternity itself would not heal. He closed his eyes. All he wanted now was the oblivion of sleep.

The tattoo, Bufo had told him, would be the first badge of membership of the Brotherhood. It would serve as a passport among Brothers whenever he encountered them, for he would encounter them in secret places far and wide until the Brotherhood resolved upon a House where he would eventually settle.

'How long must I journey?' Tobias asked.

Bufo shrugged. 'For as long as you must. You will journey through time and journey through knowledge. As you journey through knowledge, colour will be added to your badge.'

'Must I leave everything behind?'

'You know the answer to that. You have nothing left. There is nothing for you.'

'But my sister?'

Bufo studied the young man. 'What would you know?' he asked.

'Whether she lives.'

Tobias had not been able to forget the body in the cell that would have been Johanna's, but nor could he forget that according to the arrangement he now knew had been made, Johanna should have been delivered to that cell. What had happened to her? It gnawed at him that Sculldung, his sister's murderer, may have escorted him to the dungeons. That is, his sister's actual murderer had escorted his sister's would-be murderer. The bitterness was too much to countenance.

'She lives but is dead,' Bufo had said cryptically.

'Don't riddle with me, Doctor,' Tobias had pleaded.

'You know the answer to the riddle,' Bufo told him. 'To you the Maiden is dead, and must be. In a strange way she did fulfil the prophecy, for Twyll, too, is dead. Our information leads us, however, to the knowledge that somehow she was delivered from the dungeon and into the hands of the Brotherhood.'

'But that isn't so!'

'You are right. That isn't so. It is, for all that, clear that she was delivered from the dungeon and out of the hands of Twyll and out of the hands of Sculldung.'

Tobias stared at Bufo, feeling faint stirrings of hope that his sister might yet live. 'All of these hands,' he whispered, holding up his own. 'Hands of the Brotherhood, hands of Twyll, hands of Sculldung, blood on all of them. She may be out of Sculldung's bloody hands, but is she out of his reach?"

'Oh, I scarcely think Sculldung would be interested in pursuing your sister,' Bufo observed drily. 'After all, she was the one who delivered the Markgrave's chain to him.'

Tobias was silent for a moment. 'Perhaps,' he agreed, but then remembering the curved blade of the raised dagger he added: 'On the other hand,' and he paused grimly at the word, 'it could be said that I delivered the Markgrave's chain to him.'

'Oh, I don't really think Sculldung will thank anyone for his chain,' Bufo said. 'The question of how he acquired it will never arise. Such is the way of the world.'

'Who are you?'

Tobias, suddenly awake, was aware that there was another presence in his cell. He sat up in his bed, rubbing his eyes against the yellow light of a lamp. The lamp was raised and dark shadows danced about the room. There was a tall dark figure standing behind the lamp light, a figure seemingly reluctant to announce his presence.

'Who are you?'

Tobias had not long been asleep although by now it must have been very early in the morning. All night his troubled mind had raced hither and yon, always coming back to that one inescapable fact: *I would have killed her*.

Finally, the figure spoke. 'I am Brother Sheldrake.'

'Brother Sheldrake?'

'The Master thought we should talk.'

'Talk? What is there to talk about?'

'I would talk of what it means to be a Brother.'

'I am beginning to find that out,' said Tobias bitterly.

'It is a hard thing,' said Brother Sheldrake. 'We serve a hard master, but it is the price we must pay.'

'Master Bufo is a monster. I know that now. And I am to become one as well.'

'I was not talking of Master Bufo,' said Brother Sheldrake smoothly, placing the lamp on a small sideboard and lowering himself on to a stool. 'I was talking of Master Death.'

Tobias closed his eyes. 'I have seen Master Death in the face of the Markgrave. He was not something I could easily live with.'

'From now on you must, Brother Swallow. You have no choice. Besides, I understand fortune smiled on you. I understand you should have seen Death in the face of your sister.'

Tobias did not reply.

'I met her,' said Brother Sheldrake. 'She had a certain beauty and a definite spirit. It is strange that the prophecy came true. That she should have been a bringer of death.'

'I would have killed her,' whispered Tobias.

'That is your burden. Your badge. We all have our burdens. It is what sets us apart.'

'We are apart?'

'Apart and beyond. It is what gives us power. Real power. The Markgrave thought he had power because he could make men tremble. He would threaten them with death and they would fear this and be bent to his will. This Sculldung thinks he has obtained power through his treachery and your agency. But his power is as nothing to our power. He threatens death but fears it. We serve Death but have no fear of it, for how can Death harm us more than we have harmed ourselves?'

Tobias nodded.

'The Master has begun your tattoo. Are you firm in your resolve?'

'What do you mean?'

'Would you still be a Brother?'

Tobias considered the question. Now that his eyes were more accustomed to the flickering lamp-light, he glanced at his interlocutor. He saw a gaunt figure dressed in a brown habit with a cowl hanging over his shoulders. A smooth face but short-cut iron grey hair. The face was expressionless but the eyes were dark and keen.

Tobias gave a short bitter smile. 'Somebody once told me to be careful of what my heart desired, in case I gained my wish. It seems I've gained my wish. There is no going back for me.'

Brother Sheldrake sighed. 'I am glad of it,' he murmured.

Tobias gave a bitter laugh. 'Why are you glad of it?' he demanded. 'You say we each carry a darkest burden. You would have me carry this. You would have me live my life an outcast? A leper?'

'Oh no,' said Brother Sheldrake softly, 'I wasn't thinking of you at all. I am merely glad, because if you had changed your mind and decided to leave the

Brotherhood, I would have been obliged to kill you.'

Tobias stared at him, shocked not by the violence of the message, but by the calm and somewhat resigned way it had been delivered. Brother Sheldrake, appearing not to notice Tobias's consternation, quietly rose from the stool and, picking up the lantern once more, turned towards the door.

'Goodbye, Brother Swallow,' he said over his shoulder. 'It is unlikely we shall meet again before you leave. I will wish you then a good journey, wherever it may lead you.'

Before Tobias had a chance to respond, Brother Sheldrake had slipped out of the door, closing it softly behind him.

Chapter Twenty-four
TRAVELLERS

Some miles from Gleam on the road to Flintside, the three dark clad figures heard a strange sound in the air. It was early afternoon and there was a light breeze. They were negotiating a small hill and the road was bendy, the roadside wooded with ancient trees. There was a low drone and above it an eerie melody wound about and rose and fell as if it were an echo of the road they had been travelling.

Johanna stopped walking and paused, one finger raised. 'Listen,' she whispered.

'Music,' whispered Dagonet.

Hugh stood very still, not saying anything. For some seconds they listened as the two sounds, the low droning ground and the ethereal wandering melody, wove together.

'What is it, Uncle?' whispered Johanna. Behind the crudely cut slits in her headscarf, her eyes were wide.

'The Hounds of Laurel,' said Hugh Cassin.

'*No hound no hound I'll be bound*,' said Dagonet in his high jester's mode. '*The hound that sounds the sound of that hound's sound could ne'er be found*!'

'No, no,' said Hugh. 'That is the name of the song that hurdy-gurdy's playing.'

'A hurdy-gurdy?' asked Johanna. 'Does that mean there's only one musician?'

Hugh nodded. 'And I can guess who it might be,' he said.

Dagonet appeared to be suddenly very excited. He moved from side to side, cocking his head as if to hear the strain more clearly. Finally he tugged at his headscarf and then he gazed with a delighted smile down the road in the direction of the music. 'Hurdy gurdy?' he whispered. '*Foldy roldy, tirra lirra, chickety clickety, oh my dear*!' Then he turned back to his companions.

'Come on,' he called, and he set off dancing determinedly towards the sound of the music, waving his clacker wildly.

Hugh laughed, for the first time in weeks it seemed. 'The little man likes the music,' he said. He reached for Johanna's hand and together they hurried after the little jester.

Dagonet disappeared around the corner and some seconds later the music stopped altogether. Almost simultaneously, Johanna and Hugh heard a cry of alarm. Some seconds later, when they turned the corner themselves, it was to see Dagonet jumping up and down on the roadside crying to a tatterdemalion figure who had scrambled up the bank, and was crouched there staring down at the little figure in black.

'Come down! Come down again!' the jester cried, but the terrified musician would have none of him. By the side of the road lay his hurdy-gurdy, its handle still, its strange music vanished.

When Johanna and Hugh turned the corner, the man on the bank gave a little whimper of fear, and his eyes widened. The two black-clad figures must have looked unnerving, with their ankle-to-head covering and with only the two slits to reveal their eyes.

'Pippin!' Hugh called to the man who cowered ever more deeply, clutching at the long grass at the top of the bank. It was clear that if his instrument were not still lying where he'd left it by the roadside, he would have climbed up and over and scampered away. 'Pippin!' Hugh repeated. 'Master Dumky!'

At the sound of his name the man shook his head, staring fearfully from the strange little figure of Dagonet to the two taller newcomers. 'What are ye?' he whimpered.

'Friends, Pippin. Friends!' cried Hugh, pulling at his headscarf. He stood there, silver-haired and recognisable, and smiling he added, 'Your friend, Pippin. Hugh. Hugh Cassin!' And then he shrugged out of the black cloak and flung it to one side.

Taking Hugh's cue, Dagonet and Johanna too pulled their black coverings off and stood revealed, tousled and grinning by the wayside.

'Hugh Cassin, by all that's strange and wonderful,' cried Pippin on the bank, smiling in recognition, although still rather reluctant to tumble down.

'These badges are false, Pippin,' said Hugh, pointing to the heaps of discarded cloaks blotting the roadway. 'Simply our means of passing through stone walls! But what are you doing here?'

'I'm to Lamaria,' replied Pippin, finally summoning up the courage to clamber back down the bank.

Hugh nodded. 'I'm not long back from there myself. Abel Larch has made me a new lute. Even now it waits for me at Posy's place.'

'I want Abel to make me another of these,' said Pippin, gesturing to where the hurdy-gurdy lay. Dagonet darted towards the instrument and picked it up, stroking the keyboard reverently before handing it to Pippin.

Seeing the tenderness there, Pippin Dumky smiled. 'You like this hurdy-gurdy, little man?' he asked.

Dagonet nodded keenly.

'He couldn't wait to find the music as soon as he heard it,' said Johanna. 'No wonder he frightened you with his mad rush.'

'My niece, Johanna,' explained Hugh. 'And this is Dagonet.'

Pippin Dumky, all fears entirely vanished, smiled and took their hands in turn. Idly then he began to turn the handle at the front of his instrument and a low drone began, and then he began to finger the keys with his right hand. 'This song, I think you know, Hugh. I always think of you when I hear it.'

As the plaintive melody began, Dagonet's eyes shone and he nodded with recognition. 'Sing, Master Cassin, sing,' he pleaded.

It was the song Hugh had last sung in the dungeons. The song that had lulled Garth to sleep. Despite the memory of that hideous place, Hugh picked up the melody and began in his sweet tenor voice.

The geese fly
High in the sky
Their far-off voices cry
Mountains
Mountains

To his surprise, and before he was halfway through the verse, Hugh began to hear Dagonet's high-pitched voice accompanying him in wordless harmony, softly at first, and then growing with confidence. Hugh turned to the little man and nodded encouragingly as he sang, and Dagonet nodded back, pleased.

The gentian glows
Deep in the snow
Murmuring soft and low
Moonlight
Moonlight

The song continued. The two voices intertwined together, warp and weft, with the strange ground and melody of the hurdy-gurdy. However, as the words of the last verse echoed about her, the melancholy of it all reached deep into Johanna and she found herself weeping softly.

My love lies
Beneath the birch
Above the earth and sighs
Yesterday
Yesterday

As the last notes sounded, Hugh noticed her distress. 'What is it?' he asked gently, reaching for her arm.

'I don't know, Uncle,' whispered Johanna. 'Something… I was put in mind of Tobias somehow. He is gone, and things can never be the same.'

Hugh, who privately agreed but who did not want to dwell on his deepest fears regarding his nephew, merely nodded. 'We did all we could,' he murmured. 'More than we possibly know. And we were lucky to escape ourselves.'

'Oh I know,' replied Johanna. 'It's just that I have such a deep feeling I'll never see him again, or that if I do, the Tobias I once knew will be gone forever.'

'Who can tell?' asked Hugh, with far more hope in his voice than he felt in his heart.

He glanced around at the others. 'We had better go,' he said. 'We have tarried far too long already. Let's gather up these weeds,' he said, indicating the discarded robes, 'and make our way to Posy Beet's. There is still danger on this highway, possibly.'

Johanna shivered. 'Yes. We ought to hurry. Aunt Posy will be worried to grief with not knowing what has happened.'

'I'll come with you,' said Pippin, shouldering his instrument. 'For Lamaria lies beyond.'

At the mention of Lamaria, Hugh paused and looked thoughtful. 'I'm wondering,' he said. He glanced fondly at the little Dagonet, recalling his enthusiasm for the hurdy-gurdy and the surprise of his sweet singing voice. 'You know, we may make the trip back to see Abel Larch ourselves. If as you say, Pippin, you are collecting a new instrument, then we may just make an offer on your old.'

The import of what Hugh had suggested was not lost on Dagonet. He beamed with delight, jumping from one foot to the other in excitement. Pippin patted the hurdy-gurdy. 'Do you think you'd make a hurdy-gurdy man?' he asked. 'It's not easy, mind. And I'm a stern teacher.'

Dagonet did not reply. He ran up the bank until he was horizontal, then somersaulted perfectly and landed back upright.

'I think he likes the idea,' said Johanna, smiling again.

As the door of the House of the Toad shut behind him, Tobias sighed, then shrugged into his blue cloak. He was about to set out on a journey, but carried little. A small leather bag contained some clothes, some books, some tinctures and some letters of introduction from Manfred Bufo. Against his hip he had a stiletto strapped, and on his forearm he had a black tattoo with a single red spot.

It was dusk when he reached the stone quay. He would find passage on one of the small sailing vessels that crossed the Bight of Gleam and its rough waters to the town of Aser. There he would disembark and continue his journey. How long it would take and where it would take him he had only the vaguest notion. The only certainty Tobias possessed was that the journey would not end. As Bufo had told him, the passage down into the Brotherhood was a dark spiral and as yet he had only rounded the first curve. Scattered throughout the remnants of the great empire, and even beyond its borders, were secure houses locked against humanity as firmly as had been the House of the Toad in Gleam. He would visit such houses and be admitted. He would be initiated into such knowledge as the Houses possessed, and when he had taken what each House deemed necessary he would be passed on to another. Each House would represent another twist in the spiral and as he wound his way deeper into the Brotherhood the toad squatting on his arm would gain colour. He now understood that Bufo's toad, which in its painted imitation had given him a heady glimpse of power, represented a long and arduous journey.

The wind off the choppy sea lifted his hair slightly and Tobias drew his cape over his head for protection. He thought bitterly of how he had longed for that power, how he had been seduced by the serpent wine into a desperate yearning for its possibilities. Well, he had it now. What did it mean? What did it mean to be beyond fear? It meant, he now knew, to be beyond feeling. To be numb. To be possessed of nothing, by nothing.

He could not go back to that place where he had been a brother, a son, a nephew. He could not go back to any place. From now it was ever onward into the empty depths of the Brotherhood, beyond death and beyond life.

Tobias made his way down the quay to where a ship was berthed, rocking in the water, butting almost like a living thing against the bolsters. A seaman was standing in the bows checking the hawsers there and Tobias hailed him, demanding an audience with the captain. There was such a stern authority in his voice that the sailor glanced at the tall shrouded figure in some alarm, tipped his hand to his forehead, and hurried off to do Tobias's bidding.

The next day dawned shiny but cold. There had been rain in the night and the black stones of Gleam glittered in the morning sunshine. Standing in his tower, surveying the lanes and rooftops, Martin Sculldung, the new Markgrave of Gleam, could almost understand why the usually bleak and gloomy city had been given its name.

The glitter all about him simply added to his air of well-being. The tower on whose stone parapet Sculldung now leaned over with a new and compelling sense of ownership had been the private domain of Evan Twyll. No other human being had ever climbed its steep circular steps during his tenure – it would not have been worth one's life to do so – and now that Sculldung was in control this seemed to him an eminently sound arrangement. The tower was a magnification of his eyes. It allowed him to survey his domain from on high. There was a satisfaction in knowing that nobody in Gleam could be higher, physically or in any other way. Sculldung liked the poetry of this.

He scanned the roofs of the houses crouched below him. 'Pinch me,' he thought. 'How did this happen?'

He had not looked for this sudden elevation. It was as if he had been standing in an orchard when a large sweet apple fell from on high and landed precisely in his outstretched hand. The Maiden. There was a weird poetry, too, in the fact that the bizarre prediction Twyll had been cunningly contriving to forestall had in fact come true. That this very attempt had brought about his downfall. And this fact had not been lost on either the townspeople or the Citadel, who, while never holding Sculldung in any sort of regard, had nonetheless welcomed him with open arms, even celebrated his accession, simply because he was not Twyll. All that is, with the possible exception of the former Markgrave's wife and his three snivelling brats. Sculldung grinned. Soon enough they would be able to express their whining bitterness to the stone walls of the dungeons. After certain recent events, there were a number of empty rooms down there.

So, all things considered, he had a lot to thank the Maiden for. And the dead dungeon master who had half-squeezed the life out of Twyll. And the Brotherhood for the phial with the sleeping draught. And, of course, the assassin.

The assassin. Even as he thought again of that silent robed figure, Twyll's sweeping gaze stopped at the large shiny gables of the House of the Toad.

At once his sense of superiority withered, and he recalled that he was not the most powerful in Gleam, that no matter how high the tower climbed above the mortal world it would not elevate him above the dark authority possessed by that house. It came to him again that the House of the Toad enjoyed a power all the deeper and more pervasive through rarely being exercised or flaunted. A power that could afford to condescend to Evan Twyll. That would condescend to Martin Sculldung.

Sculldung felt the cold suddenly, and drew his long scarlet cape about him. His years of surviving in Twyll's service had taught him the advantages of servility, that a dog knows and does not bite his master. He breathed out more easily. The House of the Toad was a presence he had no choice about. Its door rarely opened. It did not matter. He had his bone and he knew how to keep it.

He glanced away again and out to the sea beyond the harbour. A small sailing ship was making its way towards Aser on the other side of the water. Even from his vantage point which extended the horizon many times over, Sculldung could not make out that far shore. That did not matter either. He had all that he wanted in Gleam.

Late that night Mother Grayling wearily shut the door of the Sign of the Two Fishes on the last of the topers. It had been a busy few days after the astonishment of the tyrant Twyll's sudden death. People had wanted to gather, to drink, to celebrate. Tongues had been looser than they had been for years and there had even been singing.

Mother Grayling was wise enough to know that the high spirits would not last. That Martin Sculldung was no sunrise, but just another jackal who sooner or later would shake his shaggy pelt and bare his fangs. For the meantime, though, it was good to pretend that things had changed.

Methodically, she tidied the tavern, gathering tankards from the heavy slab tables and hanging them on hooks above the bench. That complete, she went from lamp to lamp snuffing out the wicks, until at last with a single candlestick held aloft she made her way towards the narrow stairs and her bed.

Just then she heard a scrabbling noise from the little storeroom at the back of the bar. Cautiously she approached the low door. It creaked as she drew it open. She had not been in the room since she had fashioned the leper disguises for her guests to see them safely out of Gleam after Twyll had been despatched, and the noise was puzzling. In a far corner was a small pail of whitewash, and the noise, now more muted, seemed to be coming from that. When she nervously investigated, she found to her relief that the source of the commotion was only a small rat that had fallen into the bucket and had almost drowned. Mother Grayling gingerly carried the dripping bundle by its tail to the outside door, which she awkwardly unbolted. She should have put it out of its misery, but she couldn't find it in her heart after all it had been through already, and instead threw its shiny albino body into the night. It looked momentarily like a dove in the darkness, but without a dove's wings it fell to the cobbles and lay their stunned and wretched.

'One final use for the bucket,' thought old Mother Grayling grimly as she rebolted the door. 'At least I won't have the fearsome task of daubing the walls of Gleam any longer.' And then at the thought of Sculldung now wearing the Markgrave's cloak, she corrected herself. 'Not for the nonce, anyway.'

After retrieving her candle, and wiping her whitened fingertips on her apron, she climbed the stairs to her bed.

Apart from the underlying pain of having lost Tobias, the few days spent at Posy Beet's cottage by the side of Flint had not been unhappy. In the evenings there were a cheerful fire, stew and ale and music. Hugh retrieved his lute and he and Pippin played as many songs as they knew. Dagonet, as he quickly learnt the words, became ever more confident in his harmonies and he studied Pippin and the hurdy-gurdy with a happy longing. Johanna was delighted to be back in the warmth of her aunt's love and to be able to carry on with her original purpose. Baby Ellen was ever more responsive.

Gabriel Beet, too, although he would never be a man of iron will, had a merry laugh and a charm about him. He also had a wonderful fund of stories which he would embroider in bright and startling colours: funny stories, sad stories, stories that would build you up to a pitch of fear then pull a quick rug and have you laughing at your gullibility. Hugh could understand how his quicksilver tongue had won his sister Posy.

But like fresh fish, guests outstay their welcome quickly and Hugh was aware that three extra mouths were a strain on the little household. Thoughts of the Valley of Lamaria and of Abel Larch and Larissa, and the long journey ahead of him, became more insistent, so that one evening he leaned over to Posy and said, 'Sister, we must be gone in the morning for the weather looks to remain fair and we have far to go.'

Posy nodded, smiling. She knew better than to insist with hypocritical politeness that they stay longer. Instead she reached for his hand and pressed it. 'I wish you a safe journey,' she said. 'Although I'd prefer you were returning to Blackfell and our sister, Joan. There are things she must know.'

Hugh nodded. 'I'll not be that long. You'll see me back on our return to Blackfell. What Joan must hear can wait for some time yet, for it will pain her to grief.'

He stared at the fire. Posy had reminded him of the tidings he must bring his sister. That her son had decided against the University at Aser and his studies with Dr Portcullis, that he would not be a healer of the sick and a knitter of bones, that instead he had been initiated into a secret Brotherhood and was lost to them forever.

The flames licked hungrily at the birch logs as Hugh contemplated the tidings he would not bring to his sister. He could at least spare her the knowledge that her son but for a lucky happenstance would have murdered his own sister, that he had chosen death over life and power over love. This distressing knowledge Hugh would clutch tightly to himself.

He stood up, feeling the oppression of the fire, not its warmth. He opened the door and stepped out into the darkness under a bowl of stars. The shadows of trees wrapped about him as he took the path down to the riverside where the waters of Flint, phosphorescent in the starlight, rippled over the rocks. He stood there thoughtfully, enjoying the brisk chill of the night.

He had his pocket tied around his waist and idly became aware of its weight dragging at his side. He felt in it and discovered the round-shouldered shape of the wooden toad Gabriel Beet had whittled for him. He drew it out, feeling it nestle in his palm, felt its wooden wattle, its bulbous eyes and the thin line of its mocking grin.

He knew it wasn't real, that it was a bauble, a toy. He knew, too, that once on the dark streets of Gleam it had been the means of saving Johanna's life, but suddenly he felt an instinctive surge of hatred for the object gorge up inside him and he drew his arm back and he flung it far, far away into the Flint. He heard it ricochet off a rock and then perhaps a small splash amongst the ripples, then nothing.

It was a small satisfaction. Hugh sighed and turned back to the house. In the morning they would start for Lamaria once more.

James Norcliffe has previously published four highly original fantasy novels for young adults (*Under the Rotunda*, *Penguin Bay*, *The Emerald Encyclopedia*, which won an honour award in the AIM Children's Book Awards, and *The Carousel Experiment*). These were all marked by fast-moving action, cleverly engineered plots, oddball humour, and situations in which his young characters are confronted by the mysterious and the bizarre.

Much more ambitious in its themes and scope, *The Assassin of Gleam* gives his readers, young and old, an altogether darker and deeper experience and signals an exciting new direction for one of New Zealand's most imaginative writers of fiction. Conceived as the first of a series of novels in which the world of Gleam with its secrets and mysteries is examined, *The Assassin of Gleam* is to be followed by the equally compelling *The Mistress of Yewfire* and *The Witch of Aboraxus*.

James Norcliffe's work has appeared world-wide and is frequently anthologised. He has also published several collections of poetry and a collection of short stories, *The Chinese Interpreter*. Among many literary distinctions, he has been The Robert Burns Fellow in 2000 and a writer in residence in Hobart through the Tasmanian Island of Residencies Awards in 2005.